GRIFFIN HAYES

I0549282

MALICE

Trebor Books

TREBOR BOOKS

ISBN: 978-0-9878068-9-5
eISBN: 978-0-9878068-0-2

Cover design by Kit Foster

Praise for Malice

"I was **riveted** by every chapter."
—Terri, mybookboyfriend.blogspot.com

"A **wonderful** action filled story...**can't wait to read more from Griffin Hayes**."
—Emily Tuley, Greatmindsthinkaloud.com

"You MUST own this book. Do NOT walk, **RUN...and BUY IT!!** You won't be disappointed."
—Annette Nishimoto, gothicmomsbookreviews.com

More Praise for the work of Griffin Hayes

"Nail-biters beware: Griffin Hayes will have you chewing off your arm!"
—Hugh Howey, bestselling author of **WOOL**

"Hayes writes at a sprinter's pace with a new horror at every turn. Don't let your guard down for a moment because the scares are relentless."
—Joe Hart, author of **LINEAGE**

"Griffin Hayes brings to-the-point characterizations, a crisp writing style, and well-written action scenes."
—Keith C. Blackmore, bestselling author of **MOUNTAIN MAN**

Acknowledgements

Writing is a lonely business, but no one produces a book without some kind of help along the way. First, I'd like to thank Diana Cox for the great proofreading and to my editors, John Payne, who's a saint and a superhero and to Glen Krisch for helping to make sense of it all. A shout-out to the very professional and talented Kit Foster for the great cover and finally, a warm thank you to Medical Examiner, Amy Burrows-Beckham MD, for her time and expertise on blunt force trauma. Any inaccuracies in depicting severe head wounds are mine and mine alone.

Also by Griffin Hayes

Novels
Malice
Dark Passage

Novellas
Hive I
Hive II
Hive III
Bird of Prey
The Neighbors

Short Stories
The Second Coming
The Grip
Fatherland

Collections
Night Terror
Nightfall

Man... cannot learn to forget,
but hangs on the past: however
far or fast he runs, that
chain runs with him.
Frederich Nietzsche

Prologue

Millingham, 1648

The smell of burning death would soon choke the streets. The inhabitants of Millingham knew this as surely as they knew that God had sent his only son to die for their sins. By noon, the condemned witch would be burnt to ash, her evil extinguished forever.

Before long, Millingham's narrow streets were thronged with crowds from every corner of the Massachusetts Bay Colony. Two boys climbed out from a window onto the roof of their house. There they sat silently perched, awaiting the spectacle.

Governor John Winthrop arrived not long after.

In he rode at the head of a procession of selectmen, an endless stream of them from every town in the Bay area. They were greeted by squat and ruddy-cheeked Reverend Butler, who took them in hand and led them to seats with a clear vantage point. They had come from far and wide to see the witch die.

Last to arrive was the Millingham Town Council. Tall men draped in black gowns that brushed their feet, white pointed collars, wide black brimmed hats, tapered with a silver buckle. Last night, as they had rendered their verdict, a solitary voice of dissent had sounded from the young woman's mother. "You will burn in hell for what

1

you are doing!" she had shouted, but no one had been listening.

At the head of the council sat Parris Locke, a tall man with dark piercing eyes and skeletal features. As he marched to his seat, his black cloak billowed beneath him like the Grim Reaper.

When all were settled, Locke raised a slender hand and gestured to the captain of the guards. An order rang out. Soon Rebecca Goodman was led into the town square on a cart pulled by a mud-splattered white mare.

The crowd grew silent, inquisitive. Even the birds stopped squawking. From the rooftop, the two boys stared with the kind of fascination specially reserved for an insect, hobbled and flailing. She had been hideously tortured. Her face was swollen and strangely disfigured, and where her wrists were bound, a trail of blood ran down the pole. Other precautions had been taken as well. The symbol of an eye had been branded into her forehead with a hot poker, thwarting her attempts to cast the evil eye upon those gathered.

Just then the crowd erupted into a bloodthirsty roar, flinging rubbish and manure toward her. She was broken and defenseless now, and the people did not fear her anymore. Had Satan himself been tied before them, they would have done the same. There was safety in numbers, they knew that.

Two soldiers removed her from the cart and tied her to the stake on the platform. Beneath her feet, tinder and brush had been piled. A white plume of air escaped Rebecca's lips. She was shivering with cold.

A notary stood before the woman and unfurled a long parchment and the crowd grew silent. "Rebecca Goodman, by the authority vested in this council, you have been found guilty of the detestable arts of witchcraft and sorcery and hath wickedly, maliciously and feloniously used, practiced and exercised these arts in and

2

around the town of Millingham and shall henceforth be burned from this earth."

When he was done, Locke nodded and then gave the signal. Soldiers with torches approached the brush and set it alight. The pile caught almost at once, sending black smoke billowing into the air in such thick clouds that those closest were forced to take a step back. Through the blackness they could see her body writhing and they could hear yelps of fear and pain. She wore a locket around her neck, and in the sun it shone and flickered for all to see.

The flames began licking higher, and her cries became more desperate. Her screams were punctuated by moments of violent coughing, as the toxic smoke poured into her lungs. The people stood transfixed by the dying woman. Her feet and legs looked as though they had been covered in tar. In the front row, a pregnant woman buried her face in her husband's tunic. The crowd that had assembled with such glee and bloodlust now fell silent. They had never seen a living person burn before. Calls rang out for mercy. A chant was taken up. A soldier raised his musket to fire a ball through her heart, but Locke waved it away with a bony hand.

There would be no mercy today.

Slowly, the witch's head slumped forward, and relief flickered through those assembled.

The witch was dead at last.

Pleased with himself, Locke surveyed the crowd.

But the piercing cry that rang out drew his attention back to the spectacle. The witch's drooping head began to rise. Her mangled face peered out at him through the licking flames. Loathing surged out of her in almost tangible waves. Gone were her screams, her quivering frame. Gone too were her efforts to escape the flames.

Her lips began to form ugly and guttural sounds and it was suddenly clear to all present that the witch was

3

cursing them.

Locke crossed himself. *But this woman is dead*, he thought, and for the first time his hardened face betrayed a glimmer of fear.

The witch snickered and then began to laugh.

The crowd tried frantically to escape. Old women and children were flung down and crushed in the panic.

Finally, bald and blackened, the witch slumped forward for the last time and went still.

Rebecca Goodman was gone, of that there was no question, but even the young boys watching between webbed fingers from the rooftop above could see that from the witch's ghastly death, a horrifying evil had been born.

Chapter 1

Present Day

Something was terribly wrong with the town of Millingham. That was the thought floating through Lysander Shore's tired mind as he lay in bed.

Even from day one things hadn't been right. His first sense of it had come as he and his parents were passing the greeting sign on the edge of town. He was sure he had seen the sunken face of a man on that sign glaring back at him.

Below him were crooked red letters, scratched in a child's hand:

STAY AWAY

The family car had rocketed past doing over fifty, and Lysander had tried swinging around for another look, his arms bristling with gooseflesh, only to see the darkness engulfing the sign as they sped away.

There had been something especially disquieting about the look of fear on the man's face. Who was that? And did anyone else see it too? His fears were answered about a week later, when he passed that same weathered placard again. This time the strange man was gone, and in his place was a beaming, happy-looking family:

WELCOME TO MILLINGHAM!

Lysander wondered if he was losing his mind the way his Granny Pearl had after her breakdown. One day

5

something inside her just went snap. Sometimes he could hear her at night, lying in her bed at the end of the hall, speaking gobbledegook. Maybe Pearl had also started seeing things that weren't really there. Right before the men with the white lab coats and the foot-long needles came to take her away.

Or perhaps it was the barely two-week-old memory of watching his house in Hayden firebombed and reduced to a pile of smoldering ash. It must have knocked something loose inside him. If that wasn't enough to do permanent damage, he didn't know what was.

He heard a rustling in the hallway. A second later, Lysander's bedroom door opened. His mother peered inside, her hair full of curlers.

"Lysander. Wake up, honey. It's almost eight-thirty."

The door swung in a little farther, revealing a burly middle-aged man sporting a serious case of bed-head.

"Son, you're not gonna be late on your first day of school. Now get up!"

Lysander drew the covers up over his head.

He liked his parents as much as any seventeen-year-old could be expected to, which was to say he didn't like them much at all. It had become excruciatingly clear over the past year that they didn't understand him. At times they even regarded him as some kind of alien life form: a creature to be prodded and controlled, but by no means treated normally.

"I'm sick," Lysander told his father, touching his forehead and then yanking his hand away as though he had burned it. "I'm dying, Glenn."

His mother's face flushed. "Lysander, why do you insist on calling your father by his first name?" Even though she was only six months pregnant, she already looked ready to explode.

Glenn pushed past his wife and laid a clammy hand over Lysander's forehead. "You're fine. Now get up!"

6

Lysander was stuffing his lunch into his knapsack when he heard his father speaking with someone in the living room. He zipped up his bag and headed in that direction. Standing across from his father was a thin man. His hair was brown and wavy and combed back over his head. The flesh on his face was pale and tight. Lysander spotted the pin on the lapel of his suit jacket and saw that it read "Peter Hume" and below that "Zellermann's".

He was an insurance guy, here about the fire in Hayward. Lysander watched the two men talk. The house was a complete write-off and his father was going through a list of the things that had been destroyed when Peter Hume looked up at Lysander. The odd glint in his eye instantly made Lysander uncomfortable.

Glenn turned around and introduced them.

Hume offered his hand. It looked cold and bony.

"Go on, Lysander," his father, Glenn, scolded. "Shake the man's hand."

Lysander Shore's family hadn't been in Millingham much longer than a week, but he was sure somehow he had met this man somewhere before. Maybe filling bags at the grocery store or delivering mail down the street? This was going to torture him the whole day.

Lysander stuffed his lunch into his knapsack and then slowly held out his hand. The cold palm that slid into his hand a second later made Lysander's stomach turn. His father must have noticed the discomfort on Lysander's face, because Glenn's cheeks flushed with embarrassment. At least for once it wasn't about Lysander's black nail polish or matching combat boots.

"You'll have to excuse the mess," Glenn said, clearing a place on the couch where the stranger could sit. "We're still getting settled."

"Do you have any pictures?" Hume asked Glenn. "So we can take inventory of what you lost."

7

"Yeah," Glenn said, looking at his watch. "Do you need those now? I gotta leave for work."

Hume smiled apologetically. "I'm afraid so."

Glenn sighed, as he always did when asked to do something menial but necessary, and headed for the kitchen. "You want something to drink?"

"Earl Grey would be nice."

"That's the only tea we have," Glenn replied robotically. He seemed dazed. Or was he hypnotized? Lysander couldn't tell which.

Hume's eyes were shining. "Legend has it an old Chinese man gave Lord Grey the recipe for saving his son's life, if you believe that sort of thing."

His father shrugged and disappeared into the kitchen.

Now Lysander and Peter Hume were alone and the air in the room seemed to drop ten degrees. Slowly, the smile disappeared from Hume's face.

"You were warned not to come here," Hume said, his voice gravelly, almost hoarse. Lysander peered down at Hume's scalp and saw the man's translucent flesh squeezing the plates of his skull together.

Lysander's breath caught in his throat.

"He knows, Lysander." Hume's voice was more forceful. Desperate. "Knows you're here. Knew the minute you arrived. Felt you crossing the town line, just like I did..." Hume smiled, and the sight of it was chilling.

Lysander's mouth dropped open in a mixture of confusion and disbelief.

That smile...

Lysander instantly knew where he had seen this man before. It was Hume's hollow face that had been glaring back at him from the old weathered sign that greeted visitors on their way into town. And etched below him had been the words:

STAY AWAY

A tiny impression appeared in Hume's forehead, and

8

from it a thick drop of blood rolled down his face. The man's eye sockets were receding into the back of his head. A noise came from the kitchen and Hume's cavernous eyes darted over Lysander's shoulder. The fear bubbling in his voice was palpable. "He hasn't found me," Hume whispered. "Not yet. But you. He'll know you right away."

Lysander tried to say something, anything, but all that came was a moan.

Run Lysander! Turn your ass around and RUN!

"He could be any one of them out there," Hume croaked. "They all look so innocent, don't they? With their little white houses and their hybrid SUVs. Hard to imagine there's a monster coiled somewhere in all that." Hume's eyes—black bottomless chasms now—rose to meet Lysander's, and when he did the expression on his face fell flat. "You don't know what I'm talking about, do you? You haven't remembered yet."

Lysander felt the muscles in his chest knot with fear.

"He's come to finish it." The structure of his face was coming undone and Lysander tried to blink it away. "That's why he's here. To finish it..."

Lysander staggered back and nearly tripped over a moving box filled with old books. Glenn reached out a hand and caught him. He was holding a cup of tea. A photo album was wedged under his armpit. "Mr. Hume?"

Hume's gaze rose. It was gaunt and unsettling, but nothing like the monstrosity from a moment ago.

Glenn was handing Hume his Earl Grey when he turned to Lysander. "You better hurry or you're going to be late for school. It's already a quarter past."

The alarm in his father's voice rattled him. Lysander snatched his school bag off the floor and left the room as fast as he could.

"I wasn't really expecting you till tonight," Lysander heard his father tell Hume as he sped away, "so I hope

9

we can make this fast."

Lysander was trying to steady his hand over the front door handle when Hume replied cheerfully.

"Keeping you safe and sound, that's our motto at Zellermann's."

During the long walk to school, Lysander tried to make sense of what he had just seen. It had all happened so fast he wasn't sure he'd even closed the door behind him.

Whenever he closed his eyes, he'd see the stranger's face dissolving all over again.

He's come to finish it. That's what the creepy bastard had said.

Who was the *he* Hume had been talking about? But more than that, Lysander wanted to know what he had meant by *finish it?*

Chapter 2

A heavy rain had swept over Millingham the night before, leaving the roads slick and shiny. The sky was low and thick with heavy gray clouds that threatened to open up at any moment. Samantha Crow stared out the police car window. She loved the stillness, the clean feeling after a rain, the way the air smelled soggy.

A steady clicking sounded from the car dashboard. Her father, Steven Crow, the city's sheriff, made a lazy left-hand turn.

"People driving slow this morning," her father said. He sported a white handlebar mustache—a carryover from his hero, Wyatt Earp. "Good thing, 'cause it's slippery out there and we need to get you to school. Couldn't afford to be pulling anyone over, now could I?" He winked at her, twitching a matching white bushy eyebrow, and she smiled weakly in return.

"You're gonna have to think about a graduation dress, you know," he said.

Samantha remained silent, eyes closed.

"Not sure if you knew this but I asked your mother to prom. I don't think I was her first choice, though." He laughed, the way older people often laughed at the humorless things they said. "Had her eye on a boy named Billy Dobbins. But I never gave up, Sam. Went out and bought myself a nice new suit."

11

Samantha's blackened lips began to tighten.

Her father combed his mustache with the flat tips of his fingers. "She was a good woman, your mother." He glanced over and caught her change of expression. "I'm just thinking that with the way you dress. What do they call it? Goth? I just wouldn't be surprised if some nice boy might pass you up."

"I'm not a Goth." Her laugh bore a threatening edge. "And what's wrong with the way I dress?" She crossed her arms, glaring at the dashboard.

"No, not wrong…" he said. "Definitely not wrong, honey, just different. We don't live in the big city, where people wear leather trench coats and knee-high boots." His expression darkened. "I spoke to Mike Spiolis last week. You know, my friend over at the NYPD. He was telling me how a young boy and his father were waiting for the subway train when a man who lost his job as a middle school janitor came up behind them and pushed them both onto the tracks. Boy's father managed to throw his son clear in time, but he stepped on the third rail while trying to get out and jolted himself with 600 volts of electricity. When they asked the guy afterward why he had done it, you know what his answer was?"

Sam's face was blank.

"He said he wanted someone else to know how it felt to lose something they loved."

Samantha sighed, tired of her father's horror stories. "I'd rather take my chances with lunatics trying to push me in front of subway trains than spending my life living in a bubble."

"You know, your mother and…"

"Can we not talk about Mom like she's still around?"

He pushed his glasses up on his face. "The day your mother died was the worst day of my life. Thank God you're too young to know what it feels like to turn over at night and not have that person there anymore. You have

12

no idea. No idea."

Whatever pity had started welling up within her was squashed flat when she remembered what had happened at the house earlier this morning.

She had gone into her father's room to ask him for lunch money and had found his girlfriend, Sheila Evans, jiggling the bathroom door handle. The bathroom where her mother's body had been found. The one nobody went into anymore.

"What the hell do you think you're doing?" Samantha had screamed, her anger fueled more by her hatred for the woman than by what she was trying to do.

Sheila's face had blanched and one of her sagging breasts had lolled out of her satin negligee. She had fumbled it back inside, embarrassed. "I was just..."

"Going to use the washroom... He didn't tell you, did he?"

Sheila began to regain her composure, and anger was replacing shock. "Tell me what, Samantha?"

"That the day my mother died, the day someone came into our house and killed her, he stopped going in there. Betcha he forgot to mention that ol' chestnut. No, didn't want to frighten off his new lay."

Sheila's face had become a mask of disbelief. Sam could tell that no one had ever spoken to her that way before. And if Sam was lucky, it might just be enough to keep her from ever coming back.

She watched her father as he turned the corner, the memory of what happened so fresh she could still smell the trail of Sheila's cheap perfume as she'd stormed away.

"And of all the people in town, did it have to be the principal of my school, Dad?"

"Life goes on after people die, Sam. It's a tough lesson, I know, but it's one we all have to learn. Besides, your mother would have wanted us to be happy."

Sam clenched her fists. "None of us can be happy,

13

Dad, because when Mom was murdered, all that happiness packed its bags and went on vacation, permanently."

"Your mother was not murdered, goddammit." A hank of hair tumbled into his face, and he combed it back with a shaky hand. "Sam, you're gonna have to accept the truth or you'll end up a bitter and angry person."

Too late, she thought, gnawing the black polish off her nails.

"It just doesn't make sense. Who kills themselves without a note? Who slits their wrists like that? And what she did to her face—Dad, her eyes!"

"Your mother was a sick woman, Sam," her father protested, as he had dozens of times before. "There's no other explanation. Only a person who needs help would do something like that. My greatest regret is that I wasn't able to keep those details from you. No one your age should grow up with that kind of thing hanging over them."

"It just doesn't make any sense, Dad," she repeated, trying to ignore that truckload of shit about her mother's mental health that he had just tried to feed her again. "I mean, your marriage counseling was going well. You had just started loving each other again. And then this. I don't believe it. I'll never believe it," she shouted.

The car descended into a moody silence. By the time they arrived at school, Samantha had scraped all of her nail polish off. Even her father's tobacco chewing—which, for once, he had not tried to hide—had gone unnoticed and unchallenged.

Somewhere out there was proof that her mother hadn't killed herself. Somewhere the person who had killed her was still free. If there was a way, Samantha would set everything straight once and for all. That's what her mother would have wanted. Samantha couldn't understand why her dad didn't too.

14

Chapter 3

Deputy Alex Morgan knocked on the thick metal door that sealed off the autopsy room. He winced as the scent of decomposing flesh hit him. Lingering around the dead really wasn't first on his list of preferred things to do. He removed his glasses and folded them with a flick of his wrist, sliding them into a freshly starched and ironed khaki shirt pocket. Seeing that the door was slightly ajar, he took the liberty of walking in.

Dorothy Olsen was hovering over a shiny metal table, weighing what looked like a bloody piece of meat. The place gave him the heebie-jeebies. It wasn't the grotesque nature of her work or the eeriness that bothered him— Dorothy's autopsy room was so bright and sterilized you couldn't find a shadowy corner in the place. It was the loneliness, the lack of physical contact he could never tolerate. He liked a warm, breathing body next to him at all times, preferably of the female variety.

Like Samantha Crow. He pictured her great big pouty eyes looking up at him. She was just his type. Sure he was older than her by a couple of years. But age wasn't the real problem. She was the Sheriff's daughter, his pride and joy. Not to mention that Sheriff Crow had been like a father to him. He had taken a twenty-two-year-old loser under his wing and made him into a respectable cop. The

15

very thought of letting the old man down hurt.

Above him, a single rickety ceiling fan turned in lazy circles. Half a dozen stainless steel beds lined the walls like a dormitory. He wasn't sure at first whether Dorothy had even heard him knocking because of the godawful music blasting over the P.A. Some kind of opera. Alex waved at her but still got no response. She was too engrossed in her work.

"Dorothy!"

Dorothy Olsen looked up with a start from the organ she was slicing into thin strips.

"Alex, you scared the hell out of me! Shame on you."

Deputy Alex Morgan shook with laughter.

Dorothy removed her glasses and let them dangle around her neck. Rubbing the corners of her eyes, she headed over to the wall to snap the music off.

"I passed by on patrol last night and saw the light still on. Two in the morning's a bit late even for the medical examiner."

She plucked a heart from a scale suspended from the ceiling.

"The Keenans wanted to know what Grandma died of," she said dryly. "I think they're scared it's hereditary."

Alex removed his hat and brushed out his blond curly hair. He had celebrated his twenty-sixth birthday last August, but he looked more like twenty-one, which made it a hell of a lot harder to gain respect in a small town like Millingham. Alex tossed his hat on a nearby stool.

Beside it was a stack of cardboard filing boxes. Printed on each was a name and case file.

"What's all this stuff?" Alex asked, scanning the containers.

Lowery, Elizabeth: 25487.

Dorothy frowned. "No more room downstairs. Not until they finish that space age storage area." As if on cue, two men with jumpsuits and heavy tool belts strolled past

16

the open autopsy room door.

Ames, Tom: 25463

"Early lunch or another smoke break?"

"Take your pick," Dorothy said, rolling her eyes.

Crow, Diane: 25437

The box was open, and at once a chill rolled up Alex's spine as a familiar feeling crept over him. Out of nowhere, a shiny white tub appeared—smooth edges, high glossy finish. Droplets of moisture had formed at the edges. The curtain around it suddenly folded back like an accordion, pulled by an unseen hand. The tub was full, the water red and cloudy. It looked unreal, like tomato soup. A female figure lie face forward in the water, her hair floating listlessly. Her wrists were slit wide open, her body bled so clean her flesh looked nearly translucent.

"Alex!"

He looked up at Dorothy slowly, as though emerging from a long, disturbing dream.

"Are you all right?"

"Diane's box, it's still here," he said. Alex remembered reading her death certificate like it was yesterday. Suicide, it had said. At the time he had swallowed his doubts, but he had wondered if Dorothy had allowed her feelings for Sheriff Crow to cloud her judgment.

Dorothy's hand went to the glasses hung around her neck. "Are you asking me if I've been reviewing the case?"

"I'm not trying to tell you how to do your job, Dorothy." Their eyes met for a sharp moment, and he turned away. "This whole business about Diane losing her marbles doesn't sit well with me, and I've never tried to hide that. I was there when we found her, don't forget. Hell, her wrists were slashed to the bone and her eyes were torn out. Not like any suicide I've ever seen."

"No, it's wasn't." Dorothy looked away, too. Down at the box, or at Alex's feet, he couldn't tell which.

17

"I guess I've always been surprised at how quickly the decision was made," he added. "I mean, maybe if we'd spent more time. What if there was something we missed?"

Dorothy grew quiet.

That was when Alex noticed the ghostly white light coming from the conference room. On the screen was the body of a pale and naked woman in a bathtub, hunched over in a red pool.

A vicious knot formed in his belly at the sight. No matter how many instructional videos you watched, nothing ever really prepared you for the real thing. And it only got worse when it was someone you knew—even when you hated them.

There was a guilty look on Dorothy's face.

"Sheriff Crow had you change the cause of death, didn't he? Tried to get you to sweep it under the rug and you did, but you just couldn't leave it alone. Crow's wife was murdered, wasn't she? God, I knew it!"

"You stubborn bastard! You just don't know when to quit."

Alex smiled. "Show me what you have."

The projector was humming when Dorothy reached for the remote and clicked to a white sheet with the outline of a woman's body, front and back, arms and legs splayed. The one medical examiners used to identify important markings on a body. Most of it was blank, except for notes around the wrists, face and others at the top and rear of the neck. Dorothy's handwriting was characteristically poor for an examiner. Alex could barely make heads or tails of it.

"We never were able to find Diane's eyes," Dorothy said.

He nodded grimly, remembering how disturbing her face had looked.

"I know it doesn't make a whole lot of sense, but

18

judging from the evidence, she did this to herself. The tissue and blood we found under her fingernails all belonged to her."

Alex craned his head for a closer look.

Dorothy clicked a button and the slide projector went to a close-up of the wrist.

"When a person slits their wrists, the wound is normally quite superficial. But the blood flow can be pretty intense, and a quick laceration, especially with a razor, usually does the job, not to mention the pain." Dorothy moved to a close-up of the hand and wrist. She aimed a laser pointer toward the screen. "Now look here, where the laceration was made."

Alex examined the picture and shook his head. "I don't see anything."

"It's difficult to see, but the cut was made at the joint, here. The vast majority of people who slit their wrists cut themselves in the more fleshy area." She pointed just below the palm on her own hand. "Here or perhaps here."

"To get the job done."

"Right. But the lacerations in Diane's wrists are deep enough that at one point she was sawing into her radius bone."

Alex winced.

"Here's the real problem, though. By the time she hit bone, she would have severed enough tendons to render her hand next to useless."

"She couldn't have slit her other wrist unless someone else was there to do it for her."

"Not only that," Dorothy cut in, "but it looks like the eyes were the first to go."

Alex shuddered. "Get anything from toxicology?"

Dorothy's eyes fixed on the screen. "All negative. I can tell you that she smoked and drank, but otherwise she was clean."

19

"The razor we found by the tub, could it have done that kind of damage?"

"That was the initial finding, although after looking things over I'm convinced now that the incision was made with a thicker blade—an exceptionally sharp hunting knife maybe. Then again, it's hard to tell, since I don't have the body anymore or a knife to compare it to. I only have my notes and my memory to go on now."

Alex tapped a pencil against his forehead, an old schoolboy habit. "Why would she have done this to herself?" he muttered. "I don't understand."

"I don't either. But there's more." Dorothy clicked the remote again. "I found some tiny bruises behind her neck. Now initially I dismissed it since the bruising seemed consistent with what you might expect from a vigorous massage."

"I'm pretty sure the sheriff wasn't giving Diane any erotic massages. But I guess you never know. He did say they were trying to patch things up near the end."

"But it gets a whole lot weirder," Dorothy said. "Look closely at the bruise pattern."

Alex leaned forward.

"You see that?" she asked.

"A hand print?"

Dorothy slipped her right hand behind her own neck.

Alex spun to face her incredulously. "You saying she held her own head underwater?"

"Looks that way."

"It's also possible that someone else was there that night. If so, they would have had to do one bang-up job to make this look like a self-mutilation/suicide. If you're right, then she knew this person, and knew them well."

Dorothy turned the light on and gathered the pages from the file. She was wearing the reading glasses with the beaded string and for a moment she looked to Alex like an old lady clearing away her winnings after a good

20

night at bingo. She placed the bulging folder back into the filing cabinet.

Alex fished out a folder labeled death certificate.

Dorothy's eyes followed him.

"So I guess believing Diane did this to herself is kinda like believing in the magic bullet that killed Kennedy," Alex said.

Dorothy nodded.

He continued watching her, still not satisfied.

"Look," she said, her eyes narrowing. "Everyone involved, including the sheriff—hell, especially the sheriff—wanted things wrapped up in a neat little package. I guess at the time and under the circumstances, I just wasn't ready to dig any deeper." She looked up at him sheepishly. "It was a mistake, I admit that now, and it's haunted me ever since." She turned away, and her voice took on a different tone. "Alex, I don't need to explain myself to you."

"No. No, you don't." She was right. He knew of the affair. Hell, everyone did. It had been a long time in the making and had begun shortly before Diane's death. For a brief moment, a horrible thought crossed his mind. What if Dorothy and Sheriff Crow were both in on it? Maybe he had been watching too much reality TV, although he had to admit it would have been the perfect crime. One of the most powerful men in town, partnered with the only other person who could expose his crime. He swept away the idea. But the thought had left him with a startling realization. If somehow Diane didn't do this to herself, then her killer was still out there.

Alex stood, shaky at first, but trying hard not to show it. Dorothy walked him out to his cruiser and into a blinding burst of mid-afternoon sun. She held her clipboard up over her eyes.

"Alex, don't let Sheriff Crow know what you're up to."

He gave her a puzzled look.

21

"He still doesn't accept that her passing was anything but a suicide," she said.

"I might not accept it either if I was the sheriff and my wife was murdered."

"Just remember," she said, crossing her arms emphatically, "no matter how much you respect him, no matter how much you look up to him, he'll never be your friend on this one. You're alone."

Alone, Alex thought wryly. Nothing new there.

She walked over and hit him playfully with her clipboard. "Okay, now get outa here before I call the real cops."

Smiling weakly, he removed his nightstick and slid behind the wheel of his cruiser. Sheriff Crow's face had melted away, but he couldn't completely erase the picture of the sheriff's wife in the bath, slumped over, and then as the technicians pulled her out, glaring back at him from two empty sockets. But somehow the residual effect of Dorothy's slide show seemed far worse. That night, standing by the tub, the whole scene had felt surreal. He replayed the pictures of the bathroom in his head. The clinical nature of the slides—some black and white, others stark and blurry—had felt ultra real. And for a reason he couldn't put his finger on, they felt more vivid lately than they ever had.

Chapter 4

By the time Lysander found his first class, the halls had become a wasteland of crumpled papers and loose candy wrappers. He reached for the door, his pulse pounding in his neck. Not only was he late, but now he had to make a grand entrance in front of everyone. He was not getting off to a great start. As he stepped inside, thirty-five sets of eyes scanned him up and down. They were whispering, their low murmurs melding with the buzzing fluorescent lights overhead. Mr. Bennett had just finished writing his name on the blackboard, right under English 412. With an unsteady hand, Mr. Bennett flicked chalk dust out of his salt and pepper hair and fumbled through his jumble of papers.

"Mr. Shore, I presume?"

Lysander nodded.

Mr. Bennett pointed impatiently toward the back corner of the room, near an oversized map of Massachusetts.

"Over there, Mr. Shore."

With the class's attention glued on him, Lysander tripped over some smart ass's outstretched foot and stumbled into the desk in front of him.

The class exploded in a pent-up fit of laughter, no doubt brewing since his big black boots first set foot

23

inside the classroom. Only one girl didn't join them. He slid uneasily into the seat next to her, blushing and feeling microscopically small. He nodded at her in appreciation. Her large eyes flashed knowingly.

"I'll bet you and I are the only Goths within a fifty-mile radius," he whispered.

Her expression changed. "Goth? No, I'm wiccan."

"Oh. Sorry about that." He held out his hand, wondering what that strange feeling was. Déjà vu? "I'm Lysander."

She took it, and Lysander was struck by how delicate her hand was.

"I'm Sam," she said, smiling. "Ignore these assholes. They've never seen anyone with taste before."

A large, sweaty hand landed on Lysander's shoulder from behind, startling him. At the other end of it was a boy in a man's body.

"You let me know if anyone bothers you," the man-boy said.

Lysander nodded quickly, not entirely sure what to think.

Sam leaned over. "That's Derek. He's harmless. At least most of time he is."

Derek smiled. Lysander returned the gesture, not certain he had any other choice.

Slowly, the laughter died down.

Mr. Bennett stood with his clipboard perched atop his belly. "Now since we do have some students who are new to Millingham High, I would like everyone to come up, one at a time, and tell us a little bit about yourselves, your interests, what makes you tick."

The class grew uncharacteristically quiet.

Mr. Bennett fixed his hair again. "The valiant never taste of death but once," he said, quoting Shakespeare. "Are there no brave souls among us? Maybe I should pick one of you at random."

24

The students eyed one another with uncertainty.

"Fine," Mr. Bennett said matter-of-factly. "We'll start with you, then."

Lysander scanned the room, looking for Mr. Bennett's victim.

"Come now, Mr. Shore, tell us a bit about yourself."

Lysander froze and then slowly stood on numb legs, and headed toward the front of the classroom, his hands stuffed deep into his pockets to keep them from shaking.

"Name's Lysander Shore..."

"Louder!" someone shouted from the back.

"My name is Lysander Shore," he said emphatically. "Moved here from Hayward a week ago. Wasn't looking to move really, but then again, we didn't have much choice after some a-hole sent a Molotov cocktail through my bedroom window."

The class stirred uncomfortably.

He was about to elaborate, but he never got the chance. His eye caught sight of a gorgeous blonde seated before him, her hair long and golden and flowing, her skin still bronzed from hot summer days by the pool. He stammered when he saw she was staring right at him, hanging on his every word. His cheeks felt hot. She looked like a goddess.

That's when Lysander noticed the guy sitting beside her, glaring at him, his eyes burning with white hot rage. He had a bulky frame and a brush cut. He looked like he was all business and very little pleasure. In spite of the heat, he was wearing a varsity jacket, his name etched in gold and red lettering: Chad.

"You look at Summer one more time, freak," Chad growled. "Just one more time, I dare ya!" A boy sat next to Chad, broad and tanned just like him: another extra from *CSI: Miami*. Except his lips were pulled back in a dark, menacing grin.

Lysander stood immobilized, feeling the palms of his

25

hands turn wet, and the drumbeat in his neck thump wildly.

"Leave him alone, Chad," the beautiful blonde girl said. She had stuck up for Lysander and his pleasure at what she had done must have showed on his face because the next thing he knew Chad was on his feet, charging.

"Cha—" Lysander never managed to get it all out before something knocked the wind out of him. It was a left hook from Chad, right to the gut and a matching crack in the face to drive the lesson home. Lysander crumpled to his feet, hitting his head on the dusty, cool floor. He could see dust bunnies rolling around under Mr. Bennett's desk.

The next thing he knew Samantha was screaming bloody murder. From the corner of his swelling eye, Lysander could see Derek grappling with Chad. A crowd had gathered around Chad versus the giant boy. Mr. Bennett nudged between them to break it up. A skinny, awkward kid with a healthy dose of acne bent down and helped Lysander off the floor. Chad reached out a hand to grab him, but Derek blocked the move and sent him tumbling over a row of desks. Chad was about to get what he had coming to him and Lysander wanted to be there to cheer Derek on, but Lysander was quickly whisked away. He hadn't said more than two words to either Chad or Derek and it seemed more than enough for one to want him dead and the other to save his life.

• • •

Lysander awoke later that afternoon looking into a pair of yellow eyes. His new cat, Necra, perched on his chest.

"Get off, Nec," he groaned, feeling too sluggish to move her himself.

The cat hissed.

Lysander's eyes snapped open.

26

Necra hissed again. Her lips peeled back, revealing a mouthful of needle-sharp teeth.

"What's wrong girl?" A staggering fear settled over him. His arms were under the covers, trapped. If she wanted to, the cat could flick one paw and blind him. He had never seen her behave like this before. They remained eye to eye for what felt like an eternity. Then Lysander blinked and Necra meowed, almost as if to say 'you lose' and then darted off.

Lysander lay in bed, trying to convince himself to get up, when he heard his mother bellowing at him from downstairs. He ignored her for a second, and then grew curious. Had someone come over?

Please don't let it be Peter Hume again.

He heard a voice accompanying his mother's and it sounded deep and friendly and touched with a southern drawl. He dressed quickly to see who it was. Downstairs, he found his mother by the entrance, her face lit with a great big smile. A giggle escaped her lips, and the sound of it startled Lysander.

The man at the door was old and soft. The first thought that came to Lysander was that he looked like Elmer Fudd.

He lifted his head and smiled at Lysander. Deep lines formed at the corners of his mouth and eyes.

"Lysander, this is our neighbor, Reverend... oh, I'm so sorry, I've forgotten your name."

"Oh, don't be. It's Small... Reverend Nathaniel Small of the Bethlehem Baptist Church. You must be Lysander." Light from outside danced off a silver ring on Reverend Small's hand. In the center was the engraving of a fish. The same one Lysander had seen on so many bumper stickers. How did they go again?

Real men love Jesus
Are you following Jesus this close?
This fish won't fry, will you?

27

"I run a small church down on Tuslow. You folks may have seen it. Looks more like a grocery store than it does a church."

His mother nodded. "I know it. By the fire station."

"That's the one," Small said and flashed a set of mostly straight teeth. "Used to have a big old beauty three streets over, but not two years ago she burned right to the ground. 'Lectrical fire." He seemed to pause to consider this. "Would be awfully great to see you nice people down there on Sunday, so long as there aren't other matters pressing you too hard." He peered in at the packing boxes piled in the living room.
Reverend Small was still smiling when he withdrew a gold pocket watch. He snapped the lid open and gasped at the time.

"Now I'd be lying if I told you nice folks I wasn't partially here on business. Mrs. Grady's dog, from down the street, went off again last night after a raccoon or somethin' and we haven't seen him since. He's one of them husky dogs, about yea high, white coat. You folks seen him 'round?"

"No, we haven't," his mother said, concerned. "But we'll sure keep an eye out."

The reverend's gaze fixed on Lysander's black eye. "I hope you didn't let anyone get the better of you there, son."

His mother slid an arm around him and pulled him closer. "Lysander had a rough first day at school, that's all. You know how kids are."

The reverend smiled knowingly. "Regretfully, I have no children of my own, but our congregation is nearly burstin' with 'em. Most go to the local high school. So chances are good, young man, that you might just know one or two of 'em."

Reverend Small's eyes flicked over his mother's stomach. He grinned sheepishly. "My mother used to tell

28

me that I was bolder than the print on the Sunday Times, so I hope you'll forgive me, but I see you have a little one well on the way."

His mother blushed, cupping the bulge in her tummy. "Seven months," she said proudly.

"And what a beautiful little girl she'll be."

Lysander's mother nodded dreamily. "Yes, she will."

The two of them burst into a gale of laugher that made the reverend's face turn the color of a ripe tomato.

As he bid God bless and turned to leave—this time for real—Lysander couldn't help thinking about something the old man had said, about there being other kids at church.

If that were true, and not a ploy to lure unsuspecting victims to Sunday service, there was a chance that Summer might be there as well. At the very least, it was worth a shot.

Chapter 5

It wasn't more than an hour later that Lysander heard another knock at the door. He answered it and found a panicked figure before him. Sam's eyes were wide with fear and her chest was heaving in greedy gulps of air. Without saying a word, she led him around the side of the house. There, crouched behind a thicket he found Derek. His hands and fingernails were stained by motor oil or tar or... blood? Lysander took a quick step back.

"What happened?"

"Alex, one of my dad's deputies, tried to take Derek in on a parole violation. When Alex tried to push me aside, Derek knocked him out. Look, we don't have time for the details. Can you help us?" Her hands were clasped in front of her, pleading.

He owed Derek. Owed him big time.

"Yeah, of course. You wanna stay in my garage or—"

"No, no," Samantha said impatiently. "We have a place, an old house. We just need to borrow some stuff from you. I couldn't think of anyone else, and we were already on our way here to see if you were okay."

"What do you need?"

"Food, a sleeping bag, flashlight..."

"All right," he said and turned.

"Lysander," she whispered, "please hurry. We don't

30

have long."

Lysander's heart was beating a fierce racket as he went back inside to gather the things Sam had asked for. If you included his first shining day at school, he had known Derek for a grand total of ten minutes. But already both Derek and Sam had stood up for him when he was in trouble. That had to count for something.

• • •

It was drizzling when they arrived on foot. The house looked old and tired, imprisoned by the weeds and overgrowth. Over the years a thick blanket of moss had crept up its walls, until the place didn't look like a house so much as it did a living being. In the front yard, a tall pine resembled a thick and gnarled torso, its leafy branches brushing the roof. One of them intruded through a broken window. Lysander guessed the house was at least fifty years old, maybe even a hundred.

Right below the front door was a gaping hole where the planks of wood from an old porch had rotted away. A yellow ribbon was strung across the door warning all trespassers that the premises were off limits. To rip that yellow tape down and traipse in would be a clear signal to the cops that someone was inside. Might as well plop a sign out front:

Dear Pigs...
We've broken in, come get us.
Signed,
The Dumbasses

Samantha led them around the side of the house to a broken window. Below it was a sad-looking bush, its leaves shriveled and brown. She tossed the bush aside. Behind it, Lysander saw a small crate propped against the

31

wall—a makeshift step ladder.

They slipped in through the window, one at a time.

The unmistakable odor of rotting wood permeated the inside of the house. In Hayward, Lysander had been in abandoned houses before, but none this old or strong-smelling.

"Place has gone to the shits," Derek noted as he tiptoed around, testing how strong the floors were.

"Does it matter?" Samantha replied, her arms folded over her chest. "You're not looking to buy the place. Just lay low for a few weeks till it all blows over. Unless, that is, you want to turn yourself in."

Derek threw Samantha a sharp look.

The floorboards moaned under the added weight as the three came to a large foyer. The smell of old wood was stronger here.

A house like this must be teeming with history, Lysander thought.

His gaze was drawn to the spiraling staircase. He imagined a host of fancy party guests; well-to-do ladies and gentlemen, clad in evening dresses and tuxedos, drinking martinis. He saw streamers and signs that read: "Victory Europe" and another "Victory Japan." He blinked, and the image was gone. That was weird, he thought.

The second room beyond the front foyer looked mostly intact. It had a floor that was relatively dry, and three of its four windows were undamaged. On the opposite wall was an imprint from where a desk once stood. Inside it a broken chair balanced against the wall on its one remaining leg. Derek dropped the duffel bag. It clanked when it hit the floor and he sprang with surprise at the noise. He unpacked excitedly, pulling out a wad of crumpled comic books and a shiny green sleeping bag, and tossed them both aside. He came to an old lantern and examined it. His lips pursed as he whistled his

32

approval. "Wow, what antique store you get this beauty from? Does it work?"

Lysander gave him a look, and Derek went back to grabbing awkwardly inside the now supple duffel bag. Suddenly Derek's eyes grew wide. He withdrew a brown bottle with a black label. Jack Daniels.

Samantha was watching Lysander. "You mentioned something in class before Chad... well, I've been wondering about it." Sam was scratching at the nail polish on her thumb.

"What happened in Hayden, you mean?"

Sam nodded.

In spite of everything they had done for him and the almost eerie sense of ease he had felt being in Sam's company, the truth was they didn't know a thing about each other. Part of Lysander wanted to keep it that way.

"Not much to say," he said finally. "Someone set our place on fire. My dad ran out of the house with my senile grandmother draped over his shoulder like a case of beer. Everyone was safe and sound except for my dog Sandy." Lysander grew quiet and Sam put her hand on his shoulder.

"Oh, I'm so sorry. I shouldn't have brought it up."

Derek took a swig of JD and swung around so his back faced them. "Nice story, but I can beat it."

He hoisted the back of his T-shirt up over his shoulders. Stretching from end to end was a full-color tattoo of a guy on a Harley Davidson riding against the sunset in open desert.

"It's about freedom," Derek said before any of them had a chance to ask.

Lysander and Samantha exchanged a glance.

Derek spoke over his shoulder. "I got it after my brother died. It's a long story, but that's him on the chopper. He and I always talked about someday opening our own bike shop. He was real smart, my brother.

33

Maybe not school-wise, like Sam, but he knew everything there was to know about bikes." He looked up with a strained smile, letting his shirt fall to his waist.

"Can we talk about something happy, please?" Sam pleaded.

Just then a thunderous booming noise from the basement made them all jump.

"What the hell was that?" Sam whispered.

Lysander's eyes darted around the room. "Thunder," he said, hardly believing it.

The fear on Sam's face wasn't going away. She turned to Derek. "Coming here was a mistake," she said to him. "I just didn't know where else you could stay."
"Old houses make noise, Sam," Derek said calmly. "Your nerves are still frayed from earlier. And if it's that old ghost story garbage that's got you all hot and bothered—"

"Ghost?" Lysander cut in. "What ghost?"

Sam shook her head, eyeing Derek. "This house used to belong to a rich family." Her voice was trembling. "The McMurphys. They went back generations. Probably the most prominent family in Millingham. One day they disappeared. All seven of them. Not a trace. The police said they all just up and left. But that never really made much sense to most people in town, since every stitch of clothing they owned was still in their closets. No one really knows what happened to them."

Lysander let out a deep sigh. "Just like the *Mary Celeste*."

Derek's mouth fell open. "The Mary what?"

Lysander spun the bottle of JD on the floor and it made a sound like scuttling claws. "The *Mary Celeste* was a sailing ship from the eighteen hundreds, found adrift in the Atlantic. The ship was in nearly perfect condition. Filled with plates of half eaten food, pipes that were still lit. Except when they boarded her, they couldn't find a soul."

34

"What happened to them?" Derek asked.

Lysander shrugged. "Heck if I know."

"Difference here was that the McMurphys were seen again," Sam said. "At least one of them was. When I was maybe twelve or thirteen, an aunt of mine told me she had seen James McMurphy standing on her lawn." Samantha leaned forward. "She said his cheeks were all sunken in and his skin was gray like an old piece of steak that'd been sitting out too long. She opened her front door, thinking he was sick, that he needed her to call the doctor. She saw he was trying to speak, but when his mouth opened she could see right through to the other side of the road. The back of his head was gone, just as if it had never been there. Said she'd never been so scared in all her life. She slammed her front door, sank to her knees and prayed all night for the good Lord to save her." Sam looked from Derek to Lysander. "Every small town has skeletons in its closet, I think."

Derek stifled a laugh. "Amityville, yes. Salem, maybe. But Millingham? The most boring town in the world? We don't have a shady bone in our whole collective body. I'd stake my life on—"

"Don't say stuff like that, Derek," Samantha cried. "Maybe it isn't true. Maybe it is just a story our parents whipped up to scare us into being good. But what if we're wrong?"

Lysander was thinking about his disturbing encounter with Peter Hume that morning. "*You were warned not to come here.*"

Another crash echoed from the basement. This time louder.

He was pretty sure that whatever had made that noise wasn't a rat.

Chapter 6

Peter Hume was startled by the knock at his door. He glanced up from the heavy leather-bound manuscript he was reading: an original copy of Cotton Mather's *The Wonders of the Invisible World*, perhaps one of six still in existence. A tiny door on the wall sprang open, and from it a mechanical bird danced and chirped. Eight times it called out, dancing and bobbing, before disappearing out of sight.

Little late for visitors, he thought. He slipped into his yellow cardigan, with the initials PH centered over the left breast pocket.

Hume's house, dimly lit and brimming with pockets of shadow, bore a greater resemblance to something out of Ole Worm's *Cabinet of Curiosities* than it did to the home of Zellermann's top insurance rep.

Spotlights drew attention to Peter's growing collection. Historical artifacts he called some of them. Others, he called wonders. A number of his neighbors didn't think much of his hobby. Most weren't sure what to think, and it wasn't just the rank odor of antique upholstery and aging wood that got to them. Nor was it the plush burgundy wall-to-wall carpeting, which only seemed to add to the unsettling illusion that one had taken a dusty step backward in time.

In these last few months, Peter had developed an insatiable appetite for the more macabre aspects of seventeenth-century colonial life. Pursuing disturbing relics from that era was consuming more and more of his time and money.

On one glass shelf sat three dark bottles, each filled with urine, a pinch of hair and three bent pins—a vile concoction brewed over three hundred years ago as a protection against witchcraft. On a table nearby stood an eerily life-like bust of Jesus Christ, chiseled from solid oak, circa 1630. The man selling it was convinced that he had seen the eyes blink late one night. Said it had scared him so bad he could hardly look at it anymore. For that one Peter had paid cash. But it was when he added these last items that Peter's wife thought he had gone too far. They were three-hundred-fifty-year-old implements of torture used to extract confessions. The breast ripper was a particularly gruesome item said to have been used in a dozen witch trials.

Not long ago, those same strange and exotic objects had begun exerting a pull over him, a force that was growing stronger with every passing day. In a weird kind of way they were like children to him and he adored them. But their jealousy was threatening to pull his life apart. They had already done all they could to drive his wife away and what few friends he had. Before long, he would no longer be Peter Hume, salesman first class, but Peter Hume: eternal curator of living antiquities. He could feel his artifacts at night, in the darkness, watching him. Even the ones without eyes. They watched closest of all. And just yesterday he had heard one of them speak, hadn't he? Sounded like something out of a child's nursery rhyme and he had felt an odd sensation of pride at hearing it, as any father would, hearing his son speak for the first time.

He's coming...

37

It was the bust with Jesus' warm and loving face that had said the words, its eyes, half whites, peering up at him.

"Who is coming?" he had asked, feeling a touch foolish.

And that was when Jesus showed him Millingham, not the way it was now. The way it was hundreds of years ago. He showed him a man with a black gown and long bony fingers. Then he showed him a witch, writhing in blistering agony. Of course, Peter hadn't believed such things at first. How was any of this even possible? But since then Jesus had shown him lots of things. Things that had made it all clear and they had grown close, as any two people would who spent as much time together as they did. Because time was all Peter had, now that his wife was getting ready to leave him.

It was Jesus, in the end, who had told him to warn Lysander. To tell him, he was who the dark man really wanted. That Peter would be safe if he just hung low.

The bell rang again and Peter went to the door. He was alone for the moment, and because of this his body was calm and relaxed. He unlatched and opened the door.

His demeanor changed at once.

He and his new guest exchanged greetings, and Peter Hume invited his guest in for tea. Peter closed the door behind him and turned the lock. He was thinking about what excuse he might use to save himself from a long drawn-out visit.

His guest's eyes were shining.

The odd, expectant look on his guest's face did not go unnoticed. Observation was Peter's strong suit: his job at Zellermann's demanded it.

Once in the living room, the warning bells became stronger. Not sure what to do, Peter went to the kitchen, where he put a kettle on the stove and waited for it to boil. With his guest sitting at the kitchen table, things

38

didn't seem so bad. No more flashing red lights in his head, no sirens. That was one of the kinks with being alone all the time. Your mind was left to wander and the longer its leash, the wilder the ideas that stuck in your head. A few minutes later, they returned to relax in the living room. His guest was examining one of the breast rippers when Peter caught sight of Jesus' face. But this wasn't the face he knew. The face he had gazed at while they spoke for hours on end. No, this face was twisted and angry. Something had done away with the Jesus he knew and replaced it with this new one. This demented one.

His guest said something and Peter tried to force a laugh through his bubbling fear, a skittish kind of laugh that hung in the air.

When his guest approached and laid his hands on Peter's face, his body tensed. Jesus' mouth opened, and through the gaping hole came crackling static.

The room around him began to dim and with it Peter was suddenly outside himself, looking on like a voyeur through a foggy window. On the floor laying still was his guest, but it was clear, even to Peter that some part of this man had come slithering inside of him.

"I did what you said," he thought frantically, looking at Jesus' twisted face on the table behind him. "I laid low like you said, but he found me."

And then the realization slowly began to dawn that his guest had known all along. That he had only been bidding his time until that final critical piece had fallen into place. A piece that had come rolling into town only days before. A piece by the name of Lysander Shore.

Peter saw something gleaming in his hand—his physical hand. A knife, its blade long and sharp, winking shards of light at him from the breast ripper's display case. The blade touched the flesh of his left wrist and to Peter's surprise he felt the cold steel waiting to bite him just as

39

though he were doing it himself. The knife rocked back and forth splitting the flesh so that it looked like a bloody eye staring back at him. But his real eyes, the ones controlled by that monster watching now with sick delight, were white bulging orbs.

Blood ran down his forearm and fell to the floor in a thick stream. The pain was unbelievable and Peter was shrieking now, not just with agony but with the certainty that he was about to die and the sound of his screams were flat and dead in this new place. When he felt the blade begin cutting his other wrist, Peter could only hope that it would all be over soon. He had no idea that it was just beginning.

Chapter 7

Back at the McMurphy house, Derek was having trouble getting the lantern going.

"This thing have any gas?" he said, striking a match against the side of the box. The match burst into flame.

That was when Lysander heard a loud click and the room became shrouded by a deep orange haze.

There was a swooshing sound and Lysander was suddenly outside of himself, swimming, an astronaut spiraling through a vast expanse of empty watery space. The feeling was strangely familiar. The thought of death crossed his mind quickly and then vanished... he knew he wasn't dead, he could still think. Where am I? The corridor, he thought. The last thing I saw was the corridor... Two figures were hunched over him. "Mom?" he screamed... no, not Mom... this one was different. The other figure was larger like his father, but that one too felt different. He looked down and he saw a third person lying on the floor. Someone dressed in black, with big black boots covered in white dust.

Sudden blackness descended and then intense movement. He was moving at the speed of light. Trees and houses flickered by. Below him appeared two men standing in a dark living room. The shorter one buttoned up in a yellow cardigan and bent over to slide his feet into a pair of slippers. But the other didn't feel like a man at all. It felt more like a shadow pretending to be a man: something terrible hidden inside a shroud of blackness. The shadow turned and seemed to look up at him. A lump of charcoal without a single distinguishing feature... except its eyes. They were milky white and cold, like two distant stars in the vastness of space. A glimmer of light was refracted from the shadow's pocket. There was something there. Something metallic and shiny. The handle of a knife? Lysander wondered as a sharp chill shot through his veins.

The shorter man in the yellow cardigan motioned and walked into the kitchen. The shadow followed, leaving part of a shoe print behind, as if it had stepped in mud outside and was tracking it through the room. Panic gripped Lysander. Couldn't this guy see he had let a monster into his house? It wasn't trying to sell him a subscription to *Sports Illustrated* or get him to change his long-distance carrier. This thing, whatever it was, meant to kill him and Lysander was powerless to do anything about it.

The kitchen door swung open and the two men walked into the living room, laughing, the thin man with the cardigan first. They stopped by the fireplace. Then the dark man cupped the other's face. Cardigan squirmed uneasily and then settled, his eyes blinking with mute expectation. They're about to kiss, Lysander thought, puzzled. Then suddenly, the smaller man's eyes grew wide with terror and he reached for the shadow, only to have the shadow slip away and crumple to the ground. Now only the man in the cardigan was standing, but there was something different about him. Even from far away Lysander could see the difference, but didn't quite believe it. His eyes had become milky white. Somehow, the shadow had snuck into him like a fox in a henhouse. Cardigan leaned over the shadow-man, fell into his coat

42

and removed a long blade. Lysander watched with morbid fascination, utterly perplexed by the display. The thin man rolled up his sleeves and brought the blade to his wrists and started cutting. Then he cut the other wrist. The top button of his shirt was undone and he reached up with both bloody hands and ripped six buttons off so that his shirt flapped open. With the edge of the knife, he carved something into his chest, something Lysander couldn't quite make out.

The floor at his feet was now slick with blood. He shuffled over to the table, careful not to slip and reached for a strange-looking bust. Hefting it into the air, he paused for a moment, admiring it, and then brought it arcing down onto his own face again and again, until there was nothing recognizable of the man left. A stranger was destroying himself before Lysander's very eyes. He was utterly disgusted by the spectacle before him. But somehow Lysander couldn't turn away.

Shrieking, the man staggered and then collapsed to his knees. It was finally over, Lysander hoped, but he was wrong. The thin man's fingers crawled up his face and plunged them into his eye sockets. That was when Lysander finally looked away.

A moment later, the man collapsed and lay still.

An intense chill suddenly gripped Lysander. A gray mist was forming on the floor. The ghost, the creature, whatever the hell it was, was leaving the thin man's corpse and moving purposely toward the guest's form lying prostrate on the floor. They united and the fingers of the shadow's left hand began to do a subtle dance. The movement went up to his arm, then to his head. He propped himself up on his shoulder, admiring his work. Suddenly, the shadow's head snapped in Lysander's direction. His head perked up and for a moment it seemed as though he was sniffing the air. Sniffing for a scent he had found floating past him in the breeze.

Invisible icy tentacles began snaking out, probing blindly like something used to dark and damp places.

Lysander backed away, but the tentacles were closing in.

Just then he felt another presence and he tried his best to listen in spite of his gnawing fear. It sounded like a wolf, snarling low and threatening.

The tentacles approached and the growling turned to vicious snapping. Lysander swore he could hear the sound of jaws clamping shut, gnashing at dead air.

Someone was calling his name. Lysander... Lysander... Lysander. Sudden movement, like being pulled through a glass tube at high speed. Then blackness and pain. The pain racked his whole body with such intensity he couldn't remember when he ever felt anything so real. His eyes opened to a dim room. Dim was good. Anything was better than orange. Later he would remember only flashes.

Samantha was above him, talking to him softly.

Chapter 8

Alex turned left on Lincoln and into Wallace's Motorcycle Repair. Gravel crushed under his tires. He stopped in front of a steel door that framed a dilapidated sign which read "employees only."

The door swung open with a screech, and a tiny bell rang overhead. A round, misshapen man in dirty overalls glanced up from behind a large TV; antennas stretched out like the feelers of some mutant insect.

"Deputy," the man said nonchalantly. He had a cool, unhurried air to him as though the trifling world of mortal concerns was far behind him. He stood and waddled over to Alex, favoring his right leg.

Alex took off his hat. "I'm looking for Derek."

Wallace examined his watch, as though there was a new dial there he hadn't seen before.

"Well, never showed up fer work last night. Does that sometimes, that boy. Never a call or nothin', just plain doesn't show up." There was a whistle when he spoke. He looked up at Alex and his bottom lip hung down, revealing a row of empty spaces. "He's a darn good mechanic, so I let the little things go once in a while. Why? He in trouble again?"

"You could say that."

Wallace leaned forward, eyes fixed on Alex's nose. "He

45

do that to you?"

Alex shifted, and his heavy boots scuffed the wood floor. "Derek violated the terms of his parole. I was trying to apprehend him—"

"Deputy, I know Derek's a big boy, but he doesn't fight unless he's got to."

"He did today and we're looking for him now."

Wallace turned back at the TV, seemingly enthralled. "That's too bad. He's a good kid you know. One of the best mechanics I ever seen." Wallace wiped his nose with his hand again. "What you gonna do to him?"

"Depends. If he turns himself in, we'll go easy. He assaulted an officer, but we may be able to work something out." Alex was lying through his teeth, of course, but the old man had to think that Derek would be coming back to work when this was all over or else he would never cooperate.

Wallace remained silent.

"You have any idea where we might find him?" Alex asked. "We've talked to his grandmother and she has no idea—"

The room exploded with Wallace's laughter. "That ol' bitch?" He was fidgeting with the rabbit ears over the TV. "She don't know which end is up. She was ugly when Donny Thomas asked her to marry him and she's even uglier now. Not that that's possible." He flashed a toothless smile. "No, Deputy, I'm not sure where that boy is at. He may be with the sheriff's daughter."

"She's not talking." It remained unsaid, but both men knew that you didn't use the same kind of police tactics on the sheriff's daughter as you might on a regular citizen. A certain amount of delicacy was required.

Wallace's head snapped back and he exploded with phlegmy laughter again.

"Maybe you should talk to Mrs. Crow. Derek used to talk about her all the time. Talked me nearly to death

46

once, he did, told him to keep quiet or I'd—"

"Cliff," Alex said, dimly aware of the informality. "Mrs. Crow is dead."

He tore away from the TV for a moment. "Oh, sorry to hear that. Guess I woulda known if I read the papers or kept into other people's business. Just that she might have known where he was hiding. Derek talked about her all the time. They was close, you know."

A strange expression flickered across Alex's face. He had never known Diane was friendly with Derek, or any of Samantha's friends, for that matter.

"Close?" Alex asked nonchalantly. "In what way?"

Wallace's eyes found Alex's again. "Maybe I shouldn't have said…"

"Too late for that now. The circumstances of Mrs. Crow's death are still being investigated. There are signs… let's just say the case is still open."

The old man looked worried now. "Was she murdered, that poor woman?"

"Maybe."

Wallace raised an eyebrow.

"So what do you know about Derek and Mrs. Crow?"

Wallace stood with some difficulty, wiped his hands on his overalls, and then braced himself against the counter. "Derek says he used to go over there a lot when the sheriff wasn't home. Says he and Samantha were good friends, but that he and Mrs. Crow were better friends. That she used to give him money sometimes."

The old man fell silent.

Alex asked him, "That it?"

"No," he added reluctantly. "We were working on a bike together once, damn chain kept coming off, one of them foreign pieces a crap, you know. Anyhow, he told me that Samantha's mum kept askin' him over when Samantha wasn't there, but he'd always say no 'cause he had to work. But you know how women can get when

47

they got somethin' in their sights. So she kept insistin', till finally he got tired of saying no. Kid used to say that when that woman wanted something, she dang never gave up till she got it."

Alex shook his head, unable to hide the amazement on his face.

"Used to say she was real rough with him. Used to tie him up and slap his face before they… before she put it to him, as they say."

The words rang in Alex's head. He knew what was coming, the way you see an offspeed baseball, but it still nearly knocked him out when it finally hit.

"One time the sheriff came home early and Derek had to jump off the second-floor balcony." He saw the shock on Alex's face and added. "You know the way kids are. I just always assumed he was making it up."

"Yeah, he probably was," Alex lied, hoping the old man wouldn't notice the way his eyes had become thick and watery. "Anything else?"

"Sure, lots. Said she gave him a key to the house after they had done it a few times. Showed it to me, but there ain't no way anyone can tell one key from another. He did seem pretty proud of himself."

"And…"

"Well, the boy came into work pretty upset a few months later. Wouldn't tell me why. Think I was the only one he could tell about what was going on."

The old man cocked one of the antennae, then adjusted it lower. "You know how it is when you have a big secret: It's gotta come out sometime. One day he comes in and tells me she's called it off. Said her and her husband were trying to work things out. Can't remember ever seeing him that upset."

Alex put his hat back on. He couldn't believe all this had been going on. "Anything else you can tell me?"

"Truth is, I have no idea where he might be, Deputy.

48

Could be three states away by now, especially if he got himself a set of wheels. Like I told you, those hands of his were made for fixin' bikes. He's a darn good mechanic."

Alex thanked the old man and opened the door to leave. The tiny bell rang overhead. Before the door could close, he heard ol' man Wallace shouting from inside. "If you find him, you tell him he still has a job if he wants—" The door slammed shut, muffling the rest.

Alex started his cruiser and drove away.

Chapter 9

"Am I in the hospital?"

Lysander's mother crossed her arms over her belly, an expression of dismay plastered all over her face.

Samantha's eyes grew wide. "A nice man carried you home from the park and then I called the ambulance. Your parents have been worried to death over you."

Yeah, sure they have, Lysander thought.

The door opened and two men entered the room; the first wore a doctor's white lab coat, the second corduroy pants and a loose sweater. They both looked at Samantha. Reluctantly, she leaned over Lysander and whispered, "I'm glad you're all right." Then she rose and left the room.

In so many words, the man in the white coat proceeded to tell Lysander that he had suffered a seizure that very well might have killed him. The doctor's round, pudgy face made Lysander think of old women and how they loved pinching the cheeks of little children.

"Lysander," said the doctor as he turned to indicate the man standing next to him: quiet and casually dressed. "I've spoken to your parents and we think you should speak with Mr. Avery here. He's not a shrink. And he's not here to judge you. He's a therapist and he just wants to talk."

Avery approached the side of Lysander's bed slowly and threw the others a look which told them he wanted to be alone with Lysander. The others shuffled out of the room in a ragged line. The doctor was the last to go, shutting the door behind him.

Avery held out his hand. "Hello, Lysander. You can call me Jack."

Lysander kept his hands by his side.

Avery sat down. "Lemme make something clear to you. I'm not here to be your buddy, Lysander. Nor am I interested in whether or not you like me. You have a very serious condition. A lot of people don't get up and walk away from what you have, and the doctors here aren't sure what's causing it."

Lysander studied the deep lines in the man's face. He seemed weathered, beaten up by the world, but there was a wisdom hidden in those eyes that he couldn't deny.

What did he need Avery for when he knew perfectly well how the problem had started?

It might have been years ago, but the pain was still fresh in Lysander's mind. His old man had been sitting by himself in the kitchen with the lights out. The phone was off the hook, and his father was gripping the receiver in one hand.

Lysander stood there, not sure what to do.

His father ignored him until he realized he wasn't going to leave. When his gaze rose and met Lysander's he could see that his eyes were puffy and mapped with red lines.

Lysander went to the fridge. He would make his own dinner.

"Your little brother died today, Lysander."

He froze as he reached for the processed cheese.

"Dr. Johnson says a miscarriage in the third trimester could have killed her."

He didn't look back. His tiny face crumpled.

"She must have fallen when she got the call." His father

51

paused, tilted the whiskey back and then crushed an ice cube between his back molars. "The fall must have..."

The cheese fell to the floor with a clean slap. Lysander half turned, his voice quavering.

"It wasn't my faul—"

"Not your... really? Then whose fault was it, son? Your school principal calls saying you've accused the counselor of trying to molest two kids. You're a ten-year-old boy, for Christ's sake. What do you know about sex? You shoulda seen your mother's face."

His father tilted the neck of the bottle, topping his glass with a generous dollop and then some.

"I don't think you understand the impact a stupid joke like that could have. You might have ruined the career of a respected family man."

The fridge door was still open, and cool air tickled his cheek.

"But Simon Shaw said it happened in Mr. McDowell's office when no one else was around. Then Adrian Keslaw said almost the same thing, but both of them were too scared to do anything about it. I felt like I had to." His face fell. "I knew you and Mom would never understand."

His father sounded deathly tired. "If you'd just come to us in the first place, none of this would have happened. The baby... and now they're talking about firing the man and suspending you if you're lying. Goddammit, Lysander, are you lying? Is this just another one of your make-believe stories?"

"No," Lysander screamed. Fresh tears were streaming down his face.

"I don't believe you."

"But it's true, I swear it."

Glenn eyed his drink sullenly. "Get out of my sight, Lysander. I don't want to see your face right now."

Lysander didn't move.

52

"That's it, no dinner for you, get right up those stairs and go straight to bed."

But he couldn't leave just yet. Somehow in Lysander's young mind, to allow his father to dismiss him as a liar would be to prove him right.

His father rose to his full menacing height.

Lysander was suddenly aware that Sandy, their golden retriever, was at his side, looking up at him with her great sunken eyes. Glenn's booming voice had alarmed her. His father crossed the room. "You may never have felt the back of my hand, but I promise if you don't get up those stairs this minute, I'll slap you so fucking hard!"

Lysander's whole body was gripped with terror. When his father saw he had no intention of moving, his expression darkened even more. He lunged and grabbed his son by the scruff of his collar. Sandy let out a low growl, but his father wasn't going to stop until Lysander went up those stairs, even if it meant dragging him like a sack of dirty laundry. He clasped his other hand around Lysander's tiny arm and Sandy jumped between them, shielding Lysander with her great furry body, her teeth bared, that low growl now a menacing snarl. For several moments his father stood eye to eye with Sandy, the animal's hot breath lapping against his nose. Even enraged, Lysander's father had the sense to back off.

"I'm gonna put that fucking dog down!" he yelled.

As he walked upstairs, his father screamed after him: "You've cursed this family, Lysander. I don't know how or why but you have. Since the day you were born you've brought us nothing but pain." His father's words had felt like so many razors, slicing away chunks of his flesh.

From that day on, he had accepted responsibility for his mother's miscarriage, and he decided never to speak of it again. Since that day there was an empty chasm between him and his father. He might not have been able to articulate it in words at the time, but that day a part of

53

him had died.

These were wounds Lysander would never tell anyone about. But what surprised him most was that Avery did most of the talking, about his own life, his schooling, the old MGB he spent time restoring. Lysander couldn't help but notice a sense of grief—or was it guilt?—behind those eyes, filled before with such calm and wisdom. Avery had battle scars too. If nothing else, for the first time in his life, Lysander was happy he wasn't alone.

Chapter 10

"Then what *do* you want?" Samantha said challengingly.

She and Alex were the only ones in the Millingham police station. He had seen Sam coming out of the hospital and convinced her it was in her best interest to come with him.

He poked a finger in the air. "First, I want you to swear you'll never tell your father what happened when I... when Derek was resisting arrest. Second, I don't want you to think of me as your enemy. I'm not all that much older than you. If you tried, we could become friends... and who knows what else?" Alex swallowed. His mouth was dry.

Samantha's arms folded over her chest. She had felt his gaze dropping to her breasts more than once in the last few minutes. "And—"

"Consider it and I'll call off the dogs. I stop actively looking for Derek. If he leaves town then so be it. Just as long as he doesn't show his face around here anymore."

"So he's exiled?"

"For his own good, yes. Look, I know he's a friend of yours, but the kid's bad news. He's a troublemaker. He's gotten you into trouble more than once already. Consider yourself lucky your dad's the sheriff or you'd be wanted too."

55

She sighed heavily and rubbed her temples with the pads of her fingers. "Can you take me home please? I'm gonna be late for school."

"Not till your dad gets here."

How long will that be? She wanted to know. His deputy was creeping her out. Sam fiddled with a pencil on Alex's desk.

"Want something?" he asked, his hands sliding into his pockets.

She looked up at him. "Uh, sure. Got any Coke?"

Alex stiffened.

"Coca-Cola, Alex," she said, not hiding her irritation. "Wouldn't mind something to eat." She was suddenly aware of the empty feeling in her belly.

"Granola bar?" He was being nice to her now, but she knew his whole speech had been a ploy. Alex hated Derek so much, she knew he'd never stop looking for him. The satisfaction of slamming his ass behind bars would be too great.

She nodded.

"Be right back."

She watched him leave the room. Finally she was alone and the idea that struck her then was nothing short of brilliant.

If Alex had a file on Derek, maybe there was a way she could look inside and adjust the evidence against him. Like the time the receptionist had gone for lunch and Samantha had changed all of Derek's grades from Ds to B+s. It wouldn't be that hard, would it? His desk was so organized and with him downstairs making her sandwich what was the danger? She giggled with excitement. This might just work. The file folders on his desk were arranged alphabetically. She fingered through the tabs and found lots of names, but no Derek Thomas.

Next she would try his desk drawers. He had three of them. One that pulled out over her lap and two deep

56

bucket drawers by her left leg. She tried the shallow one and found it locked. Damn! Then she tried the one by her knee. It slid open easily enough. Inside was an Eldon filing unit. Could this guy get any more anal? If her heart wasn't beating so fast she might have let out a squeal of laughter. She leafed through the files, but still she found nothing.

She went to the second drawer and found more of the same. For a moment she was dumbfounded. Alex must have a file around here somewhere. At last, her focus came to rest on the shallow drawer by her thighs. In the center was a brass keyhole. Beads of sweat dotted her forehead. There had to be some way of getting it open. She lifted a corner of his desk calendar, but there was no key. She scanned Alex's desk and noticed a coffee cup filled with dozens of elastic bands and paper clips. She reached her fingers inside and wiggled them around. She heard a clinking sound. Her eyes lit up. She fumbled a tiny key out of the cup and slid it past the lips of the keyhole. She turned it clockwise and heard the tumblers release.

Sam jumped when she heard Alex's footsteps thumping noisily up the stairs. Alex appeared with a granola bar and an apple juice. His brow furrowed. "What's wrong?"

Think fast, dammit!

"I hate apple juice. Have any OJ?" she asked sheepishly.

He rolled his eyes and left again.

Sam wrenched the desk drawer open. Inside were two folders. The first was marked Derek Thomas. But the second one she hadn't expected and seeing it nearly sucked all the air out of her lungs. On it was a single name: McMurphy.

She slid the McMurphy folder out. Her hands trembled as she peeled back the tan flap. She leafed through the pages. None of them were making a whole lot of sense to

57

her. It looked like a crime-scene breakdown. There was a date too: November 1965.

We found most of the victims by the dining room table in an advanced state of decomposition. Judging by the odor and the stiffness of the bodies, they had been there for at least a week. Flies and cockroaches everywhere. Appears that the perpetrator assaulted the victims from behind with a three-foot wood chopping axe as they were seated at the table. In three cases, the victims were decapitated. Thomas McMurphy was found on the ground, pinned to the floor by an axe blow which appears to have severed the sternum and punctured the right lung. The victims all appear to be members of the McMurphy family. Upstairs, in one of the bedrooms we found the remains of James McMurphy. The man appeared to have died from a single self–inflicted gunshot wound through the mouth...
Sheriff Donald Townsend

Millingham Police Dept.

Sam's jaw fell open. Rumors had circulated for years that something awful had happened to the McMurphys. But the thought that the family's bright and shining star, James, had hacked them to pieces seemed unbelievable. He had been some kind of businessman, she remembered, with a hand in construction, bunch of buildings in Millingham, including her school. He was reputed to have brought their fledgling town into the twentieth century.

Then something else caught her eye. Below the Sheriff's crime-scene statement were two handwritten notations, penciled in almost as afterthoughts. The first read:

Surely there will be pressure from the highest levels to keep this quiet.

But it was the second that made the flesh on her arms tighten:

The lacerations to James McMurphy's arms, chest and face seem, in my opinion, inconsistent with suicide: See Medical Examiner's report. Note: could there have been someone else in the house that night?

58

She was thinking about her mother and the details of her death when she heard footsteps rapidly ascending the stairs. Alex was on his way back from the kitchen. Samantha shuffled the pages back into place and shoved the file into the drawer. She closed it and jammed the key in the lock. It wouldn't turn though. In her panic she had closed the drawer on part of the folder, and it was blocking the locking mechanism. Alex was nearly there. Heart pounding, Sam yanked the drawer open, pushed the file in properly, and then locked it. She dropped the key in the coffee cup and swore. The key landed on top of the elastic bands, not underneath as she had found it. She was about to fix it when Alex appeared, out of breath and looking sour.

"Apple's all we have, sorry."

She smiled politely, hoping he wouldn't notice the sweat on her brow. Did she look as pale as she felt?

"You okay?" he asked, genuine concern in his voice.

"I'm not sure," she said, grimacing. She *had* been famished when she'd sent Alex off to get her something to eat from the kitchen, but now, after all this, the only thing on her mind was phoning Lysander and telling him what she'd found. Bizarre lacerations. Questionable suicides. It was an almost preposterous theory, wasn't it? The possibility that there was some connection between her mother's death and James McMurphy's nearly fifty years before. But what if? There had been a reference in the police report to McMurphy's autopsy. They would need a copy of that. If for nothing else than to rule it out completely.

An image of her mother's face appeared just then. Her features were pale and waxen. Her mother seemed frightened. But of what?

59

Chapter 11

The stench spilling out from his grandmother's room was sweet and acidic with ammonia, far too much like a wet diaper for his liking. If she had sprung another leak, there was no way Lysander was gonna get stuck changing her. Not again. Besides, his grandmother weighed more than he did.

Feeding his grandmother had become something of a non-paying part-time job from hell. It wouldn't have been so bad if he could drop the food by her bed and let her do the rest, but she could barely go to the bathroom by herself, let alone eat.

Though it seemed hard to believe, she hadn't always been fat. In a wicker chest by Glenn's bed, his father kept an old family album, one of those fancy jobs in black and white where each picture is held in place with tiny white tabs. Back in the day, she had been a real beauty. After the war, a year before she would meet her future husband—Corporal Allan Thomas Shore—she had won a handful of beauty pageants all over Chesterfield County, Illinois. She was sixteen then and the envy of every girl in town.

What now lay heaped before him was a frightening contradiction to those old family albums.

In fact, just seeing her sometimes was enough to spook

him. His mother did what she could to keep the room clean, and yet it always seemed a disaster. He set the tray on the table beside her bed. Great pad for a vampire, he thought and tried to laugh. But the thought triggered an uncomfortable feeling he couldn't shake.

What the hell could she do anyway? Reach up and grab him? He looked at his grandmother, a bulbous lump under the blankets. The top of her head was barely exposed: a mat of bluish curls. He placed a gentle, tentative hand on what he guessed was her rounded shoulder and shook her lightly. "Grandma?" The mass didn't budge.

He shook her again, this time a little harder, and still there was no response. "Grandma, you dead?" he muttered, realizing how foolish he must sound.

"Granny Pearl, it's time for your breakfast."

Lysander leaned over his grandmother and began to peel the blanket away from her face. As he tugged at the covers, he half-expected to find a bloated mess staring back at him. It didn't make much sense really, considering that sometime last night his mother had probably come in to feed her. The blanket came away and he saw that his grandmother's face was whole. Her eyes open and staring blankly at the wall behind him.

"Whasmelitno." Her lips hardly moved now when she spoke.

Lysander stood, staring at the wall, wondering what it was she was seeing.

"It's dark in here, isn't it?" Lysander heard himself say. "Should we open the curtains?"

Grandma blinked.

Lysander rose and went to the heavy curtains that were blocking out the sun. They could make this place so dark sometimes it was impossible...

"Heeskhumin."

Lysander stopped, his hand gripping the curtain. He

61

could feel the dense fabric. His entire body was vibrating. Blood was rushing through his veins.

Sure Grandma didn't have her dentures in, but Lysander could have sworn she'd just said 'scuming' or was it something else?

He's coming.

The room was quiet. Except he could hear his grandmother breathing, that same labored breathing he heard late at night as he lay in bed, with the lights out. He was suddenly thinking about Peter Hume again and the cryptic warning he had given Lysander.

"Grandma…?" His voice quivered.

Her head turned and she looked right at him.

"Heeskhumin!"

The hairs on Lysander's arms were standing on end and he could feel the room pulling away from him, his grandmother's prone body telescoping into the black shapeless distance. The left side of his brain, the logical side, the know it all, swooped in to save him.

You didn't think those were real words she was speaking, did you? Can't say I blame you, but the truth is that wasn't anything other than your mind's attempt at imposing some semblance of order on the chaos swirling around you. The way Jesus freaks always seem to find His portrait in everything from dried leaves to toilet paper.

Jesus freak or not, it took him several minutes before he found the courage to circle the bed again to face her, and when he did she was sleeping peacefully.

He had read a book not so long ago where the author had suggested that people with low mental capacity lacked the psychic defenses to fend off the evil spirits always waiting patiently in the shadows for a chance to slip in and take over. He'd used a hog farmer in Virginia as a case study, but Lysander had slammed the book shut then and never opened it again. Bunch of bullshit, he had said. He wondered now with some annoyance how the thought had seeped into his stream of consciousness.

62

● ● ●

It was between math and English when Samantha told Lysander what she had found in Alex's desk.

"Fifty years ago, this guy McMurphy killed his family with a wood chopping axe and then blew his brains out."

Lysander took a step back. "That's heavy shit! But why would Alex have that locked away in his desk?"

"Good question. Maybe because if it ever got out, the town would go ape-shit. There was a sheriff, a guy named Townsend. He said he found a bunch of wounds on McMurphy's body which struck him as odd. He wondered if there hadn't been more to it."

"Wounds?" Lysander's ears perked up. He thought of the disturbing dream he had the other night, the one in which the man had disassembled his face with a block of wood. "What kind of wounds?"

"That's where you come in." Sam smiled coyly at him.

"I think I've known you long enough already to know what that smile means, and it's bad news. Stop batting your eyelashes at me. Stop!" He was trying not to laugh.

She reached into her locker and pulled out a binder. "I'd owe you big time."

"Again? But why me?"

"If I could get you a job at the medical examiner's office, you might be able to get your hands on McMurphy's autopsy report."

"Oh God, Sam, I don't know."

"Come on, I've been there before. Dorothy's got 'em all in boxes just sitting around. Nothing to it. And besides, you love all that death stuff."

"But why do you care so much about McMurphy all of a sudden?"

Sam grew sullen. "I have my reasons."

That wasn't much of a reason. "I'll think about it."

63

Samantha sighed.

Lysander licked a pair of dry lips. "Hey, have you seen Chad around?"

"No. Last I heard he was suspended."

Lysander tried to hide his relief. "What about Summer?"

Sam rolled her eyes. "Heck if I know! What do you care about Summer anyhow?"

Lysander blushed.

"Oh shit, you don't—"

"No I don't," he lied. "Well, I have noticed her looking at me."

"Lysander, she's probably wondering what planet you're from."

"I don't think so. But let's just say for the sake of argument that I did like her. What could a guy like me do about it?"

"Uh, you could pack your bags and run away."

They laughed, but a knot had formed in Sam's belly that wasn't going

away. "Lysander, you have a lot to learn about women."

His eyes dropped to the books in his arms. "I know."

"Women are complex. First things first: If you want them to notice you, you have to make them jealous..."

"Really?"

"For sure!"

A light shone in his eyes. "Maybe you're right!"

"Wha—"

"You could help me. Show me the ropes. You said it yourself, women are naturally jealous. Help me make Summer jealous. Then she's mine."

"But Chad'll kill you before the two of you even hold hands."

"Sam, you want me to go find your stupid autopsy report? That's right, you do, don't you? Then you'll do this for me."

64

The knot in Sam's belly had become a ten-pin bowling ball. "All right."

The bell rang.

Lysander turned to head for class "Sam, you're the best!"

Chapter 12

Derek hobbled up the creaky stairs of the old McMurphy house in search of a bathroom, wondering in the back of his mind whether Lysander was all right. Of course he was, he chided himself. He's with Sam.

He reached the top and surveyed his surroundings. A hallway stretched out before him. At the end of it was a door and for reasons Derek wasn't entirely certain of, he hated that room. It seemed to be pulling away from him, retracting like some living organism. He could feel the hairs on the back of his neck rise into hackles. An odd noise was trickling out from its edges, like the sound of hissing static on a radio.

But this house hasn't had power in years, right?

That was when he remembered the dream he'd had last night. He was being attacked by a shark, its teeth gnashing the air inches from his face. He could see rotting flesh between its teeth, and the smell was like a slaughterhouse on a hot summer's day. But it hadn't really been a shark. No, it had been a man, he was sure of that now—with pointed teeth, milky, pupiless orbs for eyes and a face, painted up to look like a circus clown.

Derek stopped before the door at the end of the hall and pressed his ear against the decaying wood. Silence. He turned the handle and pushed the door open. He had

66

the overwhelming feeling that something behind that room had been conspiring from the moment he ascended the staircase to lure him inside.

He entered. The room was dark, lit by a single octagonal stained-glass window which bathed him in a red glow. The corners were wreathed in cobwebs.

Doesn't every soggy house need at least one dry room? he wondered nervously.

On Derek's right were the torn-out guts of an old bed. Near the bed was an old dusty fireplace. Furniture was piled everywhere. Derek found his attention drawn toward an old rolltop desk in the corner. He went to it and pushed the top up. It slid open easily enough. The desk was filled with papers, some of them see-sawing to the ground around him.

How old was this stuff? he wondered vaguely.

Older than his parents had been when they died, he knew. His fingers registered something hard lying amongst the loose pages. He pulled it out. It was a journal of some kind. He fanned open the pages, kicking up a cloud of dust. Derek let out several violent sneezes. He wiped his hand against his pants and peeled the cover back. When he saw who the book belonged to, it nearly fell from his hands. At the top of page one, in highly stylized script, was the owner's name.

James Andre Patrick McMurphy

A door somewhere in the house slammed shut. The noise startled Derek so much that he nearly slipped on the loose papers piled at his feet.

Lysander? Sam?

He fought back the urge to call out their names. What if it wasn't them? He crammed the journal down the back of his pants and crept along the hallway and down the stairs to where he kept his things. Someone was in the house. He could hear them clearly, shuffling about in the back somewhere. He gathered what little he had and

67

threw the rest into the green sleeping bag. He tossed that into the closet by the foot of his bed. Derek was under no pretense that he was the world's smartest person, but he knew enough to cover his tracks. He was pulling on his grease-stained jeans and shirt when he heard footsteps in the room next to him. He withdrew to the front door, his heart climbing into his throat. He pushed the door open and closed it carefully behind him. Then he took off. But less than two paces away, his foot sank into the rotted hole in the front porch which sent him careening ass over teakettle. He tripped mostly because he had caught sight of the police cruiser parked out front, its engine still ticking down.

Despite the searing pain in his shoulder as he landed, he was on his feet a second later, racing past the cruiser. He was heading back to town. He'd rather take his chances there than spend another second in the belly of that rotting house.

Chapter 13

Lysander's first impression of Avery's basement office was that his cleaning lady must have jumped off a cliff in despair. Books were piled everywhere, throwing off waves of mildew and wet paper. The man's desk was even worse. It was a miracle he could find a single thing in here.

"I don't like to waste a lot of time," Avery began, rolling up his sleeves. "Do you know how this works?"

Lysander nodded. "Uh, I start babbling incoherently and after an hour you scream Eureka! and tell me why I'm so messed up?"

Avery laughed. "Your parents haven't told you?"

The confusion in Lysander's face was obvious.

"Lysander, something happened to you a long time ago, something you've buried deep within your subconscious."

Lysander's face flushed red. His eyes darted away and he vaguely spotted a marble bust of Bach by the far wall... or was it Beethoven?

"Oh, it's perfectly normal. That's the way the mind works. Call it a survival mechanism, if you will. Everyone has bad memories, but when they're, say, traumatic, the mind tries to deny them entirely."

Avery brought his hands together as though he were squeezing a ball. "A kind of pressure begins to build, you

69

see. In a way, thoughts are things, Lysander. You can't keep them down. They need free rein—they need to breathe. You get me?"

Lysander nodded as Avery's hands continued to press against the imaginary ball. "Now, if that pressure becomes too strong, something has to give."

"Hence my seizures?"

"It seems that way."

"Hmm." Lysander scratched his chin thinking. "Other therapists accept this idea of yours? I could check the net, you know."

Avery laughed again, this time a full and hardy laugh. "Some do," he said. "But not all. I'm only here to release the pressure. I'm not here to make you a perfect person or to change who you are. I'm just here to help you identify what caused your attack." Avery leaned back and rested his hands on the plush arms of the chair. "Once we do that, my man, we may have it beat."

Now it was Lysander's turn to swallow a laugh. 'My man.'

Jack, the sixties just called. They want you back.

He really was from the sixties, Lysander thought, remembering how he had found Avery in the garage as he arrived, working on his 1966 MGB. Blood red with white racing stripes. Lysander had run a hand along the car's smooth surface, admiring the dedication it must have taken to nurse the dying beast back to health.

"I'm gonna put you under hypnosis," Avery was saying.

Lysander was pulled right out of himself. "You're gonna put me in a trance and then tell me I'm a chicken?"

But no sooner had he asked the question than another, more serious concern occurred to him.

"What if I can't wake up again? What happens then?"

Avery was rubbing his hands on his knee, fighting a smile. "That doesn't happen. Can't happen. But let's say I put you in trance and then I keel over with a heart attack.

70

Eventually you would fall into a deep sleep and then wake up feeling fine."

"Would I know what was going on?"

"You would have some awareness of events going on around you, yes. If I coughed, for instance, or if there was a fire—" Avery stopped short. "Like I said, I'm here and the process is perfectly safe."

Avery leaned forward. His voice was deep and soothing, and Lysander couldn't help but feel his muscles letting go. "Let me show you what I mean," he said.

As Avery began the induction, Lysander couldn't help wondering if the man had ever been married. He hadn't seen a wedding ring. But his eyes began to grow heavier, his mind spinning in slow circles, and it soon took some effort to follow Avery's gentle instructions. He was to walk along a flowing stream, Avery had said, and watch the water as it sparkled with bits of sunlight. The water was so serene and peaceful.

Fifteen minutes later, Lysander could barely feel his arms and legs. Within thirty he had reached the deepest parts of his subconscious.

In his mind's eye, Lysander could see someone up ahead shrouded in mist. Avery's voice came again, telling him the figure before him was the Wellman—an egoless reflection of Lysander. The well was a bottomless reservoir filled with every thought, desire and emotion Lysander had ever known, and it was the Wellman's job to draw the pail to the surface, bringing forward whatever was asked for.

"Lysander, I want you to remember the seizure. I want you to go back to the cause. When I count to three you will be there. One... two... three. Tell me what you see?

"Blackness."

"Lysander, I'd like you to tell me if something is responsible for your seizure?"

He hesitated. "Yes."

71

"Is it okay if we revisit that memory?"

Lysander's head shook even as the question was being asked.

"It's important that we do so." Avery's voice was calm but insistent.

A crease of tension ran down Lysander's face. Avery sighed and leaned forward.

"Lysander, you will be completely detached from the images before you. You are an observer. You are a guest. You cannot be harmed. Now, I would like you to go to the earliest incident that is responsible for your seizures. When I count to three, you will go there. One... two... three. Tell me what you see."

Avery could see the balls of Lysander's eyes rolling around under his closed lids. In a monotone Lysander said, "I see a village. There are people in the streets. They are yelling. There is a woman in a cart. She is tied with rope and the crowd is yelling at her. She has been tortured. A young girl throws rotten cabbage and it strikes her in the head. The woman turns to shout at the girl and more food is thrown. An older woman tries to stop them. It is her daughter they are hurting, but blood is what the crowd wants and they push the old woman away."

"Lysander, where are you?" Avery asked, surprised.

"I am in Millingham."

Avery wiped a handkerchief across his forehead. The muscles in his face were twitching nervously. "What year is it?"

"It is the year of our lord sixteen hundred forty-eight."

A thin sheen of perspiration started bleeding through Avery's shirt. "Say again, Lysander. What year is it?" In Avery's voice there was a touch of incredulity mixed with concern.

"It is the year of our lord sixteen hundred forty-eight. I told you."

72

"All right. Thank you." Out came Avery's handkerchief again. "Tell me, why are the people so angry with this woman?"

"Children in town have died and she was responsible."

"How so?"

"She is a midwife. She lives on the edge of town. She has treated several people who took ill. Many of the children she treated have died."

Avery hesitated. "What is her name?"

"Rebecca Goodman."

Avery's jaw slowly came unhinged. "She's in a cart right now, you said? She's being brought to prison?"

"No, she will be burned at the stake for witchcraft. The council of elders has already determined her guilt."

"Not hanged?"

"Hanging's too quick."

Avery leaned forward intently. "Lysander, I want you to move forward now to the next important event. Again, you will be an objective observer. Nothing you see can affect you in any way. When I count to three, you will go there. One… two… three. Tell me what you see."

Lysander squirmed in his chair as though the seat itself had become intolerably hot. After several calming suggestions Avery asked the question again.

"Rebecca Goodman is tied to a wooden pole. Sticks and brush are piled at her feet. She faces the council."

"Council? The ones who condemned her?"

Lysander nods.

"Go on."

"Guards ignite the brush underneath the woman. Her face contorts with panic. The heat is unbearable." Lysander writhed in his chair again. "The flames are rising. The crowd stops hollering. Some look away. The pain… The pain is…"

"Yes, go on."

"She's mouthing words in a language I don't

73

understand. Her voice is deep and guttural." Lysander's fingers dug into the arms of the leather chair. "She's putting a curse on us. I see tiny fissures forming on the witch's arms and belly. Her skin is cracking, yawning open and closed like hungry mouths waiting to be fed."

The piercing scream that erupted a second later sent a jolt of electricity up Avery's spine. The sound had come from Lysander, there was no doubting that, but whether his vocal cords had the range to make such a shriek was uncertain.

Lysander came awake with a violent shudder, gasping for air, his hands clutched tightly about his throat. He fought to control his breathing. A thick layer of mucus rattled around in his chest.

Avery sat in silence while Lysander continued reeling.

"What the hell was that?" Lysander asked.

"Your imagination," Avery said coolly. "A fantasy. Nothing more. Listen my man, if we spent time on every flight of fancy the human brain was capable of conjuring up, we'd never get anywhere, would we?" Avery looked at his watch. "Listen, that's it for today. We're making progress, though." He stood up, walked briskly to the office door and held it open. "Next week?"

Lysander stood on wobbly legs, feeling like a guest ushered out before dessert. He stepped through the door and headed up the stairs, alone. When Avery remained in his office, the door closed firmly behind him, Lysander knew for sure that something was wrong. His sense of smell had been the one to register it more than anything. That acrid odor on Avery as he whisked him out of the office so abruptly. This wasn't damp books he was smelling. This was fear. The same fear that had emanated from his father all those years ago as Sandy had kept him at bay, growling from little Lysander's side. Plain old fear, though, didn't explain it all. Avery was hiding something.

Back at home, Lysander sat in bed with the lights out.

74

He still didn't feel completely whole yet. A residue from his deep hypnotic state remained. Visions of that woman's flesh as it turned black and peeled away seemed to be on a looped reel inside his brain.

The idea of a past life had occurred to him, that he couldn't deny, but he had squashed it mercilessly before it had a chance to germinate. The mind was a complex place that spoke in symbols buried from deep within. You couldn't take these things at face value. Shirley MacLaine had past lives, not Lysander Shore.

Avery's strange behavior after the session still bothered him, however. Why did he whisk Lysander out without so much as a good-bye? "Hey kid, you just had a fantasy so vivid you thought you were about to be burned at the stake, but if you don't mind, pull up your socks and get the hell out, would ya."

Outside, Lysander heard the muffled sound of a car door slamming. He raised himself up on one elbow and gazed out the bay window that framed his bed, happy for the opportunity to shake off that jittery feeling in the pit of his belly. Across a vacant lot was Reverend Small's house, a two-story job that looked more expensive than he could afford on a monk's salary. Through a screen of trees and brush was the good ol' reverend. He had a dog with him, German shepherd. The animal was down on its haunches, its paws dug into the manicured lawn, and the reverend was wrenching at the leash, struggling to get the animal in the house. He let out a length at the tail end of the leash and struck the dog with it. The animal yelped and Lysander flinched, wishing at that moment he had a video camera with him. The reverend turned and started walking, the leash over his shoulder, looking like an ancient Egyptian slave, tasked with moving an enormous slab of limestone. Skid marks began to appear in the grass as the shepherd was dragged along. A minute later, the animal was inside. Bit late for a trip to the SPCA,

Lysander thought, settling back into bed. Millingham was the strangest place he'd ever seen, and for a moment he debated telling someone. But who would believe him? Back in Hayward he had seen other pillars of the community do a lot worse than smack a dog, and he had certainly learned his lesson about what truths adults were willing to entertain. With great reluctance, Lysander let it go, and fell into a restless sleep.

Chapter 14

Timp, timp, timp, timp.

Samantha flicked on the lamp by her nightstand: a twisted skeletal hand that rose up from a grave, its bony fingers gripping the bulb. Against the far wall, two large candles burned, their flame's unwavering in the stillness of the room. She swore she'd heard a sound. Sam rested her head on the pillow and tried to relax. All this McMurphy stuff was getting to her.

Timp, timp, timp.

She sat bolt upright. Someone or something was tapping at her window.

"Whoever you are, get the hell out of here!" she screamed. "I've got a gun! I'll blow your head off!"

Timp, timp, timp.

She eyed the curtains for a while and then slowly swung her legs over the bed and backed away toward the bedroom door—her eyes glued to the velvet curtains.

The window. Had she remembered to lock it? Had she even remembered to close it properly? Her hand groped blindly around her for some protection. Finally it clasped around a thin wooden cane.

Timp, timp, timp, timp.

The noise sounded more insistent now. Angrier.

Something was pushing against the glass. Trying to get in.

A thought popped out at her: It was McMurphy. She wanted to turn and run, but invisible hands were holding her tight.

Fear? No, not fear. Something else. A morbid curiosity, maybe.

She forced herself toward the window.

Timp, timp, timp.

Yank the curtain open, she told herself, the way you yank the shower curtain late at night checking for serial killers. But instead her feet turned and brought her back to her bedroom

door. She fumbled with the knob, turning it frantically, forgetting that she had locked it. She looked up and saw the bolt.

Behind her, a sliding noise. The window was being opened.

She had always thought she would react bravely to danger. But now that it was happening, she realized she had been wrong. Her body was a tight ball of fear. She felt trapped. A rustling sound started behind her. Gathering every ounce of willpower, she turned her head. Something was in the room with her. It had slid in through the window and was fumbling behind the curtain now.

Her nose wrinkled, struck by the foul, pungent odor.

A corpse.

She could almost taste it. A breeze from the open window blew the candles out, leaving her in gloomy darkness. A thin glow came from a streetlight outside.

The velvet curtains parted, revealing a dark silhouette. Samantha screamed and the figure backed away fearfully, banging its head on the window.

"Samantha?"

She paused, uncertain. She knew that voice...

"Who—"

"Keep your voice down," the voice whispered. "You

78

trying to get me killed?"

She reached over and flicked the light on.

Derek stood there. His hair looked like he hadn't combed it in days.

"Jesus, Derek, I thought you were someone else." Her chest was heaving up and down.

"Shit, you reek."

Derek frowned. "Where exactly do you expect me to shower?"

"We're gonna have to clean you up," Sam said plugging her nose."

Samantha relit the candles and burned incense while Derek smelled at his armpits self-consciously. He sat on her bed, wearing a funny expression.

"The last time you had a look like that," she said, "you were heading off to juvie for three months."

"I'm leaving, Sam. Came by to tell you."

Samantha's face filled with surprise and dismay. "Leaving?"

"I can't live in that house anymore, the cops know I was there, and plus," Derek went on, "I'm tired of living off of cold cuts and stale bread."

Samantha tried to smile. Could she really blame him? Cooped up in that house was no way for anyone to live.

"Where you gonna go?"

"South. Florida. Maybe California. Gonna sniff out some work as a mechanic till I have enough cash to open my own place." Derek rubbed his hands together, trying to shake the feeling that he was deluding himself. Sometimes, talking about a plan made it sound less foolhardy. Sometimes talking was all some people ever did. This was no pipe dream, he reminded himself for the zillionth time.

Samantha's face grew warm. "Why didn't you say anything before?"

"What would it have changed? I have to go. If the cops

79

wanna come after me, fine, but I'd be willing to bet I can outrun 'em."

The smile on Derek's face waned, and it filled Samantha with despair.

"Who knows? Maybe I'll be back someday, riding into town on a custom-made chopper."

Derek turned to leave and then stopped, remembering something. "When you see Lysander, tell him to watch out for Chad's left hook." Derek threw a clenched fist into the air. "He always starts with a fake from his right. Always." He winked.

Samantha's mouth had tightened into a thin line. Part of her felt like hitting him for running away like a coward.

Derek took her by the shoulders. "You're my special girl," he told her and watched as her face hardened. "Always will be, Sam. Stop building walls around yourself, or you're gonna become a crotchety old lady." He pulled her into a tight hug.

Then he handed her a flashlight. "Won't be needing this anymore." Sam took it and tossed it on the bed. "Oh, and I nearly forgot." He produced a weathered scrapbook. "Found this at the McMurphy house."

She took it from him carefully, turning over the first few pages. She stopped with a jolt.

"It belonged to whatshisface," Derek said.

"James McMurphy."

"Yeah, that guy."

"Which room did you find this in?"

"One of the rooms upstairs. Spooked me right out of my skin."

She leafed through the pages, her mind returning to the police report.

Upstairs, in one of the bedrooms we found the remains of James McMurphy.

A picture tumbled from the journal and fell to her feet. She picked it up and studied it. Two men in suits were standing side by side, shaking hands, their faces beaming. Behind them rose Millingham High School, looking new.

As she stared at the faces of the two men, the flesh at the base of her neck began to tingle. In her mind's eye, an axe came swinging through the air, thudding into the fleshy side of a neck, severing an artery. Blood splashed everywhere. The wound was large, and blood jetted out in a great torrent. Now the man on the left was smiling. He was looking right at her, his eyes burning with hatred. A trick of the light, she thought nervously. She snapped her eyes shut, but when she opened them again, the picture was worse. The man on the right had a shotgun in his mouth, his lips stretched wide around the barrel, his eyes staring blankly. On the left, the other man's grin had grown wider still, and his arm was now draped over the man with the shotgun: old friends at a Sunday picnic.

"Oh Derek, you gotta see this."

He took the picture from her. "Yup," he said, bringing it closer. "The guy on the right looks like James McMurphy. There's a picture of him at school."

She snatched the old photograph out of his hands. In it two young men were smiling and shaking hands in front of Millingham High, just as she had seen before that horrific film reel had started playing in her head.

"Sam, your hands, they're trembling."

She looked down at her hands. They *were* trembling. She went to the door, closed a hand around the knob and shut herself in, only dimly aware that a terrible evil was closing in; born and festering from a time long before she had ever come to the world as Samantha Crow.

Outside, the wind blew up, twirling dead leaves in the air and whipping them against the house, as though they were
searching for a way in.

81

Chapter 15

At first Alex thought he had just walked into a funhouse. Old furniture, weird animal bones.

He turned toward the living room, and the odor of decaying flesh hit him like a shot to the gut. He held a sweaty palm up to his nose. His eyes watered. A man in white overalls was taking pictures of something behind the couch. He approached, walking through a small archway that separated the living room from the hallway. A curled hand poking out of a bloodstained yellow sweater came into view. Alex leaned forward and saw the rest of the body. The victim's arms and legs were spread evenly apart. What struck him was the odd way in which the body was positioned: like a drawing by one of those Italian guys, Leonardo da Vinci.

Alex guessed the body had been dead for over a day now. At least judging by the smell and the way the blood that had pooled around the man in the shape of a giant bullseye. His head was cocked unnaturally to the side, toward the far wall. A single slipper clung doggedly to the his right foot. His yellow cardigan was torn and saturated with blood to the point that it looked more like a satin smoking jacket.

A hand grabbed Alex's shoulder, and he jumped. It was Deputy Jeff Anderson, Millingham's only other and, as he liked to remind Alex, senior deputy.

"Christ, you ever seen anything like this?" Jeff asked, handing Alex a white surgical mask.

"The stiff?"

"Sure, but I'm talking about all the crazy shit this guy's got." Jeff motioned to one of the display cases. "What a collection, eh? Real nut job is what I say. Got here twenty minutes before anyone else and thought I was gonna shit myself. See those bottles up there?"

Alex looked.

"Filled with piss."

"How you know? You drink some?" "Course not, funny guy."

"Who is he?"

"Full name's Peter Hume," Jeff said, adjusting his mask. "Lived here his whole life. Hell, I remember giving that weird bastard a ticket last week."

"He married?"

"Yeah, wife's away, though. I've questioned some of the neighbors, and they said she left for Mexico more than two weeks ago. Two were having marital problems. Maybe our guy couldn't get it up anymore, eh?" Jeff was winking.

Alex looked around, ignoring him. "Any sign of forced entry?"

"No. Front door was locked when I got here. Had to kick it down."

Alex glanced back at the door and the collection of splintered wood below it. "So who called it in?" he asked.

"Paperboy came to collect and looked in the window when no one came to the door. Saw our guy lying here in a mess," Jeff said. "When I came in, I nearly lost that burrito I ate earlier."

"What about the man's office?" Alex asked, eyeing the body.

"He left there at six o'clock as always. Kept to himself mostly." Jeff grew quiet. "Weird thing is, our guy's been

83

dead for over a day by the looks of it, but there's no mail in the box. Like someone's been taking care of the place."

"That is strange. This look like a hit to you?"

A flicker crossed Jeff's face, as though he had already pondered the possibility and dismissed it. "Neighbors did mention hearing fights between him and the missus. Like I said, they were on the outs."

Just then Sheriff Crow came in, wincing at the odor. Jeff handed him a mask and filled him in on the details. Alex left them. This was Jeff's show now. He went to the front door and examined the lock.

Sheriff Crow said, "Jeff, get on any life insurance policies. See if she's been loadin' 'em up the kazoo, accidental death, you name it. I want to rule out the wife as soon as possible." Crow paused. "Have you dusted for fingerprints yet?"

"I have," Jeff said proudly. "The major entry points are covered, but I'm sure we'll find they belong to the Mister and Missus. 'Course, we'll only know when we run 'em. But if you ask me, Sheriff, looks like this sick bastard did himself in in the worst way."

Crow ignored the comment. "You find anything else?"

Just as Jeff began to shake his head, they heard Alex shouting from outside.

They rushed out. Alex stopped them with outstretched arms. "Careful," he said. Alex knelt down on the driveway. "We may have something here."

Jeff's voice registered annoyance. "In case you didn't notice, *Deputy* Morgan, the crime scene is inside."

"I got a shoe print here. Might lead through the house if your clumsy ass didn't trample it to hell when you arrived on scene."

They squatted down for a better look. By the edge of the driveway was a pile of dog shit, hard and crusted. In it was the edge of a serrated boot print. The tread looked heavy. Combat... maybe a construction boot.

"Alex, good eye," Sheriff Crow congratulated him. "Now let's get an impression." He turned to Jeff, whose face was slowly becoming the color of raw turnips. "When you're the first on scene you gotta protect the evidence," the sheriff shouted. "Even if it means pulling your head out of your ass. If this goes state, I don't want us lookin' like a bunch of cock-eyed yokels. You got that, Deputy?"

Jeff nodded sheepishly and then looked at Alex in awe. "How'd you find that?"

"Saw a trail of shit in the house. Means our guy may not have been alone."

While Jeff was left to take an impression from the dog shit, Alex and the sheriff went back inside. The sheriff turned pensive. "I don't want this out of the bag just yet, Alex. We'll let the media know as soon as the wife gets home. I don't want her coming back and being the last to find out her husband looks like a human piñata."

"It's gonna be a hard secret to keep," Alex said. "Anyone who's not standing out on their front porch is watching from a window."

"I know," Crow said. "Do your best. I don't expect miracles, just your best."

"You want me to try tracking the wife down?" Jeff offered, coming back in.

"No, I'll do that," Crow said. "You two finish collecting whatever you can and be thorough. If the state is called in, I don't wanna give 'em any room to say we haven't done a bang-up job." He sighed, looking at Jeff. "We've probably lost a ton of evidence already."

Sheriff Crow went back to the front door, following the faint trail of dog shit. By now it didn't really look like crap, more like a light brown stain on the ground, spaced evenly every few feet. Nothing more than a splotch of mud, leading from the kitchen to the living room and the body behind the couch. Crow pushed open the kitchen door, his gaze thoroughly fixed on the ground before him. He heard someone squeal and stopped suddenly. It was Dorothy and he had nearly knocked her over. She appeared to be on her way into the living room.

"Hey," he said, looking up.

She averted her eyes.

"Watch where you step," he said, deciding to try a joke on for size. "There's some important shit on the floor."

She smiled faintly, trying to brush past him but he stuck an arm out to block her.

Alex called out from the living room. "Sheriff, you might want to look at this."

Alex was kneeling over the corpse, a disturbed look on his face. Carefully he grasped the man's head and turned it. The neck cracked and groaned as it twisted. Alex shuddered when he saw the full extent of the damage.

The man's forehead and nasal cavities had been caved in. Bloody pink brain tissue surged up through the shattered bone. Where there had once been eyes, now there were only two hollow cavities. Peter Hume had bled from every hole in his face—and then some.

Jeff stood behind Alex, fidgeting. "Who would do this kinda thing to themselves?"

"You find the eyes yet?" the sheriff asked them.

"Not yet," Alex replied.

Dorothy knelt down beside the body, put on a pair of surgical gloves and examined the dead man's skull. "I see multiple lacerations and fractures, signs of subarachnoid hemorrhaging, wouldn't be surprised to find extensive cerebral contusions. I'll have more information after the autopsy but for now keep your eyes open for an object, maybe five to ten pounds. Could have been anything from a baseball bat to a large hammer to a marble statuette."

Alex noticed a cherry wood table beside them. It was covered with dust except for a circle the size of a man's

86

fist.

"If we're even going to entertain the notion that this guy did it to himself," Dorothy said, "then the object shouldn't be far."

She raised one of the victim's stiff hands. Almost immediately, a large slit opened at the wrist. A mere trickle of blood bubbled out. Hume had nearly bled dry.

She looked up and spoke to Alex as though they were alone.

"These wrists have been cut right to the bone," she said.

Carefully, Dorothy rolled up the blood-stiff sleeves of the man's yellow cardigan.

As she did so, an image flashed in Alex's mind. The man sawing into his own wrists with a long knife. The look on his face resembled something like pleasure. His eyes bulging from their sockets. Tears of blood tumbling down his cheeks.

Oh God, Alex, help me!

Sheriff Crow nudged Alex with his elbow. "Stay sharp." Alex looked up into the sheriff's stern face, shaking his head to clear away the cobwebs.

"Bingo!" Dorothy said looking at the fingernails. "We have what looks like flesh here." She put a paper bag over each of the man's hands to preserve the evidence and tied them off with a zip tie.

"So what are we looking at here, Dorothy?" Jeff asked. "Was our guy murdered or did he do this to himself?"

She looked up, first at Sheriff Crow, who pretended to be too engrossed in the body to meet her gaze, and then at Jeff. "This was no suicide, I can tell you that much..."

Alex turned back to the man's face and the empty eye sockets. Crusted blood caked the two gaping holes. *Jesus.* "What kind of a person would do this?"

Sheriff Crow's eyes dimmed. He started for the door, then planted his feet and turned around. "Jeff, lock this place down and don't let anyone near it. By tomorrow

87

morning latest, I want a solid idea what happened here and who might have done it, whether it was our friend here in the yellow sweater or... I just don't want to start a panic. So let's look sharp and do this right people. If you ask me what I think, this guy did himself in."

But even as the words were spoken, Alex could see the doubt in Sheriff Crow's eyes. Alex glanced over at Dorothy. In her face he could see that they were both thinking the same thing.

Whoever he is, he's struck again.

Chapter 16

The Bethlehem Baptist Church was hushed as Reverend Small began his sermon. Lysander peered over at Summer, sitting with her parents. He felt more animated than usual. This wasn't so bad after all. Somehow it was even pleasant.

He regarded Summer's mother; certainly a hot middle-aged momma if ever he'd seen one. She had the same long blonde hair as Summer, same fair complexion, but her mother's hair was tied into a ponytail, while Summer's was free flowing and left to dangle by her shoulders. Something prickled in his thoughts, and his attention turned to Samantha. She and her family were sitting between him and Summer. She followed his gaze to see what he had been watching and turned back, shaking her head disapprovingly.

Beside Lysander, his mother stroked the slopping edge of her belly. She was expecting any day now.

Slowly, reluctantly, the sermon drew his attention. Reverend Small was behind the podium, dressed in a simple dark suit, his eyes blazing.

Small put a tiny hand in the air. "Man, by his very nature, is susceptible to evil," he said. He eyed each of them in turn. "He is flanked on all sides by sin and demonic temptations. It is the darkness and not the light that men love because their deeds are evil." The congregation grew deathly quiet. From the front row, a group of elderly women were perched forward, nodding. Lysander stole a glance at Summer again. She was still and attentive. When his gaze shifted over to Samantha, he saw her flipping mindlessly through the hymnbook. She looked up at him, smiled, then stuck a finger down her throat. He snorted laughter, and their parents turned simultaneously to scold them. Samantha's father, his face the color of a ripe McIntosh apple, searched to see who she was looking at. When his glassy stare found Lysander, Lysander couldn't help but look away.

From the pulpit the reverend raised his hands palms up, looking from one hand to the other. "If you are poor in this life and in the service of the Lord, then in the next you *will* be rich. You cannot escape what you have set in motion by your choice to either walk with the Lord or your choice to turn your back on him." He smiled knowingly. "This Lot's wife learned the hard way. Disobedience was her sin. But do not think that because she lived long ago that her fate cannot be yours as well. Do not be fooled, Satan himself is among us. Within these holy walls you are safe. Beyond them, you have only your faith to guide and protect you."

When Samantha turned to watch Lysander she was surprised to find him listening with rapt attention. *Must be the shock from so much talk of fire and brimstone*, she thought, bemused. This was Reverend Small's favorite sermon. She had heard him perform it around the same time last year. His hands had even gone in the air at the same moment the first time around.

Then something weird happened. The podium Reverend Small was speaking from seemed to fall away. Even the great oak cross dangling from the ceiling with wires behind him vanished. And the reverend, standing there with that fire in his eyes, was no longer wearing his black blazer. Instead, perched on his head was a wide-

90

brimmed felt hat, knotted in the center with a silver buckle, and swaying at his feet, a long black cloak. When Sam was positive that she had completely lost her mind, the reverend's features began to melt away until they were gone completely, only to reform in the spitting image of Lysander.

Only problem was that this new Lysander was not the Lysander she knew and—she dared not say the word. This new Lysander came for her; his smiling face cracking and blackened. His hand was tucked behind his back and when he moved she could see something glitter in the light. She wanted to peer behind him, but before she had a chance his arm sprang into the air, clutching a long pointed knife. Samantha gasped. Lysander's doppelganger lunged with wicked speed, swinging the shiny blade in a shallow arc. It tore through her shirt and buried itself into her chest. Afterward, she would remember the pain above all else—how real it felt, how excruciating. Her initial reaction was to pull away and jerk her shoulder free, but the knife had pinned her in place, jammed in the open space between her collarbone and her neck. Lysander wrenched viciously, trying to tear her open, his wide empty smile gleaming like some hellish carnival clown. He pulled her close to him and whispered: "What do you fear most?" This time it wasn't his voice anymore. It was deeper. Older. Familiar. The voice was Reverend Small's, merged with that of her waking nightmare.

Light danced against the lids of her eyes. She opened them. Sunlight was twinkling off the ring on Small's hand. She blinked. The reverend was saying something about the hand of God. The blood had drained from her face, and Sam jumped when something touched her shoulder.

"Sam?" It was her sister Erica, an expression of concern on her tiny face. Droplets of sweat had beaded on Sam's forehead. She patted her sister's delicate hand.

"Are you okay?" Erica asked her, clearly concerned.

91

"I'm fine," Sam replied, trying to settle her breathing. "I'm just fine."

She glanced over at Lysander, remembering the expression of joy plastered across his demonic face as he had swung that knife at her, wondering why on earth he would ever want to kill her.

Chapter 17

"Getting cold out there," Dorothy said as she slid into the booth, setting a manila folder beside her. Ted's diner, home of the $8.99 heart attack special, was busier than usual. Suzie the waitress arrived as if on cue and dropped off a steaming cup of coffee for each of them.

Alex glanced outside, more in response to Dorothy's suggestion about the weather than anything. A few stray leaves, dried and fallen, were blowing across the small parking lot out front.

"You know, I'd feel more comfortable if we met at my office," she said.

Alex looked at her sideways. "The morgue, you mean?"

"People come to Ted's to eat, not to hear about stab wounds and autopsies."

"I think I've seen enough stiffs to last me a lifetime."

She fixed him with a stern gaze, the way a mother might look at a son lying about having finished his homework early. "Alex, it might not be my place, but has the thought ever crossed your mind that maybe you're in the wrong profession?"

He shifted, hoping she wouldn't be able to detect his discomfort.

"Being a cop is pretty much all I've ever wanted. It's all I know." He was becoming irritated. "Is this why you wanted to meet? To give me advice on alternative careers?"

She cleared the mounds of sugar and debris off the table with the back of her hand and dropped a folder in front of him. She flicked through crime-scene photos and bits of paper with scribbled notes. "I'm about to present my findings to Sheriff Crow tomorrow morning, but I wanted you to see it beforehand. I have a feeling he might be hesitant to act on some of my conclusions."

Alex picked up a picture of Peter Hume's dead body and stared at it, his cheeks growing warm. He wanted to switch his attention away, but he couldn't.

"So, what'd you find?" he asked, happy to let the picture flutter back onto the pile.

"First off, the lacerations to Hume's wrists match those found on the sheriff's wife."

Alex sat forward. "And the eyes?"

"In both cases, it appears the thumbs were inserted passed the zygom—uh, the outer eye sockets—and torn out."

Alex produced a file folder of his own and handed it to Dorothy. It was the McMurphy police report from more than fifty years ago.

"What's this?"

"You know that pesky habit I have of going through cold case files when things are slow?"

Dorothy gave him a queer look. "Yeah. You mean those three cases Millingham police never solved."

She was joking, of course, and Alex laughed. "Looks like we have a fourth no one ever knew about. Now, it's a long shot, I know, but I wonder if there's a connection."

Dorothy scanned the file. Her face paled. "Oh God, Alex! I never knew the McMurphy family was murdered." She flipped the page over, looking about as shocked as Alex had been when he first found out. "You hear stories growing up. You know the way it is, old wives' tales, but

94

you never really believe them. Why on earth was this covered up?"

"The man's status maybe," Alex said, shrugging. "Could a small town like Millingham handle their golden boy losing his marbles and chopping his family into tiny bits?"

"You found this how?"

"Not long after Diane's death, I got to thinking that if I went back far enough in the records, I might just find other cases with questionable suicides. I'd plugged all the parameters into the computer and nothing came up. Then I started searching the filing room. I was gonna be real methodical, since the cases in the system only go back six or seven years. Box by box if I needed to. Then I found this one little carton that had no history. Box 263. It was as if they'd collected the evidence but never entered it anywhere."

Dorothy brought her coffee to her lips and took a shallow sip. "And because of a handwritten note left by some sheriff fifty years ago, you think there's a connection with Peter Hume and Diane?"

"Maybe. Maybe not. Only one way to prove that."

Dorothy's eyes sparkled. "McMurphy's autopsy report."

● ● ●

Randy, the large-bellied security guard, found Lysander in the filing room near the back of the medical examiner's building. He poked his head in. "I'll be closin' her down in half an hour, Lysander."

Lysander was gripping his lower back, feeling as though something in his spine had been knocked out of place, but more importantly he was cursing Sam and her bright ideas.

A smile spread on Randy's face. "For what they're paying you, I don't know why you do it."

95

"I guess I'm just a glutton for punishment."

Randy's belly shook as the two of them laughed. The man's full name was Randolph Hefler III and it struck Lysander as ironic that someone with a name that could get him on a dinner list with the Queen of England tended to scratch his balls when he spoke.

"Listen," Randy said. "I'm gonna be up front filling out the log book, you just come see me when you're done."

Lysander nodded, bent down and heaved up another box.

The filing room was a misnomer if ever there was one. Nothing here was filed. Instead, over the years, documents had been dumped into boxes and shoved into a corner. Luckily, the boxes were scribbled with dates, creating some semblance of order. The chaos only made his task of finding McMurphy's autopsy report that much harder.

When he was hired, Mrs. Olsen had offered him a touch over minimum wage to lug over five hundred boxes to the basement, where this new temperature controlled storage system had been built, complete with shelves, filing cabinets and a computerized labeling system. *Welcome to the twenty-first century.*

He had agreed to it—not just to help Sam—but in part because of the promise that once this was done, other work might follow. That meant he wouldn't have to rely on his parents for handouts and the barbed strings that always seemed to come attached.

That the boxes weighed a ton didn't bother him one bit either. That the ones closest to the floor had suffered water damage and were apt to crumble in his hands did. Trying to shift under the weight of an unstable box, he had come to discover, could do more harm to your lower back than picking it up with straight legs.

Lysander had decided to start at the back of the room, with the boxes labeled 1930-1935. By the time Dorothy

96

had left for the night, he had begun approaching the 1950s. He had developed a system of stacking two boxes, one on top of another and was making good progress when disaster struck. He was near the landing when the box on the bottom split between his fingers and emptied everything before him. For several seconds the only sound he could hear was hundreds of pages spilling to the ground at his feet.

"DAMMIT!" he screamed when it was empty, but the words didn't make him feel any better. There were papers everywhere. One seesawed lazily by his feet and he kicked at it. He was getting ready to gather them together, tie them into bundles with rope and drop-kick them into the corner when the name on one of the pages caught his eye.

Delores McMurphy.

He bent down and shuffled through the pile. There were half a dozen pages with the name McMurphy on them, dated November 2, 1965. He picked up the first one he'd found and read it.

Delores McMurphy, autopsy report.

Cause of death: Homicide. Sharp force trauma.

Weapon: axe.

Lysander's heart skipped in his chest. The coldness of the words on the page left him uneasy. He let the page slip from his hand and flutter back into the pile. He grabbed another one nearby. Thomas McMurphy. Cause of death identical. Within seconds, Lysander had found three more just like it. The whole family was here, except—

Lysander stared down at the name for a long time before he stooped over to pick it up. James McMurphy. All the moisture suddenly left his mouth.

Cause of death: Suicide.

Weapon: 12 gauge shotgun.

So, the guy had blown his brains out, just as the police

97

report in Alex's desk had stated. He remembered that crazy story Sam's aunt had told her about James McMurphy's dispossessed spirit lurching around town. The way the back of his head had been gone, as if it'd been blown to bits by a shotgun blast. Lysander had assumed at the time it had been the kind of story designed to frighten little children into eating all of their Brussels sprouts. *You know what James McMurphy does to children who don't finish everything on their plate, don't you?*

But something else here made the blood in Lysander's veins drop by thirty degrees. Before James McMurphy had air-conditioned the back of his skull with a five-inch hole, he had slit his wrists and gouged his eyes out with a screwdriver.

● ● ●

"So if a nut's running around killing people," Alex was saying, "I can't believe he'd be going so far to hide his tracks. I mean, creating the illusion that the victims were doing it to themselves. Come on!"

"Keep your voice down." Dorothy glanced over Alex's shoulder. Several booths over, a large man wearing a Harley-Davidson T-shirt was staring at them. "You're right. The only real key we have are the wounds."

Alex was shaking his head. "Would a serial killer do that? Try to trick us, I mean. Wouldn't he want people to know what he had done?"

Slowly, the man at the booth returned to his meal. "Maybe he's trying to buy time," Dorothy whispered. "But that's what you have to find out."

"What else did you find on Hume?"

Dorothy searched through her papers. "I have a friend in Boston who owed me a favor. He sent me the lab report on the boot print you found. Couldn't get over the fact it was made by a pile of dog doo." Dorothy couldn't

98

help but smile as she said it.

"It was only a partial print, of course, so there was a lot he wasn't able to tell, like exact size and…"

"And…"

"It looks like a standard combat boot. Hard to tell if it's male or female, but the thing was fairly narrow." She kept glancing through her notes. "I also sent the tissue we found under his fingernails to Boston."

Alex raised an eyebrow.

"Blood traces all match our victim," she said. "Now what about the weapons? Have you found the knife yet or whatever caused that head injury?"

Alex shook his head. "Nope."

"Well, the blunt-force trauma to the midline face was fairly extensive. I found depressed fractures of the maxilla and zygomatic bones. Several of his teeth were chipped or fractured, two of them he swallowed altogether. And there was mucosal hemorrhaging in the intraoral cavity." Alex shook his head. "Speak English."

"It means that whoever did this was very angry." They both glanced at the crime-scene photo of Hume's face again, or what was left of it.

"Hume's hands had something strange I hadn't seen at first. There was bruising and chaffing on his palm and fingers. The same kind of marks left from swinging something heavy through the air."

"So what are you saying? That he bashed his own face in?"

"If you recall, the back of Diane's neck had a pattern of bruising consistent with having pulled her own head underwater."

Alex leaned forward, trying to read Dorothy's notes upside down. "What about trace signs from the weapon?"

"I found microscopic splinters of wood in the wound on Hume's face. My guess is we're looking for a bust of some kind."

"You think the killer might have taken it with him?"

"Not sure, could have been a trophy."

Alex studied a picture of the victim again, his face growing hot. "So let me get this straight. Someone shows up at Hume's door after dark, Hume lets him in. They walk around a bit and then Hume starts bashing his own face in, plucking his eyes out and carving himself up like a turkey dinner?"

Dorothy shook her head. "I don't know."

"The sheriff's gonna have a real field day with this one."

"The murderer seemed to have known both his victims well enough that they didn't panic when he showed up," Dorothy said. "Something worth looking into."

"Well, none of the neighbors we've talked to said they'd seen anything unusual. Apparently, this guy kept pretty much to himself, especially when his wife went away. We don't even know if he had any friends."

She grew quiet. "How's Steve doing with all this?"

Alex scanned the parking lot again. "The sheriff? He's stressed. I can see this whole thing's beginning to wear on him. As far as he was concerned, he'd closed the books on his wife's death. Now he's facing the possibility he was wrong."

Dorothy's eyes fell.

"And just wait until the news people get involved," Alex continued. "It's going to be a regular bonanza. They'll be withholding some stuff, though, like where he was found and the gory details that no decent person really has any business knowing. As far as I can tell, I think they're gonna call it a burglary gone bad. If people find out the guy's eyes were carved out, and his head mashed to a pulp, it's liable to start a panic."

Alex finished the last of Dorothy's coffee and reached into his pocket smirking. "Good coffee."

She slapped two one dollar bills on the table before he

100

had a chance to grab hold of his loose change.

"Next time it's your treat," she said.

Outside, Alex was halfway into his cruiser when Dorothy stopped him. "Oh, I almost forgot," she said.

Puzzled, he stood back up, leaning over the roof.

Dorothy fumbled through her papers and pulled out a black-and-white picture. She held it in the air. "Ever seen this before?"

He tilted his head. It looked like a child's drawing of an eye and suddenly a shiver ran up his spine. "Where'd you get that?"

"Found it carved into Hume's chest. Looks like you were right. Our guy does have something to say."

• • •

Lysander was still searching through the McMurphy family's death certificates—the theme from the Family Guy oddly stuck in his head when he heard the voice. LYSANDER!
He turned expecting to find Randy, telling him it was time to close up. But that wasn't the case. The room was empty. Overhead, the neon lights were buzzing away indifferently.

He paused.

The voice had been quite distinct, spoken with the delicacy of someone leaning over to whisper affectionately into—

LYSANDER!

He dropped the papers into a nearby box and went to the storage room doorway and peered down either end of the long hall. To his right, where the stairs led to the ground level, he could see a faint glimmer of light shining through the cracks of the closed door.

Thinking back, he wasn't sure how, with his arms aching under the strain of the boxes, he could have

101

closed that door even if he had wanted to. A fan of chilly air brushed his left cheek. He turned in that direction. From another room, not twenty paces away, he saw the glow from a light. Diffuse and harsh, it reminded him of the kitchen freezer and his mother removing leftovers.

Lysander crept down the hallway. He could hear the sound of his own feet shuffling reluctantly across the cold tile floor.

He came to a door with a square window and peered inside. A thick layer of condensation obscured his vision. The metallic door handle was long and cool to the touch as he grasped it and pulled. A chilly blast of air ruffled his hair. He stepped inside. Before him sat six gurneys. Five were empty. On the sixth was a clear body bag. Inside, a lump of pink flesh.

These people are dead, he reminded himself. *They can't hurt you.*

He edged toward the form in the bag, his breath billowing out in white plumes. He began tugging at the zipper. It was stuck. He pulled harder. Soon he had two hands on the bag, holding the fold with one, yanking with the other. Suddenly, the zipper broke free and went whirring down the length of the bag. Inside was a creature with cavernous black eyes. Lysander felt his heart exploding in his chest, felt himself turn and run from the room. But when he blinked, he was hit with the dull realization that he hadn't moved a single muscle. That thing on the gurney was still staring back at him through yawning holes that were once eyes and a face bashed to all hell. As Lysander's fear began to settle, he could see that this was no demon. It was a man. A man Lysander had seem somewhere before and the memory felt insubstantial and dreamlike.

He had dreamt of this man, hadn't he? It was a terrible dream. The slender man in the yellow cardigan, the one who had smashed his face until almost nothing of it

102

remained. The one who had let the shadow into his home. Into him. But it was more than that. This was someone he knew. This was the insurance salesman. Peter Hume. And his warning to Lysander that morning came back with horrifying speed.

You haven't remembered yet, have you?

A picture was drawn onto Peter's naked chest. It looked like an eye and he could feel the harshness of its gaze burrowing into him.

I SEE YOU... WHERE YOU LIVE... WHERE YOU SLEE... WHERE YOU EAT... WHERE YOU'LL DIE... WHERE YOU LIVE... WHERE YOU SLEEP...

Turning on his heels—this time for real—Lysander ran from the room and straight into a wall. The wall shouted with fright and staggered backward. Lysander looked up, his face twisted with fear. The wall came forward into the light. His belly and right shoulder were illuminated by the harsh glare spilling out from the cold storage room. This time it *was* Randy.

Chapter 18

Samantha's head dipped like a fishing pole forgotten along the muddy bank of a river. It bobbed a second time and then a third. She was drifting off and when she snapped awake, her body jerking violently. A vague disquiet settled over her. In that brief period of sleep, she had dreamed that a face had been staring at her through her bedroom window. The man's lips were stretched as if something were prying them apart. But stared wasn't even the right word because it didn't really have eyes, only two empty cavities, looking like tiny black holes swirling in the middle of its face.

But that face was unmistakable. Filled with sadness, shock and anger, all at once. Its lips were moving. This thing was trying to tell her something.

2...

6...

Its voice rose to a deafening pitch

3...

and then silence.

His lips were still moving when he turned away. Samantha felt her stomach tighten as she saw the back of his head, or what was left of it. Loose chunks of hair and flesh and fragmented bone swung lazily at the edges of a massive hole where there had once been a skull. The result of a violent...

shotgun blast.

She didn't need to see any more to know who it was. James McMurphy.

When the room around her came into sharp focus she could see two girls with teased hair pointing and giggling. She was in Mrs. Wayne's economics class. Red lines etched under Sam's eyes. The dreams had been visiting her with growing frequency, and despite slight variations, all of them were exactly the same. The snake. The room with the glowing light and then that disembodied voice begging her not to enter.

After economics, not one iota of which she could recall, she returned to her locker and found Lysander, fumbling for his books. "There's something really important I have to tell you," he said.

"Yeah, well there's something—" she began when from the corner of her eye she saw Summer and a group of her friends heading toward them. Sam threw down her books, pushed Lysander up against the locker and mashed her lips against his. Summer and her friends rolled passed with raised eyebrows. One of the girls made a catcall. As soon as they were gone, Sam pulled away, conscious of the blood rising in her cheeks. They stood blinking stupidly at one another.

Lysander wiped a hand across his lips, embarrassed. "Whad'ya do that for?"

"Well, you said you wanted to make Summer jealous."

"Oh," he said, catching sight of her blonde hair down the hall. "I guess I did."

The bell rang.

"Listen," he said, growing somber. "There's something important I have to—"

"It'll have to wait," she interrupted him. A smile filled her whole face. Her body felt light and tingly. The kiss had felt as good as she hoped it would. The problem now was how to get more of them.

Chapter 19

From far away, it looked like Lysander and Sam were caught in the web of a gigantic spider. The supports for the old railroad bridge, now green with age, crisscrossed around them. Their legs dangled over the edge, kicking back and forth. Now long in disuse, these tracks had at one time lead to the maw of the Millingham steel mill. Once the mill had closed, the town had resigned itself to a slow economic death.

Lysander had been unusually quiet since they'd come here after school. He was still trying to fit the pieces of the puzzle together in his own mind. Lysander followed Samantha's gaze down to the river below. He watched the water as it rushed by. The reflection looked like polished jewels twinkling in the sun. He reached a hand into the school bag beside him and withdrew a thin stack of old pages.

She looked up at him. "You found the autopsy?" Her voice trembled somewhere between fear and excitement. Lysander held them out to her.

She eyed the page on top. "Delores McMurphy..." she mumbled, "... Thomas." She flipped through the pages until her large brown eyes grew saucer wide. James McMurphy. She studied that one page for a long time, her face growing ashen.

107

"There's more," Lysander said hesitantly. He had never told her about what at the time had seemed like a sick dream about a man in a yellow cardigan and the dark thing that had crept in under the man's skin and killed him. He had decided to spare her the awful things the man had done to himself—plus his shame over the fact he had been unable to look away. His shocking discovery that it had all really happened and that a body sitting in the morgue had the strange marking of an eye to prove it. Things were different now, and she deserved to hear it all, no matter how much it was going to hurt.

• • •

Deputy Morgan wasn't crazy about spending such an unseasonably warm and sunny day stuck inside tracking down
leads. He had already made a dozen calls just to get the numbers he needed. Alex snatched up the receiver, checked the list he had put together, and started dialing. Barely on the second ring, he was already fumbling with his free hand inside his desk drawer, fishing out two tablets from a bottle of aspirin.

Tensions at the Millingham police department had taken on an almost surreal quality of late. Millingham's larger than life mayor, Gillis "call me Gil" Schroder, had showed up the day after the murder, offering his full support and a sprinkle of friendly advice:

It's election year, gentlemen. Find this fuck, and do it fast. Your jobs depend on it.

The steely smile on the cold sonofabitch's lips had never faltered for a second. Needless to say, the threat did not sit well with Alex. And that was when things had gone from bad to worse. Two hunters had found a homeless man, presumably a passerby, camping in the woods. When they approached him, the man was

108

nervous. Dried blood was streaked down the arms of his jacket.

Alex had jumped into his cruiser and sped to the scene. Something had been nagging at him the whole way. This wasn't the guy, the voice kept saying. The guy they were looking for was organized, methodical, not some sloppy nut bag who spent his nights spooning rabbits. But if it *was* him and the guy got away, or worse, if Jeff had arrived first, he could kiss his chances of ever becoming sheriff good-bye.

Alex stiffened against the back of his chair when the voice answered on the other end. "HCPD," a middle-aged woman said in a thick Massachusetts accent. "Detective Danforth, please." "One moment, sir," replied the woman rather blandly, dumping him into a hold pattern with terrible muzak.

Of course, Alex had taken the scraggly man into custody, but when the tests came back from the blood on the man's jacket, it belonged not to Peter Hume, but to a raccoon. The man had been living in the woods for two weeks now, surviving off whatever he could hit with a rock, which in this case proved to be a small family of raccoons. Apparently, when you killed the mother, the babies didn't run away, so he had slaughtered them at his leisure. Even long after Sheriff Crow had stopped yelling, Alex's ears were still ringing something awful.

Part of him wanted Lysander to be guilty. Tracing back Peter Hume's client list, a surprising entry had come up. Hume had paid the Shores a visit shortly before his murder.

But probably the worst part about it was how much Sam seemed to like him. The time he had picked her up near the hospital and brought her to the station, he had seen the signs as clear as day. Alex was nobody's fool. He knew a boy Lysander's age, especially one who dressed the way he did, would only ask how high, if Samantha

109

had told him to jump. He had even told Dorothy to fire the boy on account of him being a suspect, and she had refused and then proceeded to blow his entire theory out of the water with a single question: "Where was this boy when Diane Crow was killed?"

"Hayward," he had answered and dropped the subject flat. His suspicion of Lysander hadn't faded entirely though.

Alex realized his foot was tapping a steady beat on the floor. He was keeping time to a bad muzak rendition of "Get Down on It," by Kool and the Gang.

The line crackled. "Danforth here."

Alex finished swallowing the last aspirin in the bottle. "This is Deputy Morgan from the Millingham police department. I understand you've been with the Hayward County police department for a number of years now."

Danforth answered simply, "I have."

"Great." Alex was smiling now. "I've been told you might have some information for me on a Lysander Shore."

Chapter 20

A turbulent cyclone of emotions was fighting for supremacy within Samantha. At the forefront of those emotions was shock that three people nearly fifty years apart had died under such similar circumstances. First McMurphy in 1965, then her mother, and now some guy named Peter Hume—all three by their own hand, each with eyes ripped from their skull. Her body felt heavy and sluggish. Her stomach tightening and retracting painfully.

When the initial shock began to settle, she was left in a blinding fury. She was furious, of course, that her father had hidden this from her. The first *she'd* heard of it was from Lysander.

All these years she'd faced an insurmountable wall of denial over her mother's death. She wasn't sure what felt worse. That she was right or that they'd suspected all along and kept it from her.

Thinking back over the last few days, she could see now that her father had been acting strange, at times dazed, consumed with what she had assumed was a losing battle with exhaustion. But now she was realizing that the expression on his face had been something else entirely. He looked like a man haunted by what he may have missed. Her eyes filled with hot salty tears which threatened to spill down her cheeks, but she choked them back. There would be lots of time to cry later.

"You wanna head home?" Lysander asked her.

"No," she said, her mind still racing. "Nothing for me at home."

Slowly they stood and began following the rusted-out train tracks, overgrown now with spiny-amaranth and carpetweed. Ahead was a dirt road that led back to town.

"You know my father still won't go into that bathroom where she was found. He uses mine." She turned to him, pensive. "You said there was some kind of mark on Hume's body... at the morgue."

Lysander nodded.

She handed him a stick that appeared at her feet. "Draw it for me."

He took the stick from her and scratched an image into the dusty road.

She studied the eye he had drawn and took a bewildering step back. "I've seen this before," she said, puzzled.

Lysander looked at her.

She swung off her school bag off and began rooting through it. From one of the side pockets she produced a notebook. Old and worn.

"Where'd you get that?" Lysander asked, not entirely sure he wanted to know.

"Derek found it in an upstairs bedroom at the house. It's a journal McMurphy was keeping. I've only glanced through it briefly but..."

She found what she was looking for and handed the book to Lysander. He was hardly able to believe what he was seeing, felt his breath catch and the world swinging away from him. He held the book open over the etching he had drawn on the ground. The eyes were the same—watching, searching. The only real difference was that the eyes in McMurphy's journal filled the whole page.

112

Chapter 21

The elderly librarian had her hair tied into a painful-looking concoction and greeted Sam and Lysander with a keen look of annoyance.

"We need information on this," Lysander said, holding open McMurphy's journal to a page where a single giant eye had been sketched.

The librarian looked suspicious. She did not want to become the butt of some teenage prank. "Shouldn't you two be in school?"

"Are you serious?" Sam asked. "It's after four."

The gray-haired woman rolled her eyes. "Well, your picture does bear some resemblance to the Eye of Horus, so you might wanna start your, err, research in our section on ancient Egypt."

"Thank you," he managed, fighting the urge to say something nasty to the old hag, knowing it would only confirm her judgment of him. Sam, however, had no such compunction and scratched her nose with her middle finger, wiggling the tip at the woman in case she hadn't quite got the message.

They climbed a marble staircase with wrought iron railings. At the top, by a water fountain they found a computer. Sam typed the following into the search bar: Eye of Horus.

113

1054 hits.

Lysander nudged her out of the way. "Searching for stuff in the library's a tricky thing. You can't just type in exactly what you want. You gotta do it in a roundabout way, otherwise you won't get diddley-squat."

"What can we find here we couldn't get on Google?"

"Sam, any hack can put up a website or write a Wikipedia page. We don't have time to sift through mountains of crap and false leads. Besides, I try and spend as little time at home
as I can."

Sam moved aside and swung her arms in an
exaggerated motion toward the console. "I think you're just a Luddite, but be my guest. Let's see what you can do."

"What's a Luddite?" Lysander asked puzzled.

"Look it up. You're the wanna-be librarian."

He giggled as he laid his hands on the keyboard—an off-white IBM clone maybe fifteen years old—and typed: Ancient Egypt beliefs. Two generic volumes on Egyptian history came up, but nothing useful.

Sam smiled.

Lysander tried something else. Ancient Egypt superstitions.

More generic volumes.

Ancient Egypt religion was Lysander's next attempt.

The computer returned six entries. The most promising was *The Search for God in Ancient Egypt*.

Lysander winked at Sam. "See, we're getting hotter."

Then he tried something different. He typed Ancient Egyptian religion "eye of horus" and hoped that the quotation marks might single out books that were especially relevant.

The following volume came back: *The Complete Gods and Goddesses of Ancient Egypt*.

Sam threw her arms around him. "You're a genius!"

114

Lysander blushed. "It's on this floor," he said sheepishly. "Let's take a look."

They left the computer and disappeared into shadowy stacks of old books. Lysander let his fingers skim the dusty spines until he found it. The book was large, and they had to bring it to a table to open it up. Sam began flipping through the pages.

"That's not the way you do it," Lysander said. He realized then that if he'd been anyone else she might have punched him out, but Lysander didn't mean it in a bad way and was sure she knew that.

"Always check the index at the back for what you want. It'll save you a heap of time."

Sam snorted. "Yeah, well, I don't hang out in libraries much."

Lysander laughed. "You will if you intend on going to college." He drew his finger down the listings under H.

"Since we're looking for eye," Sam blurted. "Shouldn't you be looking under E?"

"No, Horus is what we're really looking for, not eye. Find Horus and we find what we're looking for."

And sure enough there it was.

"Horus, eye of, 374."

Lysander felt a surge of exhilaration. Eagerly, they flipped to the page. What they found was a hieroglyphic eye, very much like the one drawn in the journal and on Hume, but with the addition of what almost looked like long spindly legs.

They scanned the page looking for the word Horus and started reading from there. When they finished, Lysander seemed uncertain about something.

"So the Eye of Horus was a talisman used to protect people against the evil eye," Sam said, thinking out loud.

"Evil eye?" Lysander asked. "Isn't that like giving someone a bad look?"

Sam's face became grave. "Kind of," she said. "But so

115

much worse. In the old days, people believed that you could hurt someone just by looking at them a certain way."

"You mean like a spell?"

Sam nodded. "More like a curse."

"Sometimes you Wiccans scare me."

Slowly, the corners of her lips curled into a devilish smile. "Good."

"You think this is what we're after?" Lysander asked her.

She turned serious again. "I don't think so. The Eye of Horus doesn't look a whole lot like our eye. Look here. It mentions that the eye was used by more than one culture... in fact, at one time, it may have been the most popular superstition in the world."

"If the eye on Hume isn't from ancient Egypt, then where should we be looking?"

Sam kept reading. "Says here the evil eye is most commonly associated with—"

"Witchcraft," Lysander said, his finger pressed down under the word. He looked about him. "We need an encyclopedia."

Minutes later, a stack of encyclopedias were piled crookedly before them. Lysander was holding *The American Encyclopedia*, Sam the *Britannica*.

"We need pictures," Sam said.

"What we need," said Lysander, "is to find an eye that looks just like ours."

Growing frustrated, he dropped the American and picked up *The Encyclopedia of Witchcraft and Demonology*.

"Have you thought about the possibility that we're wasting our time?" she pointed out. "I mean, what are the chances of finding anything usefu—"

"Oh shit," Lysander cried. "This is it... the one I saw on Hume."

She snatched the enormous book from him and studied

116

it. "Says here that during the Middle Ages, they used a symbol of an eye to protect themselves from witches." Sam then read directly from the book. "The practice of shielding oneself from the perceived effects of the evil eye were most apparent during the trials of accused witches. The belief, a carryover from ancient times, held that by branding an eye with a hot poker into the flesh of the condemned, the act might nullify the witch's ability to curse any of her accusers. This practice carried forward even into the new world. Most notable among them was Rebecca Goodman, accused and burned in Millingham in 1648."

Sam looked skeptical. "Millingham? Our Millingham? The most boring town on earth, burning witches? I don't believe it. Lysander, what do you thin—"

Lysander's complexion had become gray and chalky. Seeing that look on his face, the stray thoughts in her mind began falling into place.

"Your session with Avery," she said.

Lysander's lips were trembling. "But he said it was only a fantasy…" Lysander's voice trailed off.

Sam looked down at the encyclopedia and the witch's name, Rebecca Goodman. "We need everything on this woman we can find."

Lysander nodded vacantly. Biting her nail, she rose and headed to the computer console, leaving Lysander half hidden behind a table piled with books.

He felt himself in some strange limbo. A great unraveling was taking place, a rescanning of all past memories, thoughts and dreams to see how they fit into this new paradigm. Conversations he had, places he visited. Was he losing his mind? Or was all of life just some unending dream with varying shades of substance and form? Lysander felt himself lost and tumbling down a long dark hole. His hands fumbled before him, feeling for something hard, something tangible. His eyes found the McMurphy journal and he could have sworn it had changed. It was happy. He fingered its cracking pages, hands numb with fear. In all the places without words, there were eyes, hundreds of them, staring back at him from the yellowed pages.

He shook his head to dispel the image and concentrated on the text. McMurphy had written diary entries.

The first began normally enough.

May 9, 1963

I never believed that a record of my life was important, in so much as I saw it as a vain and narcissistic pursuit. But as they say, a task begun will wilt if unattended, and so I know the regularity of the exercise will do me some good.

The entries went on in that vein for a few years. McMurphy was not a constant diarist.

Apparently he had written only when the mood had gripped him.

May 30, 1965

An odd and disturbing dream last night, the details of which I strain to remember, but cannot grasp. I awoke and swore someone stood at the foot of my bed. A man, dressed in a dark cloak and wearing a wide hat. I closed my eyes, thinking myself still dreaming, and when I opened them again he was still there. He was plump under his cloak and I knew this, for I could see his belly pushing against the fabric. He seemed a petulant and harsh little man, and even in the few seconds before he disappeared I felt as though I disliked him very much. I have decided not to speak of this for reasons that should seem obvious to anyone.

June 19, 1965

This journal was intended to be a chronicle of my inner thoughts and the events of my life, but has since, through no fault of my own,

118

become a catalogue of strange and bizarre occurrences. I was up late last night, working at my desk, as I have been doing of late. This business of zone development should not be left in the hands of the city council, that group of bumbling autocrats. I descended to the kitchen some time after midnight, careful not to wake any of the family. (Thomas can be so disagreeable when he's woken. If only I had the time and inclination I would find myself a wife and gladly leave this madhouse.) On my way back, a chicken sandwich and a glass of warm milk in hand, I had the strangest experience. A voice, so real I swore the person whispered into my ear, called my name. James, it whispered. And when I turned there was no one there.

July 1, 1965
Almost every night now as I begin to doze, I sense that I am being watched. It is an eerie feeling that I cannot shake. Even when I switch the light on and order whatever or whoever it is to leave, still they remain. I haven't been sleeping well of late, and it is perhaps for this very reason. Last night, when I again turned on the light and ordered the apparition to leave, something so terribly strange happened I'm hesitant to mention it even in the private confines of this journal. I've always been a religious man and know not what to make of it, but when I glanced at the cross above my bed, perhaps for consolation or guidance, I could have swore I saw Jesus' eyes scan the room before finding my own, wide and disbelieving as they must have looked. I lay awake all last night and took the cross down first thing this morning, though by all intents and purposes it appeared solid and normal.

July 15, 1965
I'm beginning to wonder at the possibility that this old house of ours, the house that's been in our family for over three generations, is beset by some restless spirit.

September 1, 1965
I was up late again last night, making myself a quick meal, when I heard that same voice whisper into my ear. It sounded strangely

119

feminine, but also masculine. I again wondered at the possibility of a ghost, since not so long ago I saw a man standing by my bed appearing as solid and impenetrable as any real thing I had ever seen. I tried ignoring it and continued back to my room and the hours of work I knew still awaited me, when I heard it speak again and this time the words were tinged with a kind of even-handed hatred I had never felt from the presence. What they pertain to and how it has anything to do with me, I have no idea, nor do I care to find out. However, if I close my eyes, I cannot help but see those words as though a placard, gnarled and battered, has been erected inside my head and will forever remain.

The voice said one simple thing: 'I'm coming.'

Chapter 22

It was nearing dusk when Samantha and Lysander reached the Millingham cemetery. The gate was bolted shut, and protecting the grounds was a stone wall ten feet high. Samantha said she knew another way in. Together they walked under the wall's creeping evening shadow.

Back at the library, she had returned with several books on witchcraft in America and had found more than one mentioning Rebecca Goodman by name. One such source came from the private writings of the Governor of the Massachusetts Bay Colony.

From Governor John Winthrop's Journal:

An Account of the Execution of Rebecca Goodman of Millingham, 1648.

At this Court one Rebecca Goodman of Millingham was indicted and found guilty of witchcraft and burned for it. The evidence against her was: 1. that she was found to have such a malignant touch as many persons (men, women, and children) whom she stroked or touched were taken with deafness, or vomiting; 2. some things which she foretold came to pass accordingly; other things she could tell of (as secret speeches, etc.) which she had no ordinary means to come to the knowledge of; 3. she had (upon search) an

121

apparent teat in her secret parts as fresh as if it had been newly sucked; 4. in the prison in the clear daylight there was seen in her arms a little child which ran from her into another room, and the officer following it said it had vanished. Her behavior at her trial was very intemperate, lying notoriously, and railing upon the jury and witnesses, etc., and in the like distemper she died.

Apparently Rebecca Goodman had been absolved and reburied here in 1712 when the practice of murdering women for being different had lost its appeal.

"Don't you see?" Lysander had whispered back in the shadowy confines of the Millingham library. "Those eyes tacked all over his journal. McMurphy wasn't going crazy. He was using them. Maybe he came to the library, just like us and found what we found."

"Using them?" she had asked. "But for what?"

"Protection."

Her body had stiffened involuntarily.

"I still don't see what good going to the cemetery will do," she said at last.

"I'm not sure either," Lysander answered truthfully, "but everything we've found so far has led us here. If those sessions with Avery are real, then there's a connection between me and these murders. McMurphy, your mother, Hume. And who knows, maybe even Rebecca Goodman."

Sam stopped to check the layout of the grounds she'd found at the library. Behind them was the stone wall they'd scaled. Past that, the small grove of birch trees and beyond that still a grouping of freshly dug graves. That meant they were approaching a part of the cemetery that was as old as Millingham itself.

Lysander swallowed hard.

Several weather-beaten tombstones stood in a crooked row. Lysander scanned each one: Mather Pell, Drake Butler, Deborah Lockwood, Samuel Tyler, Elizabeth Cabel. He had never seen graves this old before. What

122

were the bodies like? he wondered. Had they turned to dust?

Did anything of them remain—bits of clothing, strands of hair, a grisly skeleton? Or had the cold harshness of time worn them away as it had the very stones that marked their graves? Samantha checked the map one final time and then pointed at the stone marker on the ground.

"There she is."

It was hard to see in the dim light. She noticed Lysander struggling to read the inscription and pulled a small flashlight from her bag. She bathed the inscription in warm light.

Here lies Rebecca Goodman

Died November 2nd, 1648.

The words on the inscription were difficult to make out.

Burned as a witch, absolved and reburied 1712.

His breath felt suddenly labored, as though heavy stones had been stacked on his chest.

"I thought all the witches killed in America were hung," Lysander said.

"Apparently not all of them."

He looked at her skeptically.

"Most witches were hung, you're right. But maybe this one was especially mean. It was the blood they were afraid of. It had to be burned and boiled away to negate the threat."

He reached down and drew his hand across the weathered surface, smooth after all these years. He flinched at the jolt as his fingers felt the gravestone. Immediately, he was gripped by a horrible image. A woman pleading for her life, professing her innocence. Her face twisted in terror. Something about that face was strange, deformed. Her thoughts were frantic, wanting only of escape. A terrible mistake had been made. But it

123

was too late, her hands were bound behind her, pulled painfully tight around a thick wooden stake. But her locket was still with her. She couldn't see it of course, but she could feel it. Thank God. A gift from her husband, Henry. It was so precious that a part of her was happy it would go with her. Then something struck her in the face. The crowd below pitched insults and raw vegetables at her. She could not see but she heard them yelling. She was hit in the face again. A face already damaged from torture. The pain in her face was unbearable. Below her, heaped in great bundles were stacks of wood and twigs, soaked in some foul smelling liquid, making every breath nearly impossible. She did not sense the flames yet, but her hands burned as though they were on fire. She was blind, but nevertheless she sensed that the men in black, the council, were near. She knew they were watching her with self-righteousness, and their contempt only fed her hatred for them. None of these simple people ever understood her, they knew nothing about her. They knew nothing of how she had cared for that child stricken with fever day and night, nursed him until he was well. His parents were so happy, asking "How can we ever repay you?" Now they were in the crowd with the others, throwing rotten vegetables. She screamed at the judges, "How dare you pass judgment upon me! How dare you steal my life with such ease of conscience?" One judge sat at the head of the others and it was he she hated most. It was he who ordered the torture. He was the one responsible.

Tiny wisps of orange flame flickered beneath her feet. Thick black smoke was rising around her, becoming hard to breathe. The heat grew more intense. The flesh on her feet and legs began to sear with pain. Her mouth too was filled with black suffocating soot. She tried to wiggle her hands but they were bound. There was no escape. The pain was so unbearable. She could feel herself cooking.

124

She waited for death... waited for peace. But there was no peace. Only more pain, shooting through her body, a thousand knives stabbing her at once. Her nightgown had caught on fire. She screamed. The crowd was silent. Some cried out for mercy.

The pain had become intolerable, but it was miniscule compared to the anger she now felt. Her anger consumed her entire being in blackness. It embraced her and as it did, the physical pain began to fade. Her flesh was falling away in great clumps, her feet crisp and blackened beyond repair and yet she felt no pain. She had found her deliverance. She was one with the hatred.

A voice far away was screaming Lysander's name. Samantha was shaking him. He looked up at her dreamily and then back down at what he was doing. Clamped tightly in both hands was the shovel, his right foot pushing the hilt into Rebecca Goodman's grave.

Samantha's voice was frantic. "What are you doing?"

The words were coming so quick, tumbling over one another. He could barely think straight. "I saw it happen," he said hoarsely.

"You saw what happen?"

"I don't know. A woman... burned alive. It felt so real."

"Lysander, you're scaring me." Samantha sighed. She had thought maybe they were coming here and that he would kiss her and who knows what else. But to dig up bodies, especially Rebecca Goodman... this was crazy.

Her flashlight illuminated Lysander's face. Beads of sweat rolled down his cheeks and neck. His eyes were dull and protruding.

"Samantha, don't you understand?" he shouted. "I saw it happening. I was there. I was her—" Lysander stopped shoveling for a moment and touched his forehead.

Samantha's legs felt suddenly heavy. A cold fear seemed to have crawled up from the ground and grabbed a hold

125

of her. She searched around frantically, not knowing what to do. She had seen him pass out cold before. Derek had lit that old lantern and bam Lysander had gone crashing to the floor. Now he was behaving so unlike himself, she was frightened. He was digging again. She shined the light on the ground for him, although part of her wanted to leave, to run away and abandon him, but she couldn't. It was the story of her life. Yet what frightened her most was the way he kept talking to himself, repeating that same thing over and over. That he had to know. That he had to be sure it was real. He was possessed.

"Lysander, her body's gone. You know, turned to bug shit."

"Yeah, but maybe not everything."

Four feet down, Lysander's shovel clanked against something hard. He reached in and wiped it off with his hands. A large rock. He looked up with a desperate smile.

"They couldn't have buried her deeper than this. We must have missed it." He examined the pile of dirt heaped beside the grave. He hopped over the hole and began running his hands through the blackened earth. Most of it was muddy, thickened from a recent bout of rain.

The hairs on Samantha's arm stood on end as she held the light.

"There's nothing there," she pleaded. "Just dirt."

Lysander didn't answer. The beam from the flashlight flickered and then went out. She smacked it against the palm of her hand, and it came back.

"The battery's running low. If we don't leave soon, we won't be able to see a thing."

Something in the distance drew her attention. A flashlight beam was bobbing toward them. For a moment she stood paralyzed. Then she knew. It was the groundskeeper.

"Someone's coming, Lysander!"

126

Lysander didn't even look up. "Okay, just another minute."

Samantha hunkered low to the ground, dampening the beam of light with the palm of her hand.

Her heart was beating wildly. It was one thing to be caught walking through the graveyard after hours and another thing entirely to be digging up a three-hundred-fifty-year-old grave. Lysander was still fumbling through the mud, pushing back into the hole what he had already examined. There was no sign that a body had ever been here: no clothing, no bones, nothing. The earth had reclaimed every last bit. As he thrust his hand into the pile one more time, one of his knuckles scraped against something hard. Another rock, he thought at first. He groped around some more. At last he emerged with a small black object. Samantha leaned closer and lit it with the flashlight. From here, through the thin beam of yellow light, it didn't look like much.

"What is it?" she asked.

Lysander wiped it carefully with his hands. Before their eyes hundreds of years of gunk and grime was melting away. Slowly it was looking more and more like a worn piece of jewelry. Lysander's heart was in his throat. Could it be the locket he had seen around her neck? He had but touched the gravestone and the vision... no, the memory... had come.

Samantha saw that the groundskeeper's beam was much closer now. In the distance she could hear the sound of dogs barking. It began to dawn on Samantha that neither of them had worked out an escape plan. And she knew, as the only one of them still in their right mind, that if the groundskeeper released those dogs, they would be in for a world of trouble.

Almost in answer to her fear, the barking became frenzied. Samantha's eyes grew wide. "Lysander, get up! He's let the dogs loose."

127

She grabbed his arm and yanked him with everything she had. He stumbled backward, still examining the object in his hands.

"Come on!" she said, slapping the side of his head.

Finally emerging from his trance, he tucked the jewelry into his pocket, rose to his feet and staggered into a full run. They charged down the opposite side of the hill, leaping over the gravestones a second after they came into the short outstretched beam cast by the flashlight. As they clamored across the graveyard, the whooshing wind deafened them to the clumsiness of their footfalls. Sam could only hope that the uneven terrain and gravestones might delay the dogs' progress and buy them enough time to escape.

Ahead, they could just make out the cemetery's stone wall.

When they arrived, Lysander cried breathlessly to Sam: "Get on my shoulders and I'll boost you up."
Through the gloom, Samantha could see the silhouette of two tiny forms cresting the hill and racing toward them.

"Sam, get on my shoulders, quickly."

Lysander bent over and when he felt that her feet were planted firmly on his shoulders, he straightened himself. The sharp pain in his lower back was excruciating. Lysander gathered all of his strength to boost her up. Samantha scrambled to the top and draped one leg over each end. He could hear the dogs yelping. They would be on him any second now. Samantha leaned over and stuck her hand out, but Lysander backed away and took a run at the wall. He sprinted, leaping into the air at the last moment. He swung for her hand and missed it, snagging the bottom of her leather jacket instead. Samantha reeled back and nearly lost her balance. She repositioned herself and on the next pass managed to hold him. Grabbing his arm, she strained to pull him up. Just then a misplaced thought crossed her mind: For a short guy he was heavy

128

as hell. Lysander's left leg was pumping like a giant piston. His right leg however, was caught. Then he felt the burning pain as something pierced his calf. Terrified, he looked down, certain that one of the dogs had snatched his leg in its powerful jaws. He saw then that his pant leg was caught on a rusted bolt protruding from the wall.

Below him, the dogs had arrived and were leaping for him, snapping at the air with their jaws. Any moment now and they would have him. They could hear the groundskeeper huffing as he tried to catch up. Samantha saw that he had a rifle. She reached into her pocket and pulled out the flashlight. She turned it on and whipped it at one of the dogs. The animal reeled away and let out a yelp. The reprieve gave Lysander the second he needed to free his leg and scramble to the top. They swung over the edge and climbed down the tree. They could hear the groundskeeper on the other side of the wall panting furiously, trying to calm his dogs. He was swearing at them through the thick slab of stone. "You little shits ever come back, I'll blow your heads clear off. Mark my words."

Lysander started running the moment his feet hit the ground. Sam sprinted alongside him, sucking in lungfuls of air. They skittered to a stop only when the cemetery had faded from view. Lysander perched his hands on the tops of his knees, his chest expanding and contracting. His hand went inside his pocket and his fingers walked over the strange object he had found.

"What happened to you back there?" Sam asked angrily.

"I'm not really sure," was all he could say in reply.

"Well you nearly got us killed."

Lysander's hand came out with the object. His voice was unsteady as he said, "I saw that woman burn to death tonight. It happened hundreds of years ago, but it felt as

129

close to me as you are right now."

She took the object from him and examined it. "Looks like a clump of shit to me."

"There's something underneath. I've just got to clean it away."

Sam's eyes stayed fixed on him. "You're worrying me. I think this whole thing is getting way out of hand."

The turn for her street was up ahead. She would have to go home now. Sweaty and breathing like Marion Jones after the hundred meter. Not an easy thing to explain to the head of the Gestapo, Herr Crow.

Lysander pleaded with her. "We're getting closer. It's crazy, I know, but I feel it. Feel it so much stronger now than I did before."

They parted not long after, Lysander still busy with his new discovery.

As he walked, he began to see something appear beneath the layers of dirt. He stopped on a hill and stood under the dim light of a lamppost, trying to make out exactly what he was seeing. Could it be the same locket that Rebecca Goodman had worn? Lysander's heart began to race. He brushed a finger over its worn surface until a metallic gleam stared back at him. All at once, he was sure. In his hands was the locket he had seen around the witch's neck, three hundred years ago.

The voice to his left seemed to come out of nowhere and the fright sent an electric charge pulsing through his whole body.

Reverend Small's wrinkled face was hard to make out through the gloom inside the car. The passenger-side window slid all the way down. "What on earth are you doing, son? Don't you have school tomorrow?"

"I'm heading home."

Small looked at the road ahead and then back at Lysander. "Go on, get in. Wouldn't be neighborly of me to just leave you." A big smile filled his face.

130

Lysander thought about the other night, when he had seen the reverend hitting that dog. Part of him wondered if getting in this car was the smart thing to do.

If he tries anything I'll beat him down, Lysander thought with over-inflated bravado and got in.

The car moved forward and Lysander's breathing had just begun to settle when the reverend spoke.

"What have you got there?" The old guy was eyeing the locket in Lysander's hand. He had been polishing its worn metal surface without thinking. A dull shine was coming back.

Small stretched out a hand. The silver ring with the fish on it winked at him from a passing streetlight. "Mind if I see?"

Lysander hesitated.

Small let his hand fall to his lap. "That's all right, then. Where'd you find that old thing anyhow? Looks like the kinda broach my mother used to wear. Carried her heart on her sleeve for everyone to see. Bit of a cliché I suppose, but in her case it was true."

"I found it lying on the ground," Lysander said, hating the stupidity of his lie, but not feeling an ounce of guilt for having told it.

They came to a red light. "The one my mother owned had two pictures inside," Reverend Small offered, "one of her and one of myself."

Lysander fingered the lump of darkened metal in his hands, finding it surprisingly thin and light. He inspected it more closely. There was a small slit down the side, but no real way of prying it open without using something that would surely wreck it. He dug the edge of his nail into the slit and jimmied it until he heard a popping sound. As the locket opened, Reverend Small looked on with keen interest. The light turned green, but he didn't move. The light in his eyes had changed too. When he saw Lysander looking out at the streetlight, he started up

131

the car again.

"What do you see, Lysander?"

Lysander strained to make it out. There was so much sediment, he wondered if someone at a museum wasn't better suited to handle this.

"Looks like an expensive piece," Small said. "I'm sure someone's missing it. Someone who may very well belong to our congregation. I'll bet I could find them in a jiffy."

They pulled into Lysander's driveway and Small stopped the car and held out his hand. It was fleshy and smelled of discount aftershave.

Lysander knew full well he wasn't looking for a farewell shake. The honest expression on the old man's face made Lysander feel he had done something terribly wrong by digging the locket up. Regardless of everything that had happened, it didn't belong to him. But another voice was telling him he should keep it. The time wasn't right to give it up yet.

The locket hovered over Small's hand between Lysander's index finger and his thumb. Then suddenly Lysander snapped it away. "I think I'm gonna hold on to it for a bit," he said.

Disappointment registered on the reverend's face, as though Lysander had failed some significant test. "Well, let me know if you have a change of heart," the reverend said, shaking his head quietly. "I'm sure I could find the right home for it."

Lysander got out of the car, barely aware as the reverend backed up and drove away. He was still looking at the locket. There were two portraits inside. Barely visible. The first was that of a man, the second a woman. Perhaps they were married. Rebecca Goodman and her husband. Looking at the locket, Lysander realized the reverend had been right. The locket did look old and expensive. But there was something else the old man said that was making the skin on Lysander's scalp feel like it

132

was crawling with insects. Whoever lost an heirloom this precious would be looking for it. Whoever lost it would want it back.

Chapter 23

The steps outside the clinic were cold on this Hollow's Eve. Samantha shifted her nearly frozen rear. She was wrapped tightly in her leather jacket, hands pulled into her sleeves, waiting for her father to pick her up. Not surprisingly, he was late. She had come to the clinic to see her gynecologist, Gail Winters, a thin, graying woman who was a closet lesbian, if town rumors were to be believed—and Samantha knew they usually were. That didn't bother Samantha. Didn't bother her one speck. Dr. Winters did a good job. She was delicate and always made her feel comfortable.

A cold wind blew up, and Samantha watched dead leaves scatter, stacking against the tires of parked cars, some whirling willy-nilly in the intersection. A tree nearby bent in the wind, leafless and sad-looking. Samantha shivered. Things had certainly gotten chilly. There would be snow before long. She glanced up at a depressingly gray sky, unable to remember the last time she had seen the sun.

Sam licked her chapped lips, and the way her tongue slid between her teeth made her think of Lysander and that first time she had kissed him in the hallway at school. It was the most impulsive thing she had ever done. At the time part of her was actually convinced she wanted to help him get with Summer. If for no other reason than to prove to him, that once he got her, he would know what a shallow twit she really was.

A girl like Summer, Sam knew, only really cared about one person and that was Summer. Yes, Lysander was handsome, in an albeit unconventional way, but certainly not in a way that would be engaging for someone whose only realm of discussion revolved around who had fallen from the human pyramid during cheerleading practice or whether Pantene Pro V really provided the shine the commercials promised.

To the Summers of the world, guys like Lysander were only a means. A means more often than not of making boyfriends jealous. Yet she knew that a boy, never accepted for who he

was, might very well jump at the chance of being a somebody. She couldn't help but feel sadness when she thought about the way he probably saw her: as a buddy. And the thought made her stomach tighten painfully. She could see it now for the losing battle that it was.

A police car pulled up in front of her. Slowly, the window slid down. The man in the car lowered his sunglasses. In a strained voice, Alex told her she looked cold. She got up and walked, stiffly, to the passenger-side door. She folded into a car that felt as hot as a summer's day.

Alex looked different somehow, filled with a new purpose.

"Your father's busy right now, Sam," he said. "He asked if I'd pick you up." He removed his glasses and placed then on the dash. Alex turned to her conspiratorially. "Just between you and me. I think your father's with Dorothy right now."

Samantha nodded, wondering how that was any of his business.

"How do you feel about them being back together?" he

135

asked, rubbing the nape of his neck.

"Anything's better than Principal Evans."

Alex started to laugh and Samantha flashed him a wicked grin.

In no time though, Alex grew serious again, and Samantha could see the muscles in his jaw working. He looked as though some debate were raging within him.

"There's something you need to know," he said slowly. "I should have told you a long time ago. I wanted to. I tried…"

Samantha's lips drew into a thin line. Anyone who had ever started out like that never had anything good to say, she thought. Her hands fell instinctively to the brown leather seat between her legs, and she began squeezing till her hands turned white.

"You can't tell your father no matter what," he said.

"What's this all about," she asked impatiently.

"It's…about your mother." Alex spat out the words quickly, as though expecting an eruption. "I'm just gonna tell it to you the way I heard it." A single bead of sweat rolled down the side of his face. "I was with Ol' man Wallace a while back, looking for where Derek might be hiding at."

The muscles in Sam's hands tensed.

"I'm sorry you have to find out this way," he said, not sounding sorry at all. "Wallace told me Derek was bragging that he and your mother had been having an affair. That he was in love–"

The open palm of Samantha's hand struck Alex's face with such force that his ear went completely numb. The shock of it made him jerk the wheel. The car swerved a little. He slowed down and fell silent after that. His ear was ringing something awful. As he kept driving, neither of them said a word. He had an initial blinding urge to strike her back, but instead he clenched his hands into tight balls over the steering wheel.

136

Alex continued quietly. "It's important you hear this. When your mother died, I made a point of telling you how it happened. Maybe I shouldn't have, but I did. Those are the kinds of details you don't wanna find out about from a newspaper. You deserve the truth. Face to face."

Samantha sat rigid. She thought Alex had been about to confess his feelings for her and how guilty he felt about their difference in age. That would not have surprised her. But this? Where in hell was this coming from?

"The old man told me that when your mother called it off so she could work things out with your father, Derek was crushed. He showed up to work in real sour moods, pissed off, muttering under his breath. Ol'man Wallace said he'd never seen him like that, and I think it worried the old guy."

Samantha took a deep breath to steady herself. Her hands were trembling. He had been gone for nearly a month now and it was a lucky thing for Derek he wasn't there with her or there'd be no telling what she'd do to him.

Through that dense cloud of anger she suddenly thought of her father and her heart sank. Samantha watched her hands quivering. She had secrets of her own, didn't she?

"When Lysander and I were–" she stopped short, but felt a strange compulsion to continue. "Well, we found something strange at the abandoned McMurphy place."

Alex's face hardened.

"We found an old diary. Belonged to McMurphy. It's filled with these drawings of an eye. Like the whole page is covered with them." She wasn't sure if Alex was getting any of this but she said it anyway. "The same one Hume had on him."

She was right, Alex wasn't all there. But for other reasons. He was watching something on the hood of the

137

car. A gaseous vapor growing out of a hungry black hole. Alex's eyes fixed on it, the way people might fix on an approaching tornado in spite of the danger. He caught the outline of a face in the mist, looking back at him. It began to take shape, and the sight of it nearly sickened him. Diane's purple face hovered before him. Dark hair, floating in tangles. Like the tentacles of a sickly octopus tangled in a fisherman's net. The woman's bloated head turned deliberately, and Alex felt thick ropes of sweat rolling down his forehead. That face, that neck bent at such an unnatural angle, watched him through two empty sockets. The smell of rotting fish came over him. The still water in the tub became a perfect reflective surface, and suddenly that grotesque face was two faces, plastered from end to end with a wicked Cheshire grin. Wet purple lips parted and slowly words began forming in his head. She was trying to speak:

Deeeeeeeeeerrrrrreeeeeeeeekkkkkk....

Alex jerked himself back, like a man ripping himself from Medusa's petrifying gaze. The joints in his hands were cramped, he realized, stiff from the iron grip he had on the steering wheel. Consciously he willed his fingers to open.

Samantha was looking at him wide-eyed, her mouth hinged open, not saying a word.

Alex's hairline was soaked. He lifted an awkward sleeve to blot away the sweat. The red traffic light had been green for several seconds, and Alex made a right down Baker Avenue.

Five minutes of stony silence followed before they pulled into the driveway and behind Sheriff Crow's cruiser. Samantha pushed the door open and stuck a foot out. She leaned over and for a moment Alex wondered if Samantha meant to kiss him. But instead she whispered. "I hope you'll look into what I've told you."

Alex assured her he would. Of course he could only

138

recall faint threads of what she had said. Something about Hume and a book. Or was it a diary? She was about to close the door.

"Oh, Sam," he called after her.

She poked her head back in, and Alex caught himself peering into the depths of her brown eyes. They stood out like beautiful orbs against the gray sky at her back. He felt a surge of stinging jealousy at the thought of anyone setting their paws on her.

"What I told you stays between us." His face became grave. "Don't forget. Your dad will fry both our asses if this ever gets back to him. Especially if he knew you'd heard it from me."

She nodded absently.

"Oh, and the next time you need something in my desk," he said, "just ask."

A fiery blush crept up into Sam's cheeks, and the sight of it stirred Alex's desire.

"I understand you wanting to protect Derek. I might have done the same."

The look of surprise on her face couldn't have been more complete.

"I'll be by later," he said after he'd had his fill of her discomfort. "Your dad and I are gonna watch the Patriots before I go back on duty."

Samantha nodded, looking as though she wished she could be anywhere but there. She slammed the door. He could see her heading toward the house through the passenger-side window, fogged over from the combined warmth of their bodies. That's when he saw what she had drawn with the tip of her finger.

An eye. Open and all seeing.

The same one Dorothy had said she'd found on Hume's chest. Had Samantha not told him she'd found it in something related to McMurphy? A diary? He couldn't remember now.

139

He swallowed hard.

The thought of rushing out after her crossed his mind, but she was already entering the house. He flung the door open and then stopped. No, he would wait. If he where to barge in and start questioning Samantha now, the Sheriff would become suspicious for sure, and rightfully so. No, he would play it cool. Tonight when he came back, he would sneak off from the game, sit her down and find out more about this business.

● ● ●

As Sam closed the door behind her, she found herself in a dark and gloomy house. Faint daylight struggled in through the living room windows. She snapped the hall light on and was about to go upstairs to her room when she heard a noise coming from the kitchen. She paused. Even though her father's cruiser was outside, she had assumed, perhaps because of the darkness, that she was alone. She went to the kitchen and pushed through the swinging door. Her heart leapt, unsure of what she might see. Her mind was still on her conversation with Alex and she half expected to find her mother's corpse lashed to a chair, wearing a reproachful look. Instead she found her father sitting in a pool of dim light. He glanced up from the newspaper he was reading and then fell back into it.

His lackadaisical manner infuriated her. Just a few minutes ago, she had been freezing her ass off waiting for a lift and where was he? Out on some important police business? Of course not. He was at home reading the goddamn newspaper.

She went up to him with the intention of laying into her father for something he had been guilty of more than once. But when she looked down at the article he was reading she stopped dead in her tracks. Today was the fiftieth anniversary of Millingham High. On the front page was a picture taken on the day of the school's founding. Two men standing out in front of a pristine-looking high school. James McMurphy was one of them. A chill ran up her back. She had seen this picture before. The one that had fallen out of McMurphy's journal. The man beside McMurphy was smiling, but that picture had been different before. She'd seen the barrel of a shotgun stuffed into McMurphy's mouth and beside him was the other man... the one who had seemed so proud of himself. She glanced down at the caption. It was Millingham High's 50th anniversary and these were the two men who had made it happen. McMurphy was one. The other, she didn't recognize, not at first. Not from such an old picture, but she knew the name and she screamed.

"Samantha? For God's sake, what is it?" Samantha could hear her father's voice calling from far away.

She tore the paper from his hands. "I need this."

"Jesus Christ!" he shouted, eyes wide with shock and bewilderment, a thin strip of paper remaining in his clenched fist. Samantha raced up to her room to get ready for the Halloween party, leaving her father alone to mutter to himself. The idea of telling her father what she'd discovered didn't make an ounce of sense. What proof did they have, other than disturbing visions and stolen autopsy reports?

She picked up the phone and called Lysander's house. The small and tired voice that answered belonged to Lysander's mother, a weary woman set to deliver any day now. What Sam had in her hands was a matter of life or death. Lysander was at work, his mother said and from there he was going straight to Jason Gibb's Halloween party. Samantha started getting ready. There wasn't a second to lose.

● ● ●

141

By the time Lysander got to Jason Gibb's house, the sky was a deep shade of purple. Lysander stood on the street outside and fixed his costume. Inside, masses of people were crowding every window. The rule for this year's Halloween party was themed costumes only, so at the last minute Lysander had decided that his costume would be alienation. He had dug up a huge curly wig from his mother's closet, drew deep lines under his eyes—complements of her Maybelline mascara—and sported the rattiest old clothes he could find. In truth, he looked more like a bag lady, but he was unrecognizable and he figured at the very least, he'd have himself a good laugh or two.

Lysander put a hand up to his face to check his breath. He knew Summer would be here tonight, and the thought made him feel warm inside. Then he remembered that Chad and his friends were likely to show up as well. Just as quickly that fuzzy feeling withered away and died.

The front door swung open, and someone wearing a skin-colored body suit and a strap-on dildo stood staring at him. The boy was Tim Appleby from Mr. Bennett's English class. Lysander guessed by the looks of things that Tim was supposed to be horniness or something equally as crass. Either way, he didn't want to ask Tim where he got the strap-on just in case it had come from his mother's top drawer.

Tim stepped back and then doubled over, cackling. "Oh, I get it, you're Cher." Tim put a hand on his shoulder. "There's a keg in the kitchen, little buddy. Go help yourself."

Lysander waded through a sea of bodies. As he fought his way into the kitchen, he thought about the decision he had made earlier today. The decision to make a play for Summer tonight. A surge of fear and self-doubt about

142

that idea nearly convinced him he was making a big mistake. Lysander fought off the feelings of inadequacy. He would go through with it no matter what, he told himself.

He grabbed a plastic cup and poured himself a beer. He nudged the keg and it moved slightly. *Already half empty*, he thought. Something caught his eye at the other end of the room. It was Summer, wearing a flowing white gown, a halo and a pair of ivory-colored wings. The whole setup seemed a bit overdone, but she looked amazing nevertheless. To his best guess she was dressed as "angelic perfection," or something similar. She was flanked on either side by two boys Lysander didn't recognize; one in a gold suit with glasses and an oversized dollar sign necklace, his pockets bulging with fake hundred-dollar bills; the other tall and slim, hunched over with a snickering face and long fingernails—greed and envy.

Summer's eyes met his and she stared at him quizzically. Lysander threw off his wig, and a broad smile filled her face.

Her eyes sparkled. She raised her drink and he raised his own in return. Lysander threw his wig back on and mumbled to himself amid a growing torrent of butterflies: *Carpe diem. Seize the day.*

Chapter 24

"**A**re you sure there's nothing I can get for you?" Sheriff Crow asked, grinning. There was a glow about him lately, like a man who had finally swept away the cobwebs in his head. Yet Alex's awareness of the Sheriff's dramatic mood reversal was overshadowed by his need to speak with Samantha. That image she'd left him on his car window was all he'd been able to think about these last two hours.

Steve was moving past him on his way to the kitchen upstairs. The game was about to begin, a game Alex had been looking forward to for weeks, and now he couldn't have cared less. He couldn't stop thinking that Samantha was up in her room, probably listening to music through oversized headphones. Something loud and angry.

"Hello? Alex? You want a drink or not?" A frown of concern was spreading across the old man's weathered face.

Alex realized he was acting strangely. "Maybe I will have something."

"Budweiser, Coke, orange juice... or Tang," Sheriff Crow shook his head disapprovingly as he rhymed off the last one. "It's Sam's."

"One Tang then please."

Steve said almost to himself as he disappeared upstairs:

"That's more like it. Not like you to turn down a free drink."

Alex smiled uneasily. He was seized by a sudden pang of urgency. He had to speak with her immediately. When he heard the sherrif was in the kitchen, singing to himself as he opened the fridge and fumbled around inside, Alex sprung from his seat and hurried up both flights of stairs. He took them two at a time and headed straight for Samantha's room. Her door was closed. On it, an old album from Judas Priest hung askew from a single crooked thumb-tack. He knocked quietly, paranoid that Steve might somehow hear him. He waited breathlessly for a long moment, his ear pressed up against the door, hoping for movement on the other side. The room was eerily silent. She's asleep, he told himself. Asleep on a Friday night? That's about as farfetched as her having a crush on one of her dad's deputies. He went to the edge of the stairs and peered below. It would be just his luck for Steve to come up at the wrong time and catch him in Samantha's room.

When he felt sure Steve had returned to the basement, he went back to the door and knocked again, this time harder and calling Sam's name.

Still no answer.

He grasped the doorknob and rattled it, expecting to find it locked but it moved freely in his hand. He drew in a deep breath, shut his eyes, and prepared to be hollered at for trespassing as he let himself in. The door creaked open.

The room was dark. His eyes adjusted with painful slowness. Opposite him were velvet curtains drawn shut. On his right, a poster of a vampire leaning back on a cane and grinning down at him. The room was empty and Alex's heart sank. He had wanted so badly to ask her about what she had said in the car. He crossed the room to her bed and fell onto it, tucking his arms behind his

145

head. There was a lamp beside him: a skeletal hand rising up from a grave, holding a light bulb covered by a black lamp-shade.

It occurred to him that for once his intentions toward Sam had been almost completely non-sexual. The thought of sneaking into her bedroom and finding her lying in bed would usually have aroused him.

His eyes raked the room and stopped on her chest of drawers. Three half burned candles stretched skyward like so many fingery nubs. He knew she kept her underwear in that top drawer and the idea of going there now made him sick. His head began to swim, and that dizzying feeling reminded him of driving in the back seat of his uncle's Riviera as a child—a boat of a car, so big and smooth you couldn't help becoming nauseous. He heard his mother's voice bellowing after him.

You sick fuck! Is that how your mother raised you? To be a goddamned panty-sniffing pervert?

Alex rose, wavered unsteadily on his feet, and made his way to the door. He stumbled into the hallway and pulled the door closed behind him. There, he stopped cold. Something about the hallway was making him terribly uneasy. A burst of static erupted in his ears, like a radio dial rolling between stations. A feeling, like clawed fingers, began to creep up his spine and tickle the back of his neck. Someone was watching him.

He was about to run downstairs when he noticed the hairs on his arms standing on end.

He was facing the Sheriff's bedroom. He turned back to the stairs and the goosebumps went away. Like a human compass needle, he found the Sheriff's room and once again his flesh tightened.

For a moment he wondered if he was having a heart attack. Wasn't your left arm supposed to go dead numb?

As he lowered his arms, still tingling with tight and chilly flesh, he remembered something Samantha had

146

mentioned in passing once. At the time Alex had found it peculiar and sad, and he couldn't now for the life of him piece together why he had thought of it. She had told him that her father had stopped using the master bathroom altogether after her mother died. That no one had set a foot inside since it had happened.

The compulsion started out as a pinprick of morbid curiosity. Nothing more. But it morphed into a giant pair of invisible hands that propelled him before the master bathroom. He touched the doorknob. The silver metallic bulb was warm and inviting.

He turned it and pushed open the door. The air inside was thick and reeked with neglect. Against the far wall was a sink with gold handles. Hot and cold. In the large mirror Alex watched his doppelganger standing in the doorway, surveying the room with terrified awe. A heavy coating of dust layered everything. To his right, the shower curtain was pulled open, as it had been the day he arrived on the scene. Alex saw that Samantha was right: Nothing had been touched since that evening. Almost a year before the murder, Alex had been in this very room. Steve and Diane had thrown a party to celebrate his re-election as Sheriff. The air then had smelled of strawberries and lavender. The drone of voices and laughter downstairs had made this room a welcome hideaway.

Now sterility and death had replaced strawberries and lavender. He stood before the bath, gray now under a cloak of dust.

There was no sign of blood.

Yes, thank God, he thought. No more blood.

On some deeper level he had expected that horrible image of Diane's lolling body to float up before him. But nothing came. No images, no feelings of dread or panic. Only silence.

A drawer by his right leg stood slightly ajar. He opened

147

it. A box of Gillette razor blades lay inside, strewn about as though someone had fumbled one from the pack in a great hurry. He picked up one of the loose blades and turned it in his hands. A razor blade just like this was found by the tub.

Then the edge stung him. Alex's mind had wandered, and he yelped. Dropping the blade, he looked down at his right index finger. The slit was deep and white. Instantly the cut disappeared in a flow of crimson, and Alex jerked his hand over the sink, surprised by how fast the blood had come. He turned the cold water on, wanting the chill to slow the bleeding. There was a stinging pain as the water danced between the tiny flaps of flesh on his finger. Wincing, he endured the discomfort.

Looking in the mirror he saw a haggard man staring back at him. A man who had been staying up all hours of the night chasing down a link between murders that were probably unrelated. Was this business with Sam and her McMurphy diary nothing more than a red herring? She had been going through his desk after all. She might be trying to throw him off Derek's trail. And they never had found any symbol at the scene of Diane's death. Unlike Hume, no single eye was carved into her chest. No killer's calling card. The thought stung him worse than the razor's edge. There *was* no serial killer in Millingham, no lone psycho stalking the people of his sleepy little town. Somehow the thought of so much wasted time made him feel dirty. Small. He rinsed his cut furiously now, running his hands under the cold water, washing away the blood. But that dirty feeling wasn't going away. Maybe he should—

"Come in the bath. The watersssssss wwwaaaaarrrrmmmm."

Alex spun. His voice croaked: "Who's there?"

He staggered on a pair of rubbery legs.

The room threatened him with chilly silence.

He turned his attention back to his finger. Streaks of

148

blood swirled about the drain.

He had heard a voice. Heard it just as plain as day, as though someone had come up behind him and whispered into his ear. Had even felt warm breath brush against his neck.

And that voice. Certainly it was a woman's, although it sounded husky and touched with faint traces of masculinity. Looking in the mirror, he could see into the Sheriff's bedroom behind him. It was darker now. Dim light crawled in from the hallway. But hadn't the hallway light been on? He was quite certain of it.

A tiny shadow flitted past the doorway.

"All right, get a hold of yourself, Alex," he said in a strangled voice. "You're a full-grown man and you're cracking up. Get your shit and get out of here."

He looked around for something to bandage his cut, unable to stop from periodically glancing into the mirror, certain each time he would see a twisted face just behind him, wide black eyes and taloned fingers, plunging into the meaty part of his eyeballs. Blinding him. Rendering him defenseless.

"The waterssssssss waaaaarrrrrmmmm"

He looked in the mirror again, but this time he wasn't looking for bogeymen. He was looking at the glass itself. The small streak he saw there was old and barely noticeable. Looked almost like an oily finger had streaked across the mirror a long time ago. Alex thought of Sam in his cruiser earlier today, doodling on the passenger-side window. The mark it had left when all the condensation went away looked an awful lot like this. It reminded him of a game he and his older brother used to play as children. They would sit up against the bathroom mirror, writing secret messages to one another and then flood the room with steam to see what was written.

Alex's hand seemed to close around the hot water knob all on its own. He turned it as far as it would go. The taps

149

hadn't been used in so long it took a while for all the cold water to work itself out of the pipes.

Gradually the water grew warm and before long, white plumes of steam filled the room. The damp fabric of his uniform clung to his flesh. Droplets of water hung from his forehead. Alex stood staring through the thick fog, scalding water gushing out in an unbelievable torrent.

An image on the mirror was taking shape before his eyes. He could see the edges of something slowly coming into view, emerging from somewhere deep and hidden, like a great leviathan breaking up still waters.

He was so close at first, it was hard to tell what pattern had emerged on the cloudy surface. He took a step back and an almost noiseless gasp escaped his lips. No, this was nothing like the secret messages he knew as a child. His hands were suddenly encased in lead and they fell helplessly to his sides. "Oh no," he heard himself say and it sounded as though he was speaking into a drum.

Through the dense mist and streaked onto the steam covered mirror was what he had found etched into Peter Hume's flesh; what Samantha had doodled on the car window. An eye, staring back at him with singular malice. From this angle, through its hooked and jagged curves, it looked to Alex as if it were smiling at him, a giant grinning mouth. He whirled away from it and clamped his eyes shut.

The water stopped. All on its own.

The suddenness startled him.

He approached the sink cautiously, his mind working. But in a sense things had become much clearer to him. When the body was discovered, the water in the tub had been a cold and bloody broth, and any message the killer left long since disappeared. But disappeared wasn't even the right word. Dormant was more like it. Waiting for some unsuspecting sap to run the hot water for the message to be delivered.

150

As Alex turned on his heels to leave, a pink and greenish blob hovered at the edge of his vision. He stopped, fearful of turning around. In spite of the hot steam clouding the room, he felt a chill rush up his spine. The staleness of the air had been replaced by a godawful scent.

It was the odor of wet death. Something he hadn't smelled since the day Diane's body had been found and right now it was becoming almost overpowering. The shower curtain was drawn tightly closed, except for a tiny crack through which he could peer in, like a voyeur. The pale form behind the white shower curtain moved.

Someone was in the tub and they wanted him to look in.

He could hear a hoarse voice made soft, beckoning to him. That same she/male he had heard before, feminine but somehow layered with masculinity. A part of him that he wished would just shut up and go away knew exactly who it was. Like a man standing before some gruesome accident, he couldn't help but go see. He craned his head and peered down into the tub, his eyes blinking stupidly.

A jet of putrid air rushed out at him. A gaseous odor of something long dead, its full strength somehow partially blocked before by the drawn curtain. His stomach did a slow lazy roll. That head had once belonged to the Sheriff's wife. Now bloated and scaly, it was turned toward him in an unnatural fashion, glaring through vacant black sockets. It had decayed even more since the last time he'd had this waking nightmare, as though this body of pale and greenish flesh would soon dissolve completely into a floating blob with hair. Now the fishlike mouth was flapping open and closed soundlessly. But not soundlessly because clanging around inside his head was a fierce hissing. As though he had opened the lid on a basket filled with snakes. Alex's chest was thudding heavily. Beneath the static, he detected a

151

pattern. Something was being methodically spelled out for him, letter by painful letter. Just when he thought he couldn't take anymore, entire words came.

L...Y...S...A...N...D...E...R...

Alex shook his head. What about Lysander? he wanted to ask. Was he next? The hissing rose to a deafening shriek that made thin strands of blood trickle from his eardrums.

A hand touched Alex's shoulder and he jumped. It was Sheriff Crow. Gone was the glow that had accompanied him these past several days. Gone too was any trace of the perma-grin that he hadn't been able to shake free from before. The Sheriff wore the blank expression of a man who was just informed that his family had been mangled in a horrible car crash. Alex watched him, his hands still gripping the edge of the shower curtain like two steel vices. Sheriff Crow's eyes were fixed over Alex's shoulder toward the mirror behind him, toward the symbol, still visible despite the steam billowing through the room. The Sheriff's face was a jumble of emotions: confusion, fear, sadness. His mouth dropped into a question, but no words came out, only a dry squeak. Alex could see pain behind the old man's eyes, as though something long forgotten and locked away had broken free and had come running... no, slithering home. Alex glanced back at the tub. It was empty, coated again by that thin layer of dust. Yet the eye on the mirror remained in place, and even Sheriff Crow could not deny its existence. For a brief moment, part of Alex was relieved and maybe even a little overjoyed that he wasn't going mad. That at last Steve would not be able to so easily dismiss what was going on here in town. Then with brutal swiftness, that terrible warning came back to him. He grabbed Steve by his broad shoulders. The Sheriff looked unwell.

"Steve, where is Samantha?"

His bushy white eyebrows sank, but his eyes were still fixed on the mirror.

Alex repeated the question. He had a feeling that finding Sam would mean finding Lysander. He shook the Sheriff as hard as he could.

Crow blinked for the first time. "Gone…" His voice was toneless.

"I know that," Alex shouted. Time was running out. "Where?"

The Sheriff looked as though he were plucking thoughts out of the air, one at a time. "Party," he muttered. "Gibbs boy."

Alex brushed passed Sheriff Crow and raced down the stairs, hoping he wasn't too late.

Chapter 25

Samantha arrived at the party to a keg that was almost empty. She knew because of the ease with which it moved when she tilted it to one side. Tom Logan had picked her up at home in his parents' Suburban—a car far too imposing for such a skinny guy. That was her initial impression, seeing him pull into the driveway. He had been pestering her to go with him to Gibb's Halloween party since nearly the first day of school.

Someone put on "I Gotta Feeling" by Black Eyed Peas and the place exploded. But the feeling sweeping over Samantha just then was far from elation. She felt coldness seeping through her clothes and onto her skin, as though death had laid a long skeletal finger upon her. And then another sensation came, the feeling that a pair of glowing red eyes had fixed her in their sights. She could feel them burrowing into the soft flesh at her temples, tunneling into her mind...

She turned on her heels and saw Tom Logan, smiling obligingly behind her. The creeping began to fade, and she let go of it, for now.

In the corner, a boy dressed as a giant dollar bill was making out with a blonde girl in red. Stenciled on her shirt was the Soviet hammer and sickle. Communism and Capitalism. Hmm, so good to see the world coming together, Samantha thought wryly. The couple kissing triggered another thought. The very reason she had been so anxious to get here tonight in the first place. She had spent the better part of the way here being so annoyed with Tom Logan that it had actually slipped from her mind.

She scanned the party for Lysander, biting her inner lip.

He was probably the only one she knew who didn't want anything to do with cell phones. Yet another reason he was a Luddite. Finding Lysander was going to be more challenging than she initially thought. Jason Gibb's place wasn't enormous, but with everyone decked out in costumes it was difficult to tell one person from another. If she knew Lysander at all, he was wearing some unusual homemade concoction, thrown together at the last minute.

She started to leave, ready to search the rest of the house when something, or better yet someone, caught her eye. In the corner of the room was a man dressed as a clown. The kind of clown you'd expect at a child's birthday party. He was bent over at the waist, with his back to her, but he didn't seem to be picking anything up. The costume seemed weird too, out of place somehow. As if a wraith had slipped in among them, ready to...

It's a costume party, Sam, relax. Your nerves are on edge! Hell, you're dressed up too, even though I'm sure you couldn't say why you chose to come as a zombie cheerleader. Was that even a theme?

She reached inside the jean jacket she was wearing. Pulling out a flask of Southern Comfort, she brought it to her lips and tilted her head back. Her throat felt warm and tingly. She opened her eyes and the clown was still there. He hadn't moved a muscle. Something was terribly wrong. Slowly, the room began to spin in lazy circles. Now the clown was turning around.

"Sam!" a husky voice called out.

She turned, and what she saw hit her with the force of a

155

speeding truck.

Standing at the other end of the room was Derek beaming at her.

Derek's face contorted in confusion.

That bastard! was Samantha's only thought.

She was trying to swallow. But a hairball was lodged in her throat. Tom Logan leaned over her shoulder and asked if everything was all right. She didn't answer. She couldn't answer because if she did all her fury would be unleashed on poor Tom rather than on the rightful recipient. Samantha turned on her heels and stormed away. She needed a place to cool down and collect her thoughts.

She found one just off the kitchen. The room was tiny and jammed with boxes and empty mason jars. In the darkness she fell backward onto a large chest in the corner, landing hard. She would have a bruise there tomorrow, but she didn't give a rat's ass. She would sit here and calm down before she did something rash. She remembered her ride in the car with Alex earlier that day. How she swore she would kill Derek the next time she saw him. She was angry at herself now for running away.

She should have torn his...

No, it was better to cool off. She moved to close the door when the clown hand reached in to stop her. The hand was large, with long wispy fingers, painted white, nails blood red and on one of them she saw a silver ring. Searing panic rose in her throat. She opened her mouth to scream, but nothing came out.

● ● ●

"What did you call me?" Summer asked, pulling away.

Lysander sat up, still feeling her lips against his. Confusion rippled across his face. "Your name," he replied, uncertain.

156

They lay on the bed in Gibb's parents' bedroom. The party was booming beneath them. Both of them were shirtless, Summer decked out in a sexy lace bra, and yet the look on her face seemed completely at odds with that. Gone was the lusty grin from a moment ago. Her eyes were wide, her lips flat and pulled into a thin line.

"You called me Samantha!"

Summer glared at him, a smudge of lipstick streaked off the side of her mouth. "You just called me Samantha!"

Another pregnant pause, longer this time.

"No... I couldn't have."

Summer wormed out from under him, yanking her dress awkwardly until it covered her bare legs. She pulled the rest up over her chest and held it there protectively.

"Don't bullshit me, asshole!"

The words ricocheted in his head. *Don't bullshit me, asshole?*

He glanced down at his unbuttoned pants and for the first time became aware how bored he was. In fact, he couldn't remember ever really becoming aroused in the first place. He had been lying on top of Summer, all right, her shirt off, her breasts full and round and inviting, yet something had been wrong. Not physically of course. She was stunning, with a sweet voice. She was perfect. Maybe too perfect. Nevertheless, some switch in his head had never been turned on. In retrospect, even the kiss they shared hadn't been particularly good. But was it so bad that he had fantasized about Samantha?

Summer was staring at him as though he were a madman. He caught a whiff of her vanilla perfume, and it made his stomach tie up in knots. A slow epiphany was creeping into his brain. He didn't like Summer. Didn't like the kind of shallow, soulless person she was. Hell, he didn't want to have anything to do with her.

Lysander got up and grabbed his wig and the ratty old shirt he had been wearing.

157

Summer whimpered after him: "You're just gonna leave?"

"Looks that way," he said, and for once it came out as coolly as it had sounded in his head. He crossed to the door, stopped and then turned to face her. "You were right, I am an asshole."

For a moment she was stunned into silence, and then she lurched forward on her hands and knees, yelling. "You're dead meat! You hear me? Do you know who I am, Lysander? No one walks out on me. You close that fucking door and you're... Lysan—"

Lysander slammed the door and a smile spread across his lips. He could hear her whimpering on the other side.

He made his way into the kitchen, feeling a touch of euphoria, and grabbed the phone to call a cab.

An older woman with a raspy, lackadaisical voice came on and Lysander asked her to send a cab over. Ten minutes, she told him. That's all right, he replied and started to thank the woman, but she had already hung up.

He felt an urge to look for Samantha, but he decided instead to wait outside until his cab came. Shuffling through the crowd toward the lobby he pulled off his wig. He offered some half-hearted good-byes to a group hovering nearby, most of whom didn't seem to care.

I'm an asshole. You're an asshole. Everyone's an asshole, he thought as he closed the door behind him.

Had Lysander been able to hear over the blaring music, the drunken shouting, he would have heard the panicked voice yelling out for help. Had he decided to wait inside, he couldn't have missed the figure stumbling down the stairs, a girl who was dressed a lot like Summer, her mascara running down her cheeks, her dress torn and dragging partially behind her. But worst of all, he would have heard her crying out to anyone who would listen that Lysander Shore had just tried to rape her.

Instead, Lysander stood in the driveway, waiting for a

cab that was still nine minutes away, thinking how strange it was that the mere thought of Summer revolted him now.

The front door of the house burst open. Lysander turned in time to see a costumed mob flooding out toward him. Ahead of them strode Chad. The crowd formed a tight circle around them. Chad lunged forward, grabbed Lysander by the scruff of his shirt and shoved him onto the hard pavement. Lysander did a complete backward tumble and rolled up on his feet. He tried backing away. All was confusion. Chad came at him again and he threw up his arms defensively.

"What's the big idea?" Lysander yelled.

Behind the crowd, someone opened the garage door and disappeared inside.

"I turn my back for one second," Chad yelled and swung madly at Lysander, who managed to evade the blow by inches.

"Stop it," Lysander shouted back. "You're drunk."

"And you're a fucking rapist," a girl yelled from the crowd.

"What?"

His denial infuriated them even more. "I knew you were a fucking freak the first time I laid eyes on you," Chad roared and threw several wild swings, his face flushed with hatred. Someone tossed the contents of their drink into Lysander's face, burning his eyes. Chad swung again wildly and missed. Lysander rubbed his eyes, realizing one of those fists was gonna connect real soon if he didn't do something quick.

Chad was laughing. "Just wait till I'm through with you. You're gonna wish you'd never been born."

Another punch came and Lysander moved to avoid it, but this one was a feint and instead he walked right into Chad's fist. There was a crack and then the world flickered before him, threatening to go black. He

159

stumbled away, disoriented. Chad charged at him and Lysander lashed out blindly, his fist connecting with the bridge of his nose. Chad stopped, momentarily stunned by the blow. Blood gushed down the front of Chad's face. He pulled a bloody hand away and examined it incredulously. Whether Lysander liked it or not, he was in this up to his neck. This guy was gonna keep coming until one of them was dead. And Lysander decided that someone wasn't going to be him. He tucked his head down and charged, sending his shoulder squarely into the soft flesh of Chad's belly. A sound emanated from Chad that resembled a question—ugghhhh—as the wind was blasted from his lungs. The two of them tumbled backward together, Lysander on top, his arms swinging with a fury. There would be no stopping now, Lysander knew. He had been pushed to the limit, and it would end when he was good and ready. His fists numb from the pain, he continued to wail indiscriminately. Foreign hands clamored to grab hold of him. They yanked him off and Lysander managed to sink the tip of his boot in Chad's face as he was dragged away.

Chad lay on the ground with his bloodied hands covering his face. The crowd hovered over him in stunned silence. Lysander wondered if it was Derek who had yanked him off, but when he glanced behind him, he saw a skinny boy with a face full of acne who Lysander vaguely recognized as Tim or Tom Logan. Now others came to hold Lysander back, as though he were some wild animal that if set free would tear Chad to pieces. He would let them hold him back, he decided. He'd had his fill of fighting for one night.

Suddenly with a shout Chad came at him, a can in one hand, a flickering Zippo in the other. Chad raised both of them point blank, lighter first, its flame dancing in the cool air, and sprayed a fiery stream into Lysander's face. The boys behind Lysander were also taken by surprise, and they let go only moments before the explosion. Lysander, with no time to raise his arms to protect himself caught the full fury of the flames. The billowing ball of flame washed over his face. Amid the searing pain, Lysander was vaguely aware of the putrid smell of burnt hair. But far worse was what followed after he hit the ground. His body began to twitch and kick and flop around violently. He was having a seizure.

The world became deathly still... Lysander felt as though he were in a tidal pool, looking up, everything stretched out before him. He was looking through a fish-eyed peephole, bent and concave... he could hear the muffled voices of people around him... a group of boys were fighting nearby... Then with a sudden rush of airless movement he was floating above his body... and he could see himself clearly... his face blackened and distorted, his hair singed and matted in tuffs... then more movement... he was being pulled somewhere... part of him knew where... it was the coldness calling him... he prayed he was wrong... the crowd of people were fading away now... he was moving through the front door, he could feel every layer of cracking paint, pressed wood, the taste of a metal handle in his mouth and then into an empty house... colder now... he reached out to grasp the banister and his non-physical hand passed through it... empty bottles and streamers littered the floor... One read Happy Halloween...

Another: Enter the Haunted House... torn and dangling from one corner.

In a dimly lit room, someone was comforting a girl in a torn white dress, her cheeks long and black with streaming makeup... she looked up for a moment, and her eyes filled with terror, her finger pointing toward him... and he floated by like a passenger in some twisted amusement park ride.... The coldness was reaching out for him... he could feel it beckoning.

161

A dog on the other side of the room sat on its haunches and watched him with interest... who brought a dog? he heard himself ask in a hollow voice... Somehow, he knew this dog. Yes, he knew it for sure. A golden retriever, its eyes old and wise and filled with empathy, as though forced to witness something dreadful. The retriever traced his movement as he passed through the kitchen on this slow ride to hell... he turned behind him, back to the girls and saw the one in white, her face drained of color, eyes bulging, locked with his own.

He wondered whether the animal had been sent to rip his throat out. One more thing enlisted to attack him... but a calming voice inside his head told him no... and then that same voice made his day a whole lot worse.

In two days you'll be dead.

He heard himself scream and the echo made it sound as though he was shouting down the end of a long tunnel.

Why?... Why me... I haven't done anything...

He was before a door now, splintered and hanging from its frame like a crooked tooth. Blackness crackled behind it... something on the other side of that door wanted him to see... he didn't want to go inside, wouldn't go, and yet he couldn't help wondering why it wanted to show him so badly... Watching Hume's features melting away until there was little of the man that could reasonably be called human had been a strangely fascinating and exhilarating experience. He began inching closer, about to merge and then pass right through the door, as he had done before... but instead the door swung open in a great arch and a girl with a bloody face ran past—or rather through him—screaming... despite the terror stretched across her face he had felt some essential part of her being as she had gone by, and that feeling had been a familiar one. Follow her, a desperate voice commanded from within... run away... he wasn't so sure he wanted to see what was in that room

162

anymore... he began clawing at the floor, trying to get away... but the coldness wanted him... this whole display had been set up with him in mind and somehow he knew this now without a doubt... it wanted him to see... and he was being pulled...

Inside... two men were struggling... the one on top, dressed in a flared yellow jumpsuit with a painted face, a clown man, seemed to be winning... there was blood on the floor and the man underneath was grunting... the clown man, Lysander could see, was holding a knife... the same terrible knife he had seen before... and he was trying to push it down into the other man's face... into his eye... the knife point reflected a dash of light in the man's fear-stricken eye... two sets of hands were holding it now, each pushing in opposite directions... more light cutting into the room cut across the man's terror-stricken face on the bottom... Lysander gasped... he knew this man, knew him well... and he was no man at all... it was Derek... and the terror on his face was like nothing he had ever seen. A thick mat of fright took hold of Lysander and he swung out to grab the knife... to pull it away from Derek's eye... but his hands were passing through the blasted thing... he swung around before them, hardly aware of the ease with which he was maneuvering... perhaps if the angle was better, he thought desperately, it might work... The clown's head rose and for a moment his nostrils flared. He seemed to be sniffing the air. Then he looked directly at Lysander and spoke, his lips never moving. "I want it back! Do you hear me, you little shit! It's mine and I want it back!" The blood in Lysander's veins froze solid. This clown man who was killing his friend, and who had killed at least three others before him... was no stranger... But how could it be?... no, there was some mistake... there must be... but deep down he knew there *was* no mistake and the panic was suddenly too much to contain...

163

Chapter 26

Samantha had been in the back room for no more than a few seconds when the ringed hand had reached in to stop the door from closing. Once she saw the face attached to that hand, her fear had flown off the chart. The clown's wide painted grin stood in stark contrast to the man's real mouth—thin and tight with hatred. She would not have recognized him, his face narrow, angular and colored, had she not seen the ring on his left hand. It was a silver ring engraved with a fish. Or was it an eye?

Reverend Small watched her with a perverse calmness. When she saw the sightless, milky white orbs that were his eyes, she gasped and sprang up on rubbery legs, trying to leave, as though that were an option still open to her.

He put a hand on her shoulder.

SIT CHILD!

He shoved her down with unnatural force for a man of his age. Sam fell backward onto the chest with a loud thump.

His voice had changed as well. There was nothing even remotely like the cute southern drawl he had before. No, he sounded now more like an androgynous mishmash, as though a whole chorus of people were speaking through the same body.

He scanned her up and down. "I've been looking

164

forward to this."

He was fiddling with something behind his back.

Samantha's heart was thudding harder now. She thought of screaming, but she knew her voice would fail her.

"Your screams will not be heard," that thing calling itself Reverend Small said through a tight grin.

He was reading her mind. A vivid image of her mother came into focus, and she fought it away. Her mother's face was wrought with pain: *Please stop the pain, Samantha. Please stop the pain.* He grinned again, and this time she noticed the double grin: his thin crescent shaped lips against the painted backdrop of his hideous makeup. She would not let him inside her head. But it was too late. He was already there.

"Why?" she managed to say. There was fear on her breath, she knew, and he seemed to be savoring it.

Then in his sexless voice: "I want you to see something."

She saw an image of her mother in the bath with Derek. He was seated behind her. They were caressing one another. Her mother looked back over her shoulder and Derek leaned over to kiss her.

"Stop it!" Samantha yelled, and both of those terrible grins before her seemed to falter. She could feel an unbearable heat at her temples as she clutched them with both hands.

Then one of her hands fell to her side, brushing against a glass jar. And in that instant her mind cleared as though a strong wind had blown a thick blanket of clouds off the horizon. She was going to kill him. She was going to crack this bottle over his head and then cut his throat with whatever was left. Her hatred was so intense she could feel it burning the edges of her tongue, like something wet and rotting.

She grabbed the jar and swung it in a great screeching

165

arch toward the reverend's head.

In a blur he brought a huge gleaming knife out from behind his back and smashed the glass in midair. A shower of tiny razors sprayed into Samantha's face. She screamed, raising her arms to shield herself, edging away from him until she felt the crook of her back press against the wall. The reverend rose, towering over her as if on stilts, knife in hand. Eyes skull white. Dead.

His smile broadened to reveal a set of sharpened teeth.

The doorknob rattled and then a voice called out from behind it: "Samantha?"

It was Derek, and Samantha screamed to him. Outside, a pair of feet shuffled away, and in the next instant a crashing boom splintered the door. The door buckled. Then another and the door came crashing in.

● ● ●

Moments before he heard Samantha's scream, Derek had been standing in Jason Gibb's living room. It felt strange being in a house this large, he thought, sipping his beer. For the last month his time had been divided between tiny back alleys and crappy motels. He hadn't found much down in Florida. No bike shops were willing to take on a drifter, that was for sure, but more than that: he hadn't found many people willing to talk to him. The only exception had been the prostitutes—of which there were plenty in that malaria-infested swamp-turned-state. They were only more than happy to chat, so long as you slipped them a US Grant for their time.

When he finally made up his mind to come back, he hadn't dared call anyone, especially Samantha. He couldn't have risked the chance that the sheriff would have answered the phone and recognized his voice.

Derek sipped his beer again, not really caring who

166

recognized him anymore. He was tired of being on the run. He had come to tell Samantha that he was planning on turning himself in tomorrow, or at least very soon. The problem was doing it the right way. His way.

He saw Samantha again, standing before him in his mind's eye, just as she had a second ago. She was as stiff as a board, blinking at him stupidly, a skinny boy with pimples hovering behind her. Derek recalled how his own face had lit up with excitement.

He had taken a step forward. He was going to sweep her off her feet. Spin her around until she fainted, but he stopped, suddenly uncertain. Was this really Samantha? His Sam? The zombie get-up aside, she had the same large brown eyes and round face he knew and loved but this Sam seemed so filled with rage that he was positive he had been mistaken. This girl was ready to kill someone. She broke away a second later and stormed off toward the kitchen.

No, that was Sam all right, Derek knew, tilting his head back and draining the plastic cup. Then his hand tightened all on its own, crushing the cup in his grasp, making the plastic tink and pop in his hand.

He stood in the midst of people he either didn't know or didn't give a shit about. What could Sam be so angry about? His eyes flickered with dawning realization. No, that wasn't possible, he told himself. Ol'man Wallace would never have opened his mouth. But the more he twirled it around in his mind, the more obvious it became. The old man was the only person he had really confided in about Diane. The woman had practically stalked him until he agreed to have coffee with her. How was he supposed to know it was all a ploy?

Just then a shrill scream pierced the air, and Derek charged toward the kitchen. A girl in a torn white dress was stumbling down the stairs, screaming bloody murder. Suddenly, everyone was clamoring to see what the

167

commotion was about. A group began buzzing around like a handful of angry wasps. A moment later, everyone was rushing outside.

The kitchen had emptied in less than thirty seconds. Only beer bottles remained, standing sentry over half finished cigarettes, burning merrily in overflowing ashtrays. He hadn't seen Sam leave in the stampede, but he couldn't be sure. He started to follow the crowd when he noticed the door leading off from the kitchen. It was closed now, but he swore it had been ajar only moments before.

If he knew Sam, she was probably hiding away, definitely pouting, probably wanting to be alone. But wanting even more for someone to come and talk to her. Judging by the chilly reception she'd given him, Derek wasn't so sure he was the person she wanted to see right now.

He grasped the handle and shook it gently.

Locked.

He yanked his hand away, rubbing the inside of his palm. The knob was a block of ice. So cold his hand had nearly stuck there like a tongue on a metal pole in the dead of winter. Then he heard Samantha scream.

"Samantha," he called. For a second he stood before the door, dumbfounded. Adrenaline pumping through his veins. His senses sharpened, his arms and legs felt light and powerful. He took a step back and ran at the door. The frame shuddered. Staggering back again, he slammed his foot right above the handle. With a loud boom the door flew open.

The room was dark. Derek found Samantha cowering in a corner, a look of sheer terror on her face. She was pointing frantically, trying to speak.

"Look out!" she screamed.

Derek turned, but it was too late. A knife sank into his right shoulder and he howled in agony. He spun to face the source of the pain, and a horrible dread gripped him, the adrenaline suddenly expelled from his system. That smiling clown, the same one from his nightmare, now stood before him. Except this clown was worse than the one in his dreams, worse by far. Only sheer instinct saved him from a second, fatal blow. He spun away and fell backward, pinning Samantha against the wall. The clown came at him, his gleaming knife bearing down. Derek caught the arm with the swinging blade as it cut a swath toward his face. There was a searing pain where he had been stabbed in his right shoulder. His arm didn't want to cooperate anymore. The slightest movement required titanic effort. Derek clutched the clownman desperately.

"Run, Sam," he shouted. The muscles in his arms stood out like taut cords.

Sam rushed passed them, swinging the shattered door out before her, filling the house with a booming screech.

The two figures struggled on the ground. Shards of glass stabbed Derek's back. One dug into his spine and he arched his back, screaming.

The glistening knife was inching toward Derek's eye, and a knee was burying itself into his groin. The pain was unbearable. His testicles were about to explode.

Not fair, he thought. Not fair.

Then he saw those sharpened teeth, gnashing the air like a human meat grinder. They were trying to tear him apart.

Derek cocked one of his legs between them and flung the clown back against the far wall. A shelf filled with jars crashed to the floor over him.

The clownman lay curled in a ball. Derek stood and nudged him with his foot, but there was no movement, only a soft groan. Slowly, the clown looked up at him. The features of his face were coming undone. His face was melting like a waxwork dummy. Globs of thick flesh were oozing down his cheeks, dissolving and then

169

reforming into something else. Derek blinked. A moment later his brother James was curled on the floor. Derek's jaw fell open. His eyes filled with tears.

"James…?"

His brother's face was flushed with guilt. "I've done such horrible things, Derek."

"But… but you died?"

"The bike shop we used to talk about late into the night? The way Mom and Dad would rag us out for missing our bus to school the next morning? Do you still remember?"

Derek's eyes were blinking. "Of course I do. How could I ever forget that? Those were the happiest days of my life."

"Help me, Derek. Please." His brother held out his hand. "Will you help me?"

Derek started forward and then stopped himself. His head was reeling so badly he could hardly tell which way was up. Someone was tinkering inside his head. He could feel invisible hands poking around for a soft spot, monkeying with the wires and connections. His eyes dropped to his brother's hands and his fingers, stained with grease from years of work. The tension in his face relaxed and then melted away entirely. His brother would never lead him astray. Never betray him. Somehow, he seemed to know this with greater certainty than ever before. On the floor, James reached out with a single outstretched arm. Derek bent down and took his brother's hand.

Chapter 27

Lysander sat up in a blinding shot of pain. Speckled stars danced before his eyes.

An unfamiliar voice sounded above him, grumbling, cursing. He had knocked heads with someone bent over him. Through the pain, snippets of memory began swimming back, waiting to be plucked from midair. He opened his eyes and tried to focus.

The man leaning over him wore a pair of latex gloves. A name tag pinned to his chest read Frank. There was a reddish bump forming on his chin. With strained patience, he told Lysander to lie back down and not to touch his face.

Frank wasn't answering Lysander's question.

The man put a hand on his shoulder to push him back down. But in the time it took Frank to persuade Lysander to lay down, he had managed to see Samantha huddled by the stairwell, a blanket draped over her shoulders. In her hands was a steaming cup. Over by the driveway a group of girls were talking to a blond-haired man who looked a lot like Deputy Morgan—except this Alex Morgan was wearing jeans and a sweatshirt, a casual look that didn't seem to fit. The girls were crying. One of them, wearing a tattered white dress, had buried her face in her hands.

Even in his semi-delirious state, Lysander could tell that

the police and paramedics had arrived only a short time ago.

Frank, the paramedic, shone a light into Lysander's eyes, swinging the beam left to right.

"Focus on the light," he ordered.

Lysander did his best and then grew distracted when he heard a car pull up. A door opened and a pair of women's heels clicked up the driveway behind him. He turned his head—much to Frank's annoyance—and saw a silver-haired woman in a white lab coat. Dorothy! She was pulling on latex gloves and heading for the house. Lysander thought for a moment: Who called the coroner? Did it have something to do with Summer and her ridiculous accusation of rape? If that were the case, he reasoned, they would not have left him lying here on the ground soaking it up with Dr. Goodlights. He would have been crammed into the backseat of one of those brown and white jobs, facing a steel grill.

He blinked. The fog was beginning to lift. And with it, a realization. Every muscle in his body drew tight.

Derek!

The last time he'd seen his friend he was peering into the point of that knife, his terror, raw and sickening. That clown with its twisted face... no, but it wasn't a clown at all, was it?

It was Millingham's shepherd.

"Where's Derek?" The hoarseness of his voice surprised him.

No answer.

He sat bolt upright.

Samantha hadn't moved. She sat staring sightlessly into her cup. The wisps of steam were gone. The group of girls were gone too. As he decided to get up and ask Samantha about Derek, a feeling of terrible dread growing in him all the while, the light from the house was suddenly eclipsed. A form bent down and the light

172

curved around it, illuminating a face. It was Alex Morgan.

He could see Alex glancing at his left eye, and Lysander's hand went involuntarily to where a left eyebrow had once been. In its place now were a few singed hairs.

"Could have been a lot worse," Alex said matter-of-factly. "Boy comes at you with a torch like that, you're lucky to still *have* eyes."

Lysander looked down, rubbing the nub.

"Oh, and as for those rape charges." There was a stinging note in Alex's voice that Lysander didn't like. "She's dropped 'em. Something that girl saw or heard tonight scared the living shit out of her. Wouldn't say what it was either."

The subtle implication that Lysander had threatened Summer into silence hung between them. Right now, though, that was the least of his concerns. She could take that little rape charge of hers and stick it up whichever hole fit best.

Alex brought out a note pad and fired several questions at Lysander. For a moment, Lysander contemplated remaining silent. *Let the grown-ups figure it out on their own*, he thought stubbornly.

But he knew that wouldn't do anyone any good. He took a deep breath and told Alex everything that had happened that night, from messing around with Summer, and the way she had threatened him as he left the room, to his fight with Chad... and finally to Derek, battling the man with the painted face...

He glanced past the deputy and over at Samantha.

The look on her face gave Lysander gooseflesh. She knew about the reverend, just as well as he did. He could see it in her face. She looked stunned, the mug moving up to her lips as if she were underwater. He suspected she hadn't spoken a word to anyone.

Alex collected himself, scanning his notes. "You said

that the room you saw in your..." He looked visibly uncomfortable. "...your vision... was dark."

Lysander nodded, hating the way he was being made to feel right now.

"Then how can you be so certain it was Reverend Small that you saw?"

"There was *some* light," Lysander said. "I could see his face."

Alex paused to consider this. "I should probably mention that I spoke to a number of folks down in Hayward the other day," he said.

Lysander had been probing what remained of his left eyebrow and his hand froze in mid-course.

"Had some interesting conversations with a Detective Danforth and a Dr. Johnson. The good doctor says she knows you. Knows you quite well, actually. Your mother, she was in a real bad way a while ago, wasn't she?"

"What does this—" There was a sickening certainty growing in his belly that he knew where this was headed.

"Danforth also told me how you accused the mayor in Hayward of corruption and that your house was firebombed not long after. You see, here's my problem Lysander. I want to believe what you're telling me, about the visions and seeing the guy who did it and all. Strange as it seems, some of it makes more sense than it should. But your track record isn't helping me. Not to mention the fact that Reverend Small is easily the most respected man in all of Millingham."

"Well I can't help it if you don't believe me. Maybe after he's killed half the town you'll figure it out." Lysander could feel his pulse thumping wildly in his neck. "I gotta talk to Sam," he said, scrambling to get up.

Alex's eyes shifted protectively over to Samantha, who remained motionless. "Not now. Go home, Lysander. Your parents are—"

Lysander shouted past Alex to Samantha, but she

174

didn't even flinch. Specks of dried blood dotted her face. Alex reached out and grasped him by the shoulders. "Come now, don't make things worse."

The thought of knocking his hands away occurred to Lysander, of punching Alex in the face as Derek had before. He might have swung too, were it not for a hand that suddenly landed on his shoulder. He turned around. It was his father, Glenn.

Chapter 28

An hour later Alex and Sheriff Crow were heading toward Reverend Small's house. Their intention was to question the man so that, as the sheriff had so eloquently put it sliding into his cruiser, "We can move on to finding the real killer."

Samantha had barely said a word to either of them. Witnesses had seen her running from the house screaming, blood splashed across her face, some of it hers, most of it Derek's. The paramedics told them she was in shock and gave the sheriff a bottle of little yellow tablets they said would "take the edge off." She had ridden home with her father, and he had told Alex afterward about something she had said to him along the way.

She had asked him if Derek was all right. When he didn't answer, she grew morose. Then she said: "You'll know him by his silver pinky ring, Daddy. It has a picture that looks like an eye." He had tried to question her on this, but she lapsed into silence again and wouldn't say another word. He assumed the tablets had begun their numbing work.

Alex had been the first to come upon Derek, sitting upright in the back room, the door smashed in and somehow still remarkably on its hinges. When he entered,

176

jars and broken glass had crunched under his feet. The room smelled of stale beer and of death.

Beside the door handle was the crystal clear impression of a footprint. One they matched to the boots on Derek's feet.

Thick threads of blood were streaking down both sides of Derek's face, flowing from the empty sockets where his eyes had once been. His body was slumped forward but still sitting upright, and at first Alex wasn't sure how he hadn't fallen over. Until he pushed his way in a little farther and saw that one of Derek's hands was nailed to the wall, his shirt sleeve matted with blood, his wrists slit open. The index finger of his crucified hand pointed crookedly toward the ceiling. And when Alex looked up, there, in blood, was the eye Sam had drawn on the window of his cruiser, the same one they'd found sliced into Peter Hume's chest. Alex had needed to open the door to finally see it properly, but he knew just the same what it was.

He hadn't mentioned the bathroom mirror incident from earlier that evening. Alex had understood, even from the man's body language, his whole attitude toward the case was changing. Before this evening, even talking to Reverend Small about his involvement would have been unthinkable. Whoever had committed those unspeakable acts on Peter Hume and now Derek had also been the same person responsible for the death of Diane Crow and God only knew who else. Alex could see the anger building in the sheriff's gaze: the coals of a long dormant fire stirred up and glowing bright red.

Moments later they stood before Reverend Small's front door. Sheriff Crow rang the doorbell once. After the second time a light flickered on in the hall and then another one outside.

The man who finally opened the door looked more like someone out of a retirement home catalogue than a serial

177

killer, and Alex had to stifle the urge to laugh out loud. He had seen the reverend many times before. Not at church, but around town as the man went about his business. In spite of the old coot's age, Reverend Small always had a youthful and jovial air about him. But the man before them now was old and uncharacteristically disheveled, clad in a green bathrobe, his white hair skewed slightly to one side.

Can you fake bedhead? Alex wondered. The only difference here was, this bedhead was lathered in the kind of cheap aftershave old men seem to love.

Sheriff Crow removed his hat and apologized for the intrusion.

"Not at all, Steven." The reverend's smile greeted them both warmly. He waved them inside.

Alex passed over the threshold and two thoughts struck him at once, the first was somewhat comical:

Good job, Alex! You just woke up a poor old man in the middle of the night.

The second more unsettling:

No one gets out alive.

All three of them went to the kitchen together.

The house was spotless. On a table by the entrance porcelain figurines of eighteenth-century noblewomen curtsied for them.

Reverend Small put a pot of coffee on. Alex caught the sheriff scanning the reverend's fingers. On his ring finger, not his pinky was a plain gold band. It winked at Alex as the reverend pulled three mugs from the cupboard.

Alex caught the clock above the stove. It was oval and a little dated and certainly more at home in a Norman Rockwell painting.

What time is it, Mr. Wolf? he wondered uneasily.

The floor was turquoise and green linoleum. The same ones he'd seen in a church basement too long ago now to remember exactly when.

178

No matter where Alex looked, he couldn't help but notice how neat and tidy everything was. A voice called out from the backroom of his mind: *Maybe a little too neat and tidy.* He tried to ignore it, listening while the reverend explained to Sheriff Crow that he had left the church late tonight and had eaten at Kentucky Fried Chicken—one of his little weaknesses, he told them. That charming smile made another appearance.

The voice in Alex's head was growing louder, rising to an almost painful frequency. He rose and excused himself to the bathroom, and as he left the room he could have sworn he had seen the reverend's eyes flash with momentary alarm and then anger. It had lasted only a fraction of a second, and Sheriff Crow hadn't been the wiser, but Alex knew he had seen an avalanche of thoughts behind the old man's eyes.

Alex went through the living room and then down the hall and into a small study. On the desk was an old Royal typewriter and beside it a thick ream of paper. Alex flipped through what was starting to look like hundreds of typed pages. The reverend was writing a book, it seemed, but the snippets he managed to steal at a glance were hardly enough to get a handle on what it was about. He flipped back and read the title page: *The Coming Judgment.* It made him think of a bumper sticker he had seen on an old beat-up station wagon. When the rapture starts rockin', guess who's gonna come knockin'.

You gotta give it to the thumpers, he thought satirically. *Love thy neighbor. Turn the other cheek. Peace and happiness for all. Oh, and by the way, that loving hand of God's gonna sweep us all away when the judgment comes.*

Above the typewriter he saw an old black and white picture. Two men standing before Millingham High School smiling. Judging by the long hair and the lamb chops, he guessed the picture was taken in the sixties, perhaps around the time the school was first built. Alex leaned farther over the desk, his nose nearly pressed against the glass. He could see that the man on the left was a young Reverend Small. Beside him on the right, arms draped over each other's shoulder, was James McMurphy. He smiled and was about to turn away when the photograph changed. He eyed it more closely. Now both barrels of a shotgun had been stuffed into McMurphy's mouth, his lips stretched so wide they looked about ready to split. Alex's palms broke out in a sweat. A blinding bout of paranoia suddenly gripped him.

Pictures don't change on their own.

He turned back to the picture, becoming more and more certain that his imagination was doing what one would expect when running on three hours of sleep. But the picture had once again metamorphisized. Now McMurphy's face was contorted into a terrible shudder—reminiscent of that look plastered on the faces of human crash test dummies at the moment of impact. Now something new was lying at their feet and sprayed against the back wall.

He looked more closely and felt his stomach lurch. It was blood and bits of chipped bone and brain matter: an explosion from the back of McMurphy's shattered head. The man beside him in the picture, the reverend, was roaring with gales of laughter.

A deep chill pulsed through Alex's body. He could hear the laughter cackling inside his head like static. He clapped his eyes shut and put his hands up to his ears and counted to three, wishing it would all just go away. When he opened them—hesitantly at first, like a man expecting to open his eyes and find that the world around him had been flattened to the size of a crepe—he found that the picture had gone back to normal; two men standing before Millingham High, back to their old smiling selves. But what did it all mean? Was it just the confusion of a tired mind? He had been lucid enough to question

180

Lysander and deal with... what had been left of Derek. So that wasn't it. But for the life of him, he couldn't find a motive connecting Small to any of the murders.

Alex swallowed hard and his throat clicked.

From a low round table near the office door an eerie-looking bust of Jesus was watching him; the expression on its face sadly compassionate and yet pleading. Part of the bust's flowing mane was chipped away.

Dorothy's words came back to him with violent force:

"... an object, maybe five to ten pounds... Anything from the edge of a baseball bat... to a marble statuette."

A ready-made weapon within arm's reach. Taken from Hume's house after the murder and maybe kept by the killer as a sick token of a job well done. Alex grabbed the bust in his two hands. It wasn't enormous, but certainly large enough to kill a man if it struck him with sufficient force. He shoved it down the front of his pants, pulling his loose sweater over the bulge to conceal it. At that moment a voice nearly made him wet himself.

"Can I help you, Deputy?" Reverend Small said from the doorway. He was struggling to pull his bathrobe tight. Gone was the warm, charming smile.

Sheriff Crow was scowling at him from behind the reverend, just visible over the reverend's thin shoulder.

"I went to find the washroom and must've strayed a little."

The reverend remained stoic.

Sheriff Crow laid a hand on the reverend's shoulder, and Alex wondered if he meant to arrest the man. But instead he said: "I think we've taken up enough of your time tonight. Again please accept our sincere apology for waking you."

The reverend stared at Alex, and Alex felt his face flush with guilt. The man's gaze was shattering, like having a thousand suns suddenly turned toward you. He couldn't help but look away, and he hated himself for letting some

181

scrawny little man do that to him.

The reverend saw them to the door. Alex and Steve went to their respective cars. All the lights in the house went out. But even so Alex was sure he could see a shadow staring out at them. He slid into his cruiser feeling a chill that was not just from the coldness outside. He removed the bust from under his belt, threw it on the passenger seat and turned the ignition. The car hummed to life and he turned on the heat. A cold gust of air blew into his face. Slowly it warmed. He backed his cruiser out of the driveway and waited for the sheriff to do the same.

Alex glanced over at the bust.

Jesus' head was tilted to the side, looking up through the car window toward the sky, dark and starless. An inscription on the base of the bust read: Vengeance is mine: I will repay, saith the Lord.

Alex lifted his radio.

"Sheriff, I know it's late, but there's something I gotta do."

The sheriff's car pulled into line with his own. "The next time you go playing detective, be a little quicker about it," Crow replied. His voice was strained. "That man in there's one of the most influential, law-abiding citizens in town. We can't go treatin' him like a two-bit thug."

Several replies came to mind, but Alex said none of them.

"Roger that, Chief," he answered instead. "See you in the morning."

He drove away, thinking about the autopsy report he'd found on James McMurphy not long ago. It had disappeared for a short time from the morgue, but had turned up eventually, filed away in Dorothy's new storage facility. It was beginning to look like this sonofabitch had just taken his fourth victim tonight.

● ● ●

The Hume house was an icebox. Mrs. Hume, stashed temporarily in a motel on the outskirts of town, had insisted they turn off the furnace to save on her heating bill. At the time, Alex had gone to the fuse box uncertain which switch would do the job. Ten minutes later and severely ill-tempered, he had opted to simply shut the whole house down.

Now he was standing before that same fuse box, trying to read the labels beside each switch through the yellow glow of a flashlight, looking like an overweight man comparing low fat yogurts.

A part of him was grateful the box was on the main floor and not in the basement. That unsettling feeling he'd gotten in the reverend's office still hadn't faded away entirely, and even more unwelcome was the prospect of having to paw his way around a musty cellar. If the living room was anything like the basement, then he would gladly pass. He swung the beam of light before him, illuminating the kitchen and found a disturbing tableau of normality. A kettle sat askew on the stove, as though deposited there only moments before. On the counter, a teapot still donned its cozy; a brown smiling cat, its tail curled around its haunches like an Egyptian statuette. Shining the flashlight ahead of him, he went through the kitchen door and into the living room. He flicked the light around, trying to ignore Hume's collection of voodoo shit. A patch of sweat was gathering on his stomach, in particular around the bust of Jesus wedged against his pubic bone.

He stopped suddenly, and his head perked up. The odor of Hume's decomposing body had vanished, but something else had taken its place and it wasn't the smell of rotting antique furniture. This was something entirely new and it hadn't been there before.

183

You're tired. The quicker you do this, the quicker you can go home.

He brought the light up to illuminate the fireplace mantle and saw the shrunken heads with their sewn eyes that still seemed to be peering out at him. So where had he seen that missing piece again? There was so much creepy shit on every table, this would take longer than he thought. Every bloody inch was spoken for... except...

On a cherry wood table against the far wall, Alex spotted a vacant space between two medieval depictions of hell.

He angled Jesus out from under his belt buckle and crossed the room. A circular, almost dustless depression was visible on the tabletop where something had been before. Even measuring visually, the dimensions appeared to match. He angled himself so he could place the statuette, feeling a little like Indiana Jones preparing to swap the golden idol for that bag of fine sand.

Alex's head snapped up.

That smell was back. It had skated right past him before. Cheap aftershave was what it smelled like, and he remembered now where he'd encountered it before. He turned quickly and flickered the beam of light across the room.

The beam cast long, twisted shadows that scurried from the light. Alex's pulse quickened. That sense of being watched was almost unbearable now.

He's here! He's in the house with you!

But Alex turned his back, trying to smother the rising panic.

There was no way a seventy-year-old man could have gotten here before he did. He had broken nearly every speed limit out there. Nevertheless, a scream was on the verge of slipping free. He swallowed it down with a strained, dry gulp. He was imagining things again, the way he had imagined Diane Crow's bloated body in the bath

184

and that picture on the wall, moving on its own. In spite of the apparent nonsense of it all, his hand clutched the flashlight tightly.

He caught threads of cheap aftershave again, stronger now than before. He tried to ignore it. The same way he was trying to ignore the feeling of ghostly hands reaching from out of the darkness, clawing at the back of his neck.

He slowly lowered the bust onto the table—fighting the sickening urge to glance behind him. It had to be exact, precise.

Jesus slid into place.

The fit was perfect.

Well I'll be damned...

Course, lots of things could fit there, couldn't they? Besides, he had never heard of a jury convicting anyone on the basis of a clean spot on a table.

But this wasn't for the jury, was it? No, this was just for him—the only jury that mattered. Besides, who knows what kind of trace evidence Dorothy would be able to find. He grabbed the bust and turned just in time to see the gleaming edge of a hatchet cutting through the air. He screamed and the crotch of his trousers became a warm glow. The glow trickled down his leg and onto the floor.

The flashlight fell from his hand and smashed onto the floor, doing a full three-sixty. For a moment, it flickered on and off, painting the wall with ghastly shadows. Then the light went out. Alex raised his hands defensively in the dark, waiting for the strike that he knew was coming, but never did. He waited and then slowly opened his eyes, allowing the darkness to creep in. He groped on the floor desperately for the light, and when he snapped it back on, the room was empty.

There was no hatchet. Just a man in a dark house scaring the shit out of himself. "Next time," he whispered to the empty room, if there ever would be a next time, "I'll turn the power back on first—every light in the

185

goddamned house."

Alex looked down at the bust of Jesus again. The smell of aftershave was so far gone, it might never have been there in the first place. He shook his head.

I'll be damned, he whispered again.

Chapter 29

"I don't want us to be enemies anymore," Glenn was saying as they drove home in the dark. Lysander's head, pounding like something out of a Stomp concert, was leaning against the window. He had no intention of talking to his father. That had already been decided. Until a moment ago, the only question unanswered was how long he was required to fake sleep before his father left him alone.

But the plea his father was making. This was new, wasn't it? Let's not be enemies? No, he had never heard that one before. Lysander remained quiet, listening.

"Your mother and I... we feel that... well, I'm just gonna come out and say it. We feel you're drifting away, son. There was a time when you and me were pals and..." His voice trailed off. "And I guess I'm asking how we might fix things." Lysander could see Glenn's fingers tapping nervously against the seam of his faded Levi's.

"I don't think you're ready to have me back," Lysander said. The headlights from a passing car made shadows rush across the ceiling.

Lysander could feel a momentary flash of anger rise up in his father. He hadn't meant to be condescending. It was the plain and simple truth.

187

"I've just picked my son up from a fight where some kid tried to burn his face off and he might have died from another seizure. No, I think I'm ready, 'cause this has got to stop!"

Lysander snapped upright. "Then promise me you'll stop going to Reverend Small's church. Don't even let him in the house anymore. No, I'm serious, Dad. You have to trust me."

Glenn's chest rose and fell. "You asked us to trust you back in Hayward and look what happened. We lost everything." He let out the last remnant of a smoker's cough and wiped his lips with the back of his hand. "Of all the people in the world, why Reverend Small? What has he ever done to you?"

A support beam somewhere deep within Lysander was giving way.

"He killed Derek tonight, Dad," Lysander said it with such matter-of-factness that Glenn's face turned pale. "And for some reason I don't quite understand yet, he's after me too."

"Lysander! Reverend Small's a good ma—"

"No, that's where you're wrong. He's not a man. Maybe he *was* a man once, but not anymore. He's something else now. And the more I think about it, the more I see that he's been after me for a long time. Maybe ever since I was born."

Lysander was breathing heavily, waiting for Glenn to cut in with a good old-fashioned dose of common sense, but he never did. His father was listening, maybe for the first time in his life. Then Lysander decided to tell him everything, from the old picture of McMurphy Sam had seen to the clown man hunched over Derek with that look of demonic glee....

Behind them, a car honked impatiently. The light had been green for nearly a minute. Glenn pulled ahead,

188

driving like an old woman on her way to Sunday service. Lysander could see he was so deep in thought, his lips were working soundlessly.

Why shouldn't he be? In the span of a few minutes, he had been told that everything he held to be true about the world was a lie.

When Glenn spoke, every word felt weighed and measured. "So you've gone to the police then?"

"The police here don't believe me any more than they believed me in Hayward."

Glenn started fiddling with the radio, searching through abrupt walls of hissing static. The crackling sound made Lysander uneasy and he reached over and snapped the radio off.

"Not one good goddamned station in this whole shitty town," Glenn said. His face was pale and angry. "I want to believe you, Lysander. As hard as what you're telling me is to swallow, I'm trying." Glenn's foot pressed down on the gas, pushing Lysander back in his seat.

"Where you going?"

"Reverend Small's," Glenn said ominously. "See if he'll answer a few questions for us." The smile that was growing on his face was the first genuine expression of pleasure Lysander could remember.

"No, we can't! This isn't a game."

There was a plan brewing in Lysander's head. Something he had been turning over secretly for a few days now, prodding carefully for holes. Feeling more certain with every passing day that it would work. Certain it was the only way.

"Lysander, you can't tell me that the man who lives next door is trying to kill you and not let us do anything about it. I'm glad you told me—no, that's not it. What I'm glad for is that you felt you could trust me enough. This is between you and me. Something your mother can never know. She's a wreck as it is these days, and

189

something like this would destroy her." His father looked somber. "We can't risk another...accident."

A needle pressed into Lysander's heart. He swallowed it down as Glenn continued...

"But you can't expect me to just sit by—"

Lysander was rubbing the patch of tender flesh above his eye. "You said that you were glad I had enough trust to tell you?"

After some hesitation, Glenn nodded.

"Then you have to keep trusting me. Give me a couple of days and I'll have enough to bring to the police."

A car went by, and in the gleam Lysander could see that Glenn was shaking his head.

"Please," Lysander whispered.

His father hardly glanced at him, but Lysander could see that for the first time his father's normally hardened expression had changed. Perhaps it was the light or maybe not, but something had changed.

"I know I'm not the kind of father I thought I would be," Glenn began. "There were mistakes my own father made and I swore to God I'd never repeat them. There have been times, too many to name, where I've caught myself doing to you exactly what I hated my father for doing to me. Maybe I knew I was doing them all along. I just..." Glenn stopped and bit his bottom lip.

His father's vulnerability caught him off guard. For a moment the impenetrable veil between father and son was drawn back. His father didn't need to explain any further because Lysander already knew.

Adversaries? No. That, he felt, was something they had left behind them tonight, shrinking away in the distance with every mile put between them and Jason Gibb's place.

But friends? Perhaps the next two days would tell.

● ● ●

190

Three quarters of an hour later, despite the exhaustion that was overtaking him, Lysander snuck off to Samantha's. Thirty minutes had passed before he had heard the steady rhythm of his father's snoring and had felt it was safe enough to inch the garage door open and sneak his bike out.

Pulling away, Lysander failed to glance over his shoulder as his house faded rapidly in the distance. Had he done so he might have caught the hideous face in the window of his grandmother's room watching him as he left.

At Sam's he found a thick drain pipe that led up onto the roof over the garage. Sam's room was on the other side of the house, and he would have to pass several windows, perhaps even the sheriff's, before he could get to hers. Two cars were parked in the driveway. One of them, he knew, belonged to the sheriff, and it served as a reminder that the slightest misplaced step would end in a lot of unpleasant questions. His heart pounding, he shimmied up the pipe and then carefully maneuvered across the roof's front lip, hoping his clumsy combat boots wouldn't betray him.

Riding on his bike through the deathly quiet streets, his hands frozen to the bone, he had passed a TV news truck, barreling toward the center of town. KPXG News in trailing red letters. It had looked more like a blur since the truck had raced past him doing over seventy. They had probably heard about Derek: the advance guard from the realm of bloodsuckers out to cash in on the world's misfortunes. Voyeurism dressed up nice and pretty. Lysander snickered at the thought that Sam's cynicism was rubbing off on him.

But he knew the sheriff would have a hard time explaining this latest murder. No more of his old faithful wandering hobo routine: "Folks, the assailant is just a

191

transient. I assure you, the killer does not live in Millingham."

Lysander angled underneath a large paint-chipped window, trying to crab-walk so he wouldn't be seen. As he angled his back to the roof, a patch of rotting shingles gave way like a grouping of loose rocks on the edge of a cliff. He was sliding toward the edge of the roof and a steep twelve-foot drop. Perhaps not enough to kill, but certainly enough to snap your femur right out of your pant leg.

Lysander jerked himself backward and spread out his arms. His fingers clawed at rotted shingles. In desperation, he pressed his hands flat against the roof and pushed down with everything he had, hoping the friction would slow him.

He felt the flesh on his palms tearing away as he slowed and then came to a stop, his combat boots dangling over the edge. A light came on in the room above him. The top of his head was bathed in yellow light as he clung to the roof with every ounce of his failing strength. A face peered out. Silver hair and mustache.

Please God. Don't let him see me. I'll do anything...

He waited for what felt like a lifetime, holding his breath, his cheeks ballooned.

Eventually, the light flickered out.

Lysander remained motionless, legs dangling. Then, with the utmost care, he edged himself back up and continued, sliding one tenuous foot in front of another until finally he reached Sam's window. He knew Derek had made this same trek several times in the past, and he couldn't imagine how the big oaf had done it.

The thought of Derek made his bottom lip quiver and he held it between his teeth until the taste of salty blood told him the feeling had passed. "Men don't cry," he told himself. "Besides, how are you gonna do Sam any good if you're a blubbering mess?"

192

He tapped at the window and waited.

No answer.

He tapped again, and as he did a thread of doubt began working into the conscious part of his mind.

This is Sam's window, right?

He thought so. But he wasn't so sure anymore. It was dark and he had only heard stories of Derek crossing the roof to see Samantha.

He tapped the window pane again, more tentative now.

Finally a weak light flickered on from behind the curtain. The heavy fabric parted and Sam's face, weary and pale, peered out at him. Her dour expression broke slightly when she saw who it was. She unlocked the window latch and lifted it up. Lysander snuck in and drew the thick velvet curtains closed behind him. The window he left open, however, just in case he needed to make a run for his life.

Samantha's face was sunken and haggard. He could see she had been through hell.

He drew close, pulled her face to his chest and stroked her long black hair. They had never hugged before. He felt as if a powerful magnet were pulling them together, sucking him into her and her into him. Had he not felt this from the very beginning, though? And yet this feeling, natural as it was, had gone swooping right over his head. How could he have been so blind?

That surge of energy continued to spike through his body.

This was something else, bigger than both of them. Even in his semi-dazed state, one question kept poking away at him: What took you so long?

She peeled her head away from his chest and looked up at him. Her smile filled her entire face, as though she was thinking the same exact thing. She squeezed him tighter.

"Did they give you anything?" he asked. "Medicine... sleeping pills?"

193

"They did." She spoke into his jacket. "I didn't take them."

If this moment had lasted forever, he would be the happiest man on earth. But he had come for a reason.

"You saw him tonight, the reverend?"

A dance of emotions flashed across her face. Lysander's own complexion darkened. "We have to do something," he said. "I was hoping it would be tonight, but it may have to wait till tomorrow." He didn't tell her that he had seen his old dog Sandy tonight and that somehow she had told him he would be dead in two days time.

"We need to get inside the reverend's house."

Her face went ashen.

"There's gotta be something in there," he said.

"Okay, and if we find this *thing*, then what?"

"We go to Alex." Lysander's face became hard and for a moment his expression reminded Sam of her father.

She shook her head.

He was fighting to keep his voice to a whisper. "I don't like it either, but I think Alex is beginning to see."

"Lysander, I'll help you with whatever you want, but people here have their minds made up. Look at us. We're every parent's worst nightmare, and we're accusing one of the most trusted people in town of—"

That look of defiance on Lysander's face was back. "We're just gonna have to unmake their minds, that's all." He brought his hand up to his mouth and yawned. Exhaustion was starting to catch up with him.

"You're tired."

"No, I'm all right."

"You shouldn't bike back like that."

"I'll be fine, honestly."

Her eyes fell to the floor. "Why don't you stay and help me fall asleep?" She suddenly looked more beautiful than she ever had. "Every time I doze off I see that clown face, staring back at me." She blinked. "Once I'm asleep

194

you can go." She held out one of her tiny hands and led him to her bed.

They stopped short, and she suddenly brought her lips up to his, exploring the fullness of his mouth. She peeled back the covers and Lysander kicked off his boots and slid under the covers. Samantha followed and cinched her body up to his.

Lysander buried his face in the crook of his arm. "Are you trying to kill me? I think you're trying to kill me."

She smiled as she reached a hand over and turned out the light.

Later, lying in bed with Samantha, snuggled under her warm blankets, he looked into her deep brown eyes. Watching her, he could tell he was beginning to lose himself. No longer was he Lysander Goth, foreigner and outcast, and no longer was she Samantha who believed that all men were idiots.

Not long after, tucked into the fold of Lysander's arm, Samantha fell into a restful sleep. For the time being, not a thought appeared of that gleaming clown with his sharpened teeth.

Chapter 30

When he finally arrived home, Lysander closed the garage door and glanced at the clock above his father's workbench. Four in the morning.

Jeeezus!

He turned on the light in the laundry room just off the garage, and the bright flash jogged something loose in his memory. Had he not seen the light on in his grandmother's room when he turned onto his street? And had it not been snapped off as he approached?

He couldn't be sure. When you were slogging home in the middle of the night, you couldn't really be sure of anything.

He made his way into the darkened kitchen, groped along the wall for the light switch and when he couldn't find it, he was struck by another thought. Years ago his family had spent a July weekend in a beach house in Nantucket. A telescope had sat neglected in a corner on the back deck, and he had spent hours peering out at what he could only guess was Neptune or Jupiter.

Searching the night sky, he had seen an infinite number of stars blinking back at him, billions of fiery balls of light. The universe was a pretty bright place. Lysander had thought about God then. With a sky so densely packed, surely God must be up there someplace. Then

196

Lysander had pressed his eye to the lens and swiveled the long barrel of the telescope toward a dark patch of starless sky. The darkness he found there was so cold and frightening that he had shuddered. He had come to discover that day that if God really did exist, he was not the ubiquitous being priests would have you believe. It was clear to Lysander now that there were places from which God was absent. Dark places he didn't dare go.

Lysander turned the kitchen light on, and a subtle smell greeted him. So faint that when he twisted his head the slightest bit it was gone. It reminded him of his father. Early mornings as a young child, scrambling onto his Winnie the
Pooh riser, struggling to prop himself against the bathroom counter so he could watch his father shave.

Yes, that was it. Aftershave. That brief moment of nostalgia passed, and he let the thought slip from his tired mind, ignoring the fact that his testicles had inexplicably retracted up into his body.

This business of being the last one awake wasn't so appealing to him anymore. What was stopping Reverend Small, or whatever that thing called itself, from hiding in his closet and waiting for him to fall asleep?

The answer to that was nothing. Nothing was stopping him, except perhaps the man's sick delight in letting fear and panic build to such a screaming pitch that you were begging him to come in and end it. Or—

A heavy thud from upstairs. Directly above him. Sounded like something heavy falling over. Or someone falling out of bed.

He glanced up at the ceiling.

His Grandmother.

Had they forgotten to feed her? he wondered dully. Or had she slipped out of bed?

For the first time he became aware that the cat had not greeted him at the door. Necra was always awake, waiting for him to come home, nearly tripping him as she weaved between his legs.

He stumbled through the darkness toward the spiraling staircase, a looming form before him. He started up it sluggishly, stair by stair, and he couldn't help but glance over his shoulder, to be sure no one was behind him. He arrived at the top riser, his breath coming in quick shallow spurts. Grandma's door was ajar. Her light was out.

A prickly sensation tickled his spine.

He flicked on the bathroom light and started for his grandmother's room. He would just check in on her, he told himself. Make sure that she had been fed and that she wasn't... he looked down at his feet and saw that they weren't moving.

Mush! he ordered.

It was as though eight-hundred-pound sandbags had been strapped to his ankles. The strain was almost painful. He struggled to advance, one lumbering step at a time.

The scent of aftershave was becoming stronger. With a trembling hand Lysander pushed open his grandmother's door. It gave a few inches, creaking lightly in protest, and then stopped.

The room seemed so dark that an image came immediately to mind: a black hole, churning like a cosmic garbage disposal full of grinding teeth, eager to liquefy anything that strayed too close.

He held his breath and pushed the door open all the way. By the dim glow of the bathroom light, he could just make out a large oval lump underneath the covers. From here, it was difficult to be sure if he saw the steady rise and fall of her breathing, but he wasn't going any farther to find out. An empty plate of food sat on her side table.

"No problems here officer," he said scratchily, his blood pressure cringing below the red line.

198

He gripped the doorknob, colder to the touch than usual, he noticed, and pulled it closed.

Only after he shut the door and started for his bedroom, his eyes stinging and begging to be closed in sleep, did he see the trail of blood. Thin and almost unnoticeable, it seemed to lead from his room, down the hallway and under his grandmother's door, now closed tight behind him. *It's after four in the morning and your eyes are playing tricks on you.* He stroked the scorched remains of his eyebrow, evidence that he had already been through enough tonight to justify the illusion. It was a remarkable illusion too when you thought about it, since no amount of seeing the blood made it waver or disappear. He bent down, dabbed his finger onto the wet carpet and rubbed his slippery fingers together until they grew thick and sticky. He brought them to his nose. The stench made his muscles bunch up like taut cords, all five senses jacked on full alert.

Blood!

He spun to face his grandmother's room, a growing dread foaming into his mouth, like some bitter pill.

Her door was closed, just as he had left it.

His bedroom was open, though, accessible and safe, and a voice was screaming that he should barricade himself inside.

Put your bed against the door and don't open up no matter what they say or how much they beg you.

He tried to slow his mind before it spun out of control. No, he would not do that. He would tell his parents. There was really nothing else to do. Then it occurred to him that the blood might belong to them. If he knocked, they might not answer. They too might have been lured into that room never to come out again. First his mother, exhausted and in a pissy mood, but responding on instinct to some noise she had heard. And later, after she had not returned for some time, his father.

199

A second later, he was standing before his parents' door, about to start pounding, his fist poised at eye level, when he glanced behind him. Through the gloom cast by the bathroom light he could make out an unusual form in his room. A form he hadn't noticed before. He took a step closer, incredulous. There was an irregular lump under his covers. Someone was in his room, in his bed. He looked over at his grandmother's bedroom door.

Her door was ajar.

His fists clenched tightly. Not possible, he thought. She hadn't walked in years. He looked back at the bloodstain on the carpeted floor. It was smeared now, as though in those few seconds when his back was turned, something had been dragged across the carpet. No. That wasn't it. He knew that wasn't it, but he couldn't bring himself to admit what his senses were telling him. That smear on the carpet, the one which led to that thing lying in his bed, hadn't been made by something inanimate being pulled along the ground. No, not a something, but a someone, a someone who had dragged a pair of useless legs behind them, down the hall, and right past him.

● ● ●

Samantha came awake screaming. She had been trying to warn the man in her dream of some terrible danger. Her thoughts were still fuzzy, but she was awake enough to know she had been dreaming again, and this one was worse than the last. No clown this time. Only an old woman. An old decrepit woman and she was crazy, her fingers long with sharpened claws reaching out to snatch and tear. And Lysander had been there. She looked at the depression in the mattress beside her. He was gone. Just as well, she thought exhausted, he needed to get his sleep. She rolled over and smelled the pillow he had been sleeping on. It smelled of clean laundry. She smiled to herself in the dark. Already she had begun to forget about her bad dream and that horrible woman. She sighed and drifted off again, still uneasy.

● ● ●

Lysander stood by his bed. His trembling right arm was cocked over his head. In that hand was the only weapon that had been within arm's reach: the conciliatory trophy he had brought home after his defeat with the Hayward Junior Comets. He was holding it by the tiny silver figurine.

Gold is for winners, son, his father had scolded at the time.

The heavy base wobbled in his hand.

The mangled lump under his covers looked more like a pile of old, rotting clothes than it did a human being. The smell of things wet and moldy that hovered about his bed in a fine mist did nothing to disprove that. He waited for the covers to rise and fall with the rhythmic pattern that accompanied sleep, but the form in his bed wasn't moving at all. He wiped the sweat from his forehead with the back of his left hand and reached for the blanket. He would flip it back, and if it turned out to be anything other than a pile of dirty clothes he would swing this trophy with everything he had...

until there's nothing left but a mashed, blood-jetting stump!

The ferocity of the thought made him recoil.

He was about to grab the covers when he heard something behind him. He turned quickly, half expecting to see Reverend Small scrambling out of the closet, his hand glittering with six inches of steel. But there was nothing there. A branch outside was scratching at his window.

He turned back to see the covers peeled back and a

201

maniacal face staring up at him. Its eyes were bulging and wild, wrapped in bursting red veins. Its mouth opened in a half expectant smile. It had a pleased look, as though it were happy to see him. Blood was smeared around the open edges of its mouth. Bits of fur—cat fur?—clung to the blood around its face, some of it jammed between its blackened teeth.

It looked vaguely like his grandmother—her hair was the same, a mess of bed-flattened curls—but gone was the old dullness in her eyes, the serenity of her once peaceful existence. Something had snuck into her poor weakened mind and set up shop. Something had put a cold killing gleam in her eye and the smell of death on her lips.

He opened his mouth to scream. He could feel his abdomen tighten, the air rush from his lungs. That thing that looked oddly like his grandmother grabbed his hand with the trophy, squeezing it with dizzying force, crushing the bones in his wrist, until he couldn't help but drop it.

It was saying something, but its lips weren't in sync with the sound he was hearing. That thing was trying to pull him closer, its smile broadening with delight. He struggled to escape its iron grasp. It flailed out with its other hand, clawing at him. He drew his free hand back and punched it in the face full force. It shook off the blow and let out a perverse laugh. Blood was running from its nose now. He punched it again, and again and finally that thing that was once his grandmother let go, its nose split wide open and bent to one side. Lysander wrenched his arm away and ran toward his parents' room. He shot a terrified glance behind him and saw that it was sitting bolt upright. He turned the handle and shouldered the door open, but it was locked. Behind him, he could hear it slipping out of bed, landing on the ground with a wet fleshy sound. Could hear it slithering toward him. He wanted so badly to turn around, but he couldn't, because

202

he knew that if he saw what was behind him, he would be immobilized by terror. He stepped back and sent his aching shoulder into his parents' door again and nearly went sprawling as the door gave way. The scream locked behind his lips was finally let loose, jarring his parents from their sleep. His father propped himself up on his hands, his eyes wide and cloudy. His mother, still on her back, head cocked at a sharp angle, was glaring at him. The fear of God was in her eyes.

Lysander turned around, slammed the door shut and leaned against it with all his weight. He could hear it on the other side, wheezing, its long fingernails scuttling along the bottom of the door, clicking up toward the handle.

A second later his father was behind him.

"Jesus Christ, Lysander, what the hell is this all about?"

Lysander's breath was skipping in his throat. He was hyperventilating.

"Calm down, son. What's going on? Is there someone in the house?"

Lysander nodded vigorously, his face so milky white they might have mistaken him for an apparition.

His mother wrapped herself in her bathrobe. She was rubbing her enormous belly, her face stricken with weary terror. "Oh, Glenn. What's happening? Is there someone in the house?... Glenn!"

Glenn disappeared into the walk-in closet. They could hear him swearing, the sound of things being scattered and tossed about. A second later he emerged with a silver .45.

"No, Glenn, don't do something silly. Call the police."

Lysander's eyes grew wide when he saw the gun.

"I *will* call the cops, but not before I find out what's going on."

Glenn turned sharply back to his son. "Lysander," he shouted, prying his son's hands from the doorknob.

203

"Move!"

Lysander fell back and Glenn swung open the door, his gun stretched out before him. His mother got on the phone to the police, frantic. He followed his father as he crept down the short hallway toward his bedroom. His door was still ajar, exactly as he had left it a moment ago. But his bed was perfectly made, the covers pulled tight the way his mother set it every morning. A tidy room breeds a tidy mind, she always said.

Gone was the trail of blood, smeared as his grandmother had clawed her way along the floor.

Glenn made his way toward the grandmother's room and Lysander stopped dead in his tracks.

"Dad, no. He's in there."

Glenn waved him away. "Just stay where you are, Lysander."

He entered her room and Lysander saw the light flicker on.

A moment later, his father re-emerged, his voice, brushed with concern: "I'm going downstairs."

"But—"

"Don't worry, she's fine."

It's not her—anymore—I'm worried about, Lysander thought darkly. The woman just tried to eat me for breakfast.

His father brushed past him and headed for the stairs.

The light in his grandmother's room was still on.

"Dad, you—" But he was already gone.

Lysander approached her room, and as he did he became aware of a prickling sensation against the pads of his feet, giving his step an odd stilted rhythm. Her door was open a crack. He decided he would only slip a hand in and snap the light off, but he found himself pushing in her door. It gave easily. No creaks or groans this time. She was sleeping like a baby, a lump under a rug, just as she always was, her head tucked beneath the covers. At least most of her head was tucked. He could see a bushel of matted hair and part of her face. He blinked and his eyes felt terribly heavy. He rubbed them hard. He was beginning to wonder if they were playing tricks on him, because from here it looked like one of her eyes had opened and rolled down to watch him. He flicked off the light and shut the door.

For the next twenty minutes, Glenn searched the rest of the house, but Lysander knew his father wouldn't find anything. All the windows were shut, and the doors, including the garage, were locked from the inside. For a while afterward, Lysander couldn't get his heart to stop pounding. He would sleep with his bed nudged against the door tonight all right, only after he checked his closet a second time that is. And after he had words with the cops who were no doubt on their way, more than likely a tired and cranky Deputy Alex Morgan. Yeah, he would sleep behind a barricaded door tonight. If he slept at all.

Chapter 31

Samantha had lain hunkered behind the large maple tree for what felt like an impossibly long time. The sky, gray and lifeless all day, was growing darker now. She wrapped her arms about her. Even in the gloom she could see her breath pluming out and then disintegrating before her. She was sitting alone in a patch of empty land between Lysander's and the reverend's house, waiting for Small to leave. Every passing second put her more on edge. From somewhere behind her, a branch snapped, then feet rustled through dead leaves. She turned to see a dark form approaching.

"Lysander?" she croaked.

"Yes," he whispered back.

"You nearly scared the shit out of me."

In the distance, they heard the sound of a door slamming shut. Lysander dropped to the ground. Through the darkness they saw the distinct shape of Reverend Small heading toward his white Cadillac. The motor hummed to life a second later, and he backed slowly out of the driveway. The headlights washed over them as the car straightened onto the road. Samantha ducked behind the thick maple. Then like a hearse in a long procession, the car lumbered away slow and deliberate.

Lysander ripped open the bag he had brought from his house and pulled out a long, fur-lined jacket. Samantha took it from him and angled herself into the sleeves without getting up. She wrapped it tightly about her, appreciating the insulating warmth.

Lysander handed her a thermos filled with coffee and a walkie-talkie.

"What's this for?" she asked, shaking the walkie-talkie in the air.

"So you can warn me if he comes home."

Her face became stubbornly set. "I thought we were going in together."

"No, it's better this way."

The smug expression plastered across his face made her wonder if he was trying to be a hero.

As if in response Lysander said: "I've never been so nervous in my whole life."

She smiled weakly and kissed him. Her lips were tight with worry.

"Be careful," she said.

He nodded briefly.

She turned on her walkie-talkie and he did the same. He brought it to his mouth. "Testing one, two, three. Testing."

"Gotcha," she replied.

"I'm gonna get what I need and then vanish. Quick in and quick out."

She tried to smile but couldn't entirely hide her concern. "And if he comes home?" she asked.

"Just give me enough warning to get out in time."

"Do you even know what you're looking for?"

"I was kinda hoping to find a sign somewhere with flashing neon lights that says 'I did it!'"

Lysander took her face in his hands and kissed it. Then he stood and gave her perhaps the world's worst Arnold Schwarzenegger impression. "Ay'll bee bach."

207

He started off toward the rear of the house. She lifted the walkie-talkie and spoke into it, "You better *bee bach*, asshole, or I'm coming in after you. He turned and nodded. She watched him until he disappeared behind the backyard fence.

Sam undid the thermos and took a sip of coffee, swished it in her mouth and then spat it onto a pile of leaves beside her. She hadn't eaten all day. Her stomach had been so unsettled, she knew she would only throw it up. Whether or not it was because of her father's pills she had finally decided to take this morning, Samantha didn't know, but things had been hazy and dull since Derek had been killed. With the notable exception of Lysander's visit last night. For a while, the warm feeling she got replaying that evening over in her mind had helped her forget what was really bothering her. But when that failed to hold back the tide of shadows and flashes of memory, the pills had come out.

Her eyes focused in front of her. Two young lovers had scratched their names into the bark of the maple next to her and circled it with a heart.

Paul luvs Trish

At any other time, that kind of wishy-washy sentimentality would have made Samantha stick a finger down her throat, but now it made her flush. She searched her pockets for a knife or a key. She felt a sudden overpowering urge to make a mark of her own: Lys luvs Sam. As if the very act would make it eternal. This was not the strong ball-busting Samantha she knew and loved. The same Samantha she could trust not to lose her head and go get herself hurt.

Since her mother's death she had been preparing herself for the day when her father's death would mean she was completely alone. She had decided then that she would not let herself be hurt. Then along came Lysander.

She lay on her stomach and brought the walkie-talkie to

208

her lips. She pressed the button, was about to speak, and then released it. No, she thought, fighting the urge to check up on him. She watched the road for the reverend's white Cadillac.

● ● ●

Above the reverend's nondescript single bed hung a large wooden cross. Soft light came in through a large window that looked out onto the street. The room was dark and the gloom cast a sickening glow on the cross. There was something odd about the Jesus that was nailed to those two tiny beams of wood. Something Lysander couldn't quite put his finger on.

He went to a nightstand and a small drawer. He would start his search here. He nudged the drawer open and narrowed his eyes, slowly becoming accustomed to the darkness. Inside was a package of blue pens, a single cigarette, a Zippo, a deck of nudy playing cards and a pile of faded gas receipts. For some reason, the cigarette surprised him the most. The reverend seemed like the kind of guy who would tsk at anyone with a Marlboro clamped between their teeth.

To think that he had petty vices—besides that nasty little habit he had of torturing and killing people—was almost absurd. Lysander closed the drawer and glanced over again at the statue of Jesus on the wall. The statue's pained, pleading face was turned toward an open closet.

He went there, his body tightening with the thought that something was waiting behind that cracked door, some insane clown man with sharp claws. Slowly, he drew it open. There were no red eyes peering back at him, only a series of dark suits, all identical. Below them, shoe boxes stacked one on top of another with glaring precision.

There's the sicko we know and love.

Lysander rifled through each one, finding nothing. He tossed them aside. Then his hand brushed against something that gave at the edges. He grabbed hold and pulled. An old leather-bound book.

No, a planner.

A planner that went back to the year 2000, but there were more underneath, each in five-year blocks, right back to 1960. Lysander grabbed one marked 1965. The pages were musty and discolored. He wiped the dust from the cover and opened it over his lap. He flipped through the pages, stopping at random. His eyes were straining to see. Noticing a light bulb in the closet above him, he flicked it on.

The gnawing urge to look behind him had begun the moment he opened the first planner. But he had pushed the feeling aside, figuring it for nerves. Now it was back, and it was more than just gently persistent. It had become a command.

See me!

He glanced over his shoulder.

Nothing there. The room hadn't changed one bit.

He returned to the book, unable to shake the odd sense of disquiet and then swung around again.

Something wasn't quite right.

Red warning lights were flashing inside his head.

Everything seemed to be the same—

Except...

Jesus. From here in the closet, he could see the statue's chrome features, but something about the eyes made the skin along Lysander's arms begin to creep.

They were moving.

Stop messing around, he told himself. This nut job's got you seeing things. He wiped a thin layer of sweat from his forehead with the back of his hand and returned to the reverend's daily planner. There was a note on June

210

9, 1965, reminding him to see a Dr. Stephens. Similar notes appeared for two or three weeks. Then visits with Doctor Stephens ended, replaced by visits with another doctor. Dr. A. Who was Dr. A?

Lysander began flipping through the pages, and what he saw next made him gasp.

Dr. A.

Doctor A.

Doctor Avery.

"Why in hell was Reverend Small seeing Avery?" he wondered aloud, only dimly aware of the queer ring in his voice. He lifted the pile of planners and shoved them back in place. They hit the back wall and made a hollow booming sound. For a moment he stood stiffly in place, aware of the icy blood pumping through his veins and then he slid his head into the closet. Either he was much stronger than he thought or that back wall wasn't really a wall. He reached out with a trembling hand. The wall swung back, opening into another room. It was the size of a walk-in closet. The air inside was tinged with formaldehyde. Lysander peered behind him. Through the darkness he could see Jesus' silver eyes fixed on him. A look of pleasure suffused its face, as though there was something back there it wanted him to see.

He would have to hurry. The reverend might be home any minute. Lysander grabbed the walkie-talkie from his back pocket and wondered for a moment if the cheap thing had died on him. Fresh batteries aside, they were toys that he had grabbed from under the basement staircase, crammed for years in a box labeled, "Lysander's stuff." But no, the little red light was still on and that meant he was fine.

"Sam, you there?" He listened to the crackle of static.

Then: "Yeah, I'm here. Find any neon signs?" The tension in her voice was unmistakable.

211

His eyes dropped to the ledger, now stacked back in place and then into the dark room behind the closet wall. "No, but I may have found something else."

"Something else. God, Lysander, hurry up!"

He paused and looked over his shoulder.

"Okay. Two minutes." Lysander slid the device into his back pocket and stepped inside the closet. The smell of fur was strong here. Before him, a white string dangled in shadowy darkness. He pulled at it and when the light came on, he nearly screamed.

An enormous ram's head scowled at him with sightless glass eyes, its horns curved downward like two ancient blades.

Above the stuffed ram's head was the eye.

Animal heads glared down at him accusingly from wooden mounts.

Four cats and nearly a half dozen dogs, stacked one on top of the other. One of them looked disturbingly like a Siberian Husky. His face twisted sourly when he realized the husky was probably Mrs. Grady's dog. The one Small had come asking about on that first day they met. The eyes gazed at him and he turned away. Beside it was the shepherd Lysander had seen him dragging across his lawn that night.

On a set of shelves to his left were vials filled with a cloudy liquid. Inside were pale, almost translucent body parts. He couldn't tell if they were human or animal.

Before him was a raised platform draped with a black sheet. It might have been an altar or an operating theatre.

And on this altar was the body of a dead rabbit. White fur stained red. Its insides were torn out. Lysander leaned closer. The brown patch of fur on its head looked familiar: the same kind of patch Necra had, and the sudden stinging certainty filled him with rage. His hands curled into fists.

You sick bastard!!

212

In his mind he could hear the reverend's laughter.

A knife lay on the table. He forced himself to examine the blade. For a tantalizing second, his spirits rose. Was this the weapon that murdered Derek and the others? If it was, he would snatch it and present it as evidence. But it was a small paring knife and not the large one he had seen the reverend use before. Muttering to himself, he threw it back onto the table with a clatter and tugged out his walkie-talkie. He was about to tell Sam what he had found, about to ask her what he should do with the cat. He paused instead and rested the walkie-talkie on the table. No, that kinda news would only upset her, he knew. He would find the evidence the cops were too incompetent to find on their own and help put this sonofabitch away forever. Through the darkening storm cloud of anger that was rolling over him, Lysander failed to notice the tiny red light on his walkie-talkie flicker and then go out.

Chapter 32

When Samantha saw the white Cadillac drive down the street and then pull into the driveway, she felt the hairs on her neck stand on end. She fumbled inside the deep pocket of the fur coat and came out with the walkie-talkie.

The reverend got out of his car and stood there, looking up toward a second-floor window.

She struggled to keep her voice cool and collected. "Lysander, he's back! Lysander!"

It was too dark to tell for sure what Small had or hadn't seen, but something about the way he was staring told Samantha it wasn't an overflowing eave that had caught his attention.

The reverend started briskly toward the back of the house.

Sam began to panic. She said urgently, "Oh God, Lysander. Can you hear me?"

The reverend reached the fence at the rear of the house, and when he turned, his eyes raked the overgrowth.

She dropped to the ground. Had she been too loud? He must have heard her, she was sure of it. But her body was abuzz with adrenaline, and it was difficult to be certain. He stood at the edge of the woods now, scanning. She

214

lowered herself even more and held her breath. If he started running after her, she didn't know what she'd do: die of fright or trip over the long-ass jacket she was wearing. Jittery laughter trickled out of her and she clapped a hand over her mouth. When she was sure the feeling had passed, she peered out again and saw that he was gone. She spoke into the walkie-talkie:

"Lysander, if you can hear me, get out now. He's coming inside the house. He knows you're there."

The ninety seconds that followed were the most agonizing of Samantha Crow's life.

She bit her nails furiously, spitting out black polish in clumps.

I can't just leave him in there.

She sprang to her feet and made her way to the reverend's back door. It was swaying back and forth when she found it. She stepped tentatively into the darkness. She let her hand slide along the wall to guide her. First over smooth painted walls, then to a doorway and a new room. She came to a set of wooden cupboards and heard a sudden clank and a rattle as she hit a rack of kitchen knives suspended from a magnetic track. She groped at the knives, removing what felt like the largest one, gripping it in her right hand. Her breathing must have sounded like a violent gale screaming through a deep canyon, broadcasting her location to everyone in the house. But she was inside now, and there was no turning back. On her right, she found a flight of stairs that led to the second floor and past that, a living room cluttered with old furniture draped in white sheets.

Her eyes were beginning to adjust.

Somewhere in the house, a grandfather clock was clanging. It chimed ten times, deep and hollow. She stood suspended, clutching the knife.

She noticed a shadow at the end of the hallway. Fear slipped around her neck like a noose and cinched tightly.

215

She waited, staring.

The shadow didn't move.

She blinked and still it remained.

Had she not seen a coat rack in the hallway with a long garment hanging from one of the hooks? And hadn't it been in the corner, between what she thought was a bathroom and an office? The dark mass took on the form of a coat rack and the realization that her mind was spinning her in circles helped to ease her fear. The grip on the knife in her hand slackened a little.

She could hear movement upstairs. A warm trickle of light was coming from one of the rooms.

"Lysander," she called out softly, hesitantly.

The sound of rustling footsteps. But not from upstairs.

She glanced down the hallway and a hot panic gripped her.

The coat rack was gone.

She looked behind her and screamed when she saw the face.

A closed fist struck the side of her head, knocking her off her feet. Samantha stumbled backward, hitting the small of her back against one of the risers. A flash of pain shot up her spinal column. Hands grabbed her ankle and yanked her down the stairs. Panic blunted the pain and she lashed out with her feet and then swung wildly with the knife until she managed to break free. She sprang frantically to her feet and reached for the banister. She was going to run upstairs and shut herself inside the room with the light. Surely Lysander was in there. But before she could get more than a stair length away, a hand closed around a clump of her hair and wrenched it back. Her head snapped, and for one terrible moment her legs dangled in mid-air. She screamed in wretched agony and her voice resounded through the house as she crashed onto the tiled floor.

He was standing above her now and she could see him

216

clearly.

The light from a passing car outside turned the reverend's face into a skull with two cavernous sockets.

Pain flared high in her right leg. She looked down and saw that the tip of her own knife had bitten into her thigh. The reverend reached behind him and produced a long bone-handle blade of his own. His thin, cracking lips parted with anticipation. She screamed as she tore the knife from her leg and sank it into his left knee where the joint met the kneecap. The knife made a popping sound as it sliced through muscle and tendon. The form wailed and crumpled on top of her, smacking her head onto the hard linoleum tiles, and with that the world faded into darkness.

● ● ●

Lysander was just emerging from behind the closet, Necra's mutilated body cradled in his arms when he heard Samantha's voice calling him faintly from downstairs.

Then a scream, like a gust of violently cold wind, shot up the stairs. Lysander dropped Necra and lunged for the door.

With a shuddering boom, the door slammed shut in his face. He grasped the knob with both hands, rattling it back and forth. The door was jammed. He backed away and lowered his shoulder. He charged the door with his full weight and heard a loud boom and a splintering crack.

He took a step back and went at it again. Any second now the door would give. From behind him came the sound of hissing static and Lysander didn't dare turn around to find the source.

Instead, he put his shoulder down and ran blindly

217

ahead. He hit the door and it collapsed before him, sending him stumbling onto a bed of splintered wood. He scrambled to his feet and tore downstairs, jumping two risers at a time. At the foot of the stairs lay Samantha: her hair matted and a streak of thick purplish liquid splashed across her face.

No, God. No!

He turned her over. Her eyes sprang open: two peeled grapes in a sea of blackness. And with a chilling scream she swung the bone-handle knife at his face.

• • •

The reverend was standing over her, shaking her. The knife was somehow still in her hand, and she shrieked as she swung it at him again. She missed, but she knew he had felt the wind against his face. The reverend was screaming for her to stop. The very idea of him pleading confused her. Something different about his voice deepened her bewilderment. Slowly, Lysander's face, pale and terrified came into focus. The tension went out of her like air out of a balloon, and she fell back to the floor with a dull thump. Lysander bent down, slid his hands underneath her and grunted as he heaved her up and over his shoulder. His frame staggered for a moment as he took her weight onto him and then stabilized as he began moving sluggishly toward the front door.

A trail of spattered blood led off toward the kitchen.

"I got him," Samantha said hoarsely. "I nailed that bastard!"

She could hear Lysander fumbling with the locks on the front door. In her dazed state it sounded to Samantha like there were dozens of them.

"Oh, please hurry up!" she begged him.

The reverend came around the corner like an angel of

218

death. Black suit. Pale, dead face. His left pant leg was turned up at the knee and dressed with a tattered and bloodstained dishrag. In his right hand he carried a long knife. His left tugged at his wounded leg, nudging it forward like a sack of rotting food.

Bent over Lysander's shoulder, Samantha felt her heart catch in her throat. "Oh God, Lysander, he's coming!"

The locks were a chaotic mass of confusion. Some turned and clicked, others just spun round and round in useless circles. His mind was racing. 'The big tall ship goes round and round. Round and round. Round and round...' He shifted Sam's weight on his shoulder and nearly fell backwards.

With sickening dread, the thought of Jeffrey Dahmer came to him. The way the serial killer had used a host of dummy locks to confuse his victims as they tried to flee.

Samantha was wiggling so much now he was certain he would drop her. His trembling hands fumbled over the locks.

"Lysander!"

He looked back and what he saw made him blanch. The reverend was ten feet away, limping toward them determinedly. His face a mask of sick pleasure. His lunatic eyes wide and pallid. Lysander reached the bottom lock and turned it. It rotated and clicked. The reverend raised his knife and brought it down, cutting through the air. Samantha screamed. The door began to open and then stopped abruptly. There was a chain Lysander hadn't seen. The blade bit into hard oak, not an inch from Lysander's right ear. The reverend struggled to free it as Lysander, still carrying Sam, staggered away.

They got maybe fifteen feet before Lysander felt his legs give in.

"Can you walk?" he screamed.

"Maybe..."

Lysander stopped and leaned forward. Samantha

219

stumbled onto her feet. They were heading for the kitchen, the way they'd come in, but the reverend was ready for this. He had gone around the other way to cut off their escape. He stepped out in front of them. Lysander skidded to a stop and they ran the other way.

Samantha's voice was electrified with fear. "We're trapped!"

Through the dimness, Lysander made out a room down the hallway. It had a window, he was sure of it. They could barricade themselves in and break the glass.

"This way!" he shouted.

She followed, staggering behind him.

They slipped inside and slammed the door. They hadn't bothered to check whether the reverend was behind them or not. Lysander leaned against the door. Beads of perspiration rolled down his forehead blotting his vision. Both of them breathing heavily.

Throbbing pain thumped in every part of Sam's body. She looked down at her right thigh and saw the hole in her jeans where the knife had stung her. Her entire leg felt like it was on fire.

Lysander's eyes were adjusting to the dimness of the room. There was no window, only three walls cluttered with old photographs.

He cursed under his breath.

Sam came near. "I don't hear him. Do you think he's still out there?"

Lysander tried listening, but deathly silence reigned outside.

"There's no way out of here," he said gravely. "Except through this door." He scanned their surroundings. "Sam, check for a phone. We'll call your dad."

She found one almost at once, on a mahogany desk by the far wall. Above it was a picture of two men standing together—the same she'd seen in McMurphy's basement. She lifted the receiver and began to dial. In the middle of the second ring the line went dead.

"I don't have a tone anymore," she said, fear curdling in her throat.

Lysander's spirits began to sink and then suddenly his expression changed. "He could only have cut the line from outside."

Sam looked puzzled. "So?"

"So, it means he isn't standing behind this door. If we move quick we can sneak out before he comes back."

"I don't know, Lysander."

He grabbed her hand. "Do you trust me?"

Her eyes met his. "I trust you."

"Then let's go."

He flung the door open, half expecting to find a knife arching toward his head, and they fled into the hall. The house was dark and eerily silent.

They came to the kitchen and a pair of sliding doors. Lysander jiggled them and found that they were locked.

A noise like the closing of a door sounded from over by the garage. The reverend had come back inside. Then they caught sight of him, staggering in the gloom, ready to finish what he had started. The kitchen counter stretched out to divide the room in half and they crouched behind it. They could hear his footsteps drawing closer. Step, drag. Step, drag.

Sam's heart was hammering wildly in her chest.

They could hear him as he approached, muttering under his breath.

It sounded as though he was carrying something heavy and metallic. A wood-chopping axe thudded against the floor right before them. He was going to chop down the door and then hack them to pieces, the same way he'd done to the McMurphys all those years ago.

Through the darkness they could see him clearly, standing before them. He seemed to be peering down the hallway. His labored breathing seesawing in and out. The reverend only needed to turn in their direction, and he would see them, huddled together like little piglets hiding from the big bad wolf. Sam was on the verge of a scream, but her hand found its way to her mouth just in time. All the muscles in Lysander's body tensed.

Only after he'd disappeared did they hear him bellow. They'd forgotten to close the door behind them and now he knew they'd escaped. Lysander tugged on Sam's hand and they straightened, sprinting for the back door. They could hear the reverend swiveling his axe head, striking a whole in the drywall as he did so.

"Allie, ollie oxenfree!" he yammered drunkenly, as though intoxicated with the idea of chopping them up into little bits.

They took the corner at full throttle and came to the back door. There was a single bolt lock there. Lysander turned it, heard it click and yanked at the door.

It wouldn't move.

Step, drag. Step, drag. Faster now.

In his panic, he thought they were finished. That this door too was little more than a decoy. Then Sam stuck a hand past him and fumbled with the doorknob. She gave it a half turn until she felt the push button come unlatched. The door flung open and they went spilling outside.

Lysander didn't stop until he was behind his own front door, locked tight. He stood by the window for awhile to be sure the reverend hadn't followed them. His parents' car wasn't in the driveway either. He remembered his father saying that they were going to a movie at the Davenport. Sam's leg was still bleeding. He went to the laundry room and emerged a moment later with a rag.

Lysander tied the rag tightly around her upper thigh, and when he was done, he fell back against the stairs, his chest heaving up and down.

The full consequences of what had just happened hit

them both at once. Samantha's hand loosened until the knife left her fingers and fell clanging to the floor. The noise startled Lysander. "Where'd you get that?" he asked, pointing at the knife.

She glanced at it, and her eyes turned to pinpricks. "I... huh..." She knew at once that this wasn't the knife from the kitchen she had pulled from the magnetic rack. That had been a cutting knife. The knife Lysander held was a white handled hunting knife. Bone handle.

"He must have dropped it when I stabbed him in the leg. Must have taken the one I had by mistake."

Lysander smiled and kissed her lips hard. He pulled away and flicked a string of bloody hair out of her face. "This may be it."

She shook her head. "May be what?"

"The evidence we need."

Samantha fixed him squarely. "What did you find upstairs?"

He paused, remembering the room with the formaldehyde, the stuffed animal heads, the jars crammed with the gore, Necra's body, mutilated. There was no need to tell her that. He did tell her about Avery and the daily planner.

"I don't understand. What's the connection?" she asked. Her eyes were still puffy and red.

"I'm not sure. But that first time Avery brought me back, all those hundreds of years, I knew something wasn't right with him. His face went pale, like a ghost had come up and bitten him in the ass." Lysander rose. "You've got to bring this knife to your father."

"Wait a minute," she said, laying a worried hand on his shoulder. "What are you gonna do?"

He smiled, but she already knew.

223

Chapter 33

When Lysander arrived at Avery's, he found the basement window unlocked. Not that it really mattered much since he was ready to put a rock through it if need be, but there was no sense in drawing any unnecessary attention to what he was about to do. He slid through the narrow opening face first, his ribs squeezed by the tiny window frame. A misplaced thought came to him then. About how a newborn baby must feel, birthed into the world, cold and cramped, knowing fear for the first time. Fear of the strange and the unknown. And more than one unknown was running through Lysander's head just then, as his hands scrambled for a wobbly bookshelf propped below him. That Avery was somehow involved in this whole business was an idea he found hard to grasp. Harder still was the notion that some invisible clock was ticking away and when that clock reached zero, the curtain would fall forever on his one-man play, its working title, Lysander: alienation and true love found too late.

With difficulty, he swung his mind back to the task at hand. With Samantha on her way to her father, wielding the only solid piece of evidence they had, he felt strangely certain that something here would explain why the reverend was trying so desperately to kill him. Just as that last thought blinked on in his head, an image of a man's face flashed before his mind's eye in such vivid detail he might have reached out and touched it. The face was stern and marked with deep intersecting lines. But in spite of the wrinkles, this was not an old man. A silver-buckled hat rested squarely on his head. Dark, ancient thoughts drifted from the old man and seeped into Lysander's awareness, forming into a single word. Blood dripped from the edges.

Power

As quickly as it came, the image was gone. He had seen the thin man's face many a night as he skated along that ill-defined ledge of semi-consciousness. It was the man Avery had showed him in the regression. The one with the broad-brimmed hat sitting at the head of other men also in broad-brimmed hats, looking on as that poor woman, tortured and bleeding, was burned to a crisp.

The chilly mist that emanated from the man's aura was a familiar one. It occurred to Lysander that if there was such a thing as past lives, the wrinkled face must have belonged to the reverend.

Another time. Another life.

A nervous laugh skittered out of him, and he clamped a hand over his lips. He wanted to chase the thought away, but he couldn't hide from it any longer, in part because he couldn't help wondering if it were true. Supposing, just for the sake of argument that the reverend and the skinny man in the long black cloak were one and the same, would that not make Lysander the witch condemned to death? The crushing sense of alienation fit. So too did the feeling he had carried with him all his life of being damned out of hand for not conforming. But was the universe that cruel? Were we destined to return again and again, he wondered, clad in a rotating wardrobe of costumes so that some remote and aloof deity could

225

watch reruns of the same pathetic cosmic play? It seemed insane. Or maybe just insane enough to be true.

Lysander flicked his light over a pair of filing cabinets tucked behind Avery's wide oak desk. The room had become a lot more disheveled since he was last here. Papers were heaped and littered on every available surface. On one table a half eaten apple had become a browning paperweight. He opened the cabinet and found, to his surprise, files that were neatly organized and alphabetical.

Allcott, Jim
Aloe, Sarah
Babich, Dora

He shut it and opened the bottom one.

Reynolds, Eric
Roberts, Jack

He was getting close.

Sims, Kathleen
Small, Nathaniel...
Bingo!

He yanked the reverend's file with the cold efficiency of a banker pulling up a loan application. With the back of his hand he swept everything off Avery's desk. He set the file down, opened the cover and scanned the pages. The paper smelled like an old sock. The print had faded with age and was hard to make out in places. It didn't help that Avery's handwriting looked like something right out of a kindergarten arts and crafts primer. He opened the file to 1965. He found it divided according to visits. Notes followed each visit.

"Subject: Nathaniel Small... complaining of bouts of extreme rage... outwardly he seems composed and gentlemanly... flashes of deep-seated anger... his eyes... uncanny... spoke of a dream he had last night that a boy came to him, lost. He took him in to stay the night and couldn't fight the urge to touch the boy. When the boy

226

resisted his advances, he killed him and kept his head in the fridge until the flesh fell away…"

Lysander skimmed through a number of entries, looking for Avery's reaction to the confessed murder, but all he found were clinical recountings of his visits with Small.

"Still no clear source for Small's uncontrollable anger. We spoke of his childhood today. Subject described how his mother, a devout Baptist, would hold a smoldering cigarette to his eye and oblige him to recite the book of Revelation. A small circular scar over this right eye is consistent with the burn from a cigarette. Prescribed 10 mg of Miodeen, twice daily. Suggested hypnotherapy for root cause of Small's condition. Patient accepted."

Lysander continued to skim through pages until something caught his eye.

"Regressed Small to childhood. Not much there. When asked to return to the cause of his feelings of anger, the patient lapsed into a fantasy where he saw himself in colonial Millingham. Asked him to repeat the name and he confirmed it was Millingham… described a stake surrounded by wood saturated in a flammable liquid. Says the town had gathered to witness an execution. A woman charged with practicing the dark arts (witchcraft?)… was about to die… noticeable change in the patient's voice…"

The noise from the office door made Lysander jump. "Would it help if I turned on a light?" Avery asked. He was standing in the doorway, his face darkened.

Lysander held the file in the air. "You never told me about Reverend Small… you—"

"I told you, my man. Fantasy. At least that's what I thought it was before you came along. Harmless fantasy, played out by a mind eager to respond to hypnotic suggestions. The mind will do almost anything to please, to camouflage a person's pain, to dress it up in whatever way it can."

227

"This is no fantasy."

"No, you're right," Avery replied reflectively. "This is no fantasy."

"Then what is it?"

"I shouldn't be telling you… patient confiden—"

"Cut the crap, Avery! People are dying… and I'm next. You could have stopped this fifty years ago and you didn't."

Avery slumped into one of the plush leather chairs. He swallowed and his throat made an audible clicking noise. "Kids out of college are so full of piss and vinegar, you know that? No, you probably don't. Well, they are. I sure as hell was. Twenty-six, my own practice, a head the size of a carnival balloon.

"Then along comes a man who would one day become Reverend Small. Bethlehem Baptist's finest. A young guy from the deep South with one hell of a chip on his shoulder. He had assaulted a police officer. Did you see that when you were snooping through my things? No? Court ordered him to see me for a temper that had put him before a judge on more than one occasion. In those early days I thought I could do anything. Fix anyone. Change the goddamned world!" A contemplative smile formed on his lips and remained there a second before fading away. "School in the sixties had a nasty habit of doing that to people."

Lysander stood behind the desk unable to move, eager to hear more.

Avery went on. "When he came to me, I could sense the darker parts…" He paused. It didn't last more than a second, but it was enough to make the skin on Lysander's arms rise in tiny hackles. "I could see the struggle going on within him. The evil, begging for release. We delved into this past-life fantasy of his for weeks. I thought living them out in a controlled environment might free him from them, but the grip grew tighter. As though his true

228

self was stirring awake. I could see glimpses of what was happening, but I didn't do anything to stop it. Not until the momentum was too great. He took up God not long after. I didn't quite understand it at first, and now that I met you, it's beginning to make sense."

Lysander's face was burning. "You motherfucker! *You* started this. You wound this crazy asshole up like a ticking time bomb, and now he's after me."

Avery laughed. "No, Lysander. It wasn't me who started this, it was you."

Lysander frowned, feeling suddenly numb from the neck down. He swallowed hard, his eyes blinking stupidly. He shook his head.

"After McMurphy and then Sheila Crow," Avery went on, "I believed it *was* me. I thought I had spun things out of control. All these years carrying around the guilt. Do you have any idea what that kind of guilt does to a man my age? You should see my medicine cabinet." His fingers played with a pleat in the leather chair. "Wasn't until that day I had you in my office that I realized it wasn't me at all and some horrible little voice inside me said: *Thank God! Thank God, Jack, 'cause now you're free. A free man.*" The muscles in his face seemed to settle all at once. "No, Lysander, you started this, a long, long time ago, and now it's come full circle."

Lysander stepped back and his heel hit the trash can, making a hollow sound. He wobbled and caught the edge of the desk. His other hand went to his temple. It was throbbing wildly. "But how?" he asked. "I don't understand."

"You know, Small said the same thing." Avery pointed at the chair in front of him. "I'll show you."

"Another regression?" Lysander asked.

Avery nodded.

The induction took some time. Lysander's mind was a churning mess as he sank into the soft leather chair, and

229

he had to let all that go enough to fall into a suitable state. Avery brought him deeper and deeper. Finally, when Lysander relaxed, the room settled into a dull haze. His body felt heavy and distant.

The Wellman was back. Lysander could see him up ahead, pail in hand—a twin brother in almost every respect. He stood before the deep reservoir of everything Lysander had ever known, ready now to pull up whatever was asked for. First, Avery brought Lysander to his youth, then to the security of his mother's womb, and finally, back to that other life.

"You will no longer be a detached observer as you were before. You are a participant now and you will report to me exactly what you see."

Lysander nodded sluggishly.

"Tell me your name."

"Parris Locke."

"Where are you?"

"I am on a hill overlooking town."

"What town?"

He laughed incredulously. "Millingham, of course. Where else?"

"Go on."

"I am with Anna. The tanner's daughter." Lysander snickered, and his voice had become deeper. "She is below me socially. She thinks we will marry. I have told her we will, but I know my family would never allow it. They have already picked out my wife. She is the governor's youngest daughter. She is round and uncouth, but at least she is my equal."

"The girl you are with now, the tanner's daughter. Do you recognize her from your current life?"

There was a slight hesitation. "Yes. It... it is Samantha."

"Move forward to the next major event in your life. Tell me what you see."

230

Lysander stiffened in his chair. "I am Millingham's head selectman. My job is to maintain order and report to the governor on the state of the town."

"And how are you faring in your new role?"

A long pause, then, "Not well. There is drinking and unlawfulness. Many prefer gambling in the taverns to attending mass."

"So what effect does this have on you?"

"The governor is unhappy. If the people are not following God's laws, they are easy prey for the Devil. The very existence of the colony depends on obedience. The governor has threatened to remove me unless I can regain some measure of control."

"Did you marry the tanner's daughter?"

His shoulders drooped. "No. I married Governor Winthrop's daughter, that ungrateful wench. And she knows I did it only to become governor one day myself."

"Tell me, who is Governor Winthrop's daughter in your life now?"

"Summer."

"And what became of the tanner's daughter?"

"She married Hugh Parsons. I think she too is unhappy." Lysander's face grew pained. "There are rumors that he beats her."

"How does this news make you feel?"

"I should have listened to my heart. I know that now."

"Sounds like you've gained some perspective from the experience. What did you do with this new wisdom? Did you try and win her back?"

"How can I? She's married now!"

"Let's go back to the governor. How is it you intend to please him?"

"I am not sure. But I must find a way of frightening the people into obeying me. Into obeying God."

"Move to the moment when something important happens. Tell me what you see?"

"A crowd has gathered to hear the sentence. I sit at the head of the town council."

"Sentencing for what?"

"Witchcraft. A young woman, Rebecca Goodman. She is a healer who lives on the edge of town. It is said that her look can kill. All those she has treated have died. Even in her jail cell apparitions of children are said to have conversed with her and then fled through walls of solid stone."

"Do you believe this?"

There is reluctance in Lysander's voice when he speaks. "No. But it has united the town in a way I had never foreseen. This woman is innocent, but it is the perfect opportunity to show the governor that I am able to rule with law and order."

"If this woman is innocent then how can you sentence her?"

"She has confessed."

"Confessed? Why?"

There was a long pause and Avery wondered whether Lysander would answer the question.

"Several were accused," he said finally. "She was the only one who confessed."

"Was she tortured?"

"Of course."

"How?"

"A burning poker was inserted into her eyes and her wrists were slashed. Not enough to kill, just enough to weaken her resistance."

"Apart from Rebecca Goodman, how many others were accused?"

"Four."

"Those others, do you recognize any of them from your current life?"

A long pause, then, "Yes."

"Who are they?"

"Sheriff Crow, Glenn Shore, Deputy Morgan. Pearl Shore."

"Pearl?"

"She is my grandmother now. She was the witch's mother then and her attempts to save her daughter drew the suspicions of the council."

Avery sighed heavily. "Did you burn the eyes out of these four?"

"There was no need. Rebecca seemed in my judgment the most likely to confess."

"Confess to something she was innocent of."

"Yes." The look of guilt on Lysander's face was unmistakable. "I did not create this mess. It was brought to me."

"But you knew she was innocent and still you continued. You tortured her!"

"It wasn't me." There was pleading in Lysander's voice.

"Who then?"

"Another member of the council did it."

"Who are they in this life?"

"Peter Hume."

Avery fell back into his chair. His head was reeling.

"Events were all happening so fast," Lysander was saying. "I hoped she would be left in jail for a while, until tempers cooled, but the entire town was clamoring for blood. They're animals. Even the council wouldn't listen to reason. I was in charge and they looked to me for action. If I had backed down, my career would have been finished."

Avery laid his clipboard down. "Go to the time when Rebecca Goodman is executed. What do you see?"

"I am sitting at the head of the council. There are five of us. We have convened and rendered our decision. Rebecca Goodman will be burnt before us. The announcement is a formality however. Already the pit and stake have been erected. Things had gone too far.

233

Someone had to die. The town would have accepted nothing less."

"And you didn't try to call it off."

"I did." A dispirited look suffused Lysander's face. "I tried, believe me, but they wouldn't listen."

"Describe what you see."

"Rebecca is led out in a cart. People are pelting her with rotten food. She looks very weak. In my heart I hope this will all be over soon, but I must not show it. I must remain stoic and confident in the decision. Her forehead bears the mark of the condemned. The all-seeing eye. After she is tied to the stake I signal to the guards, who light the brush beneath her. Black smoke begins to rise, swirling around her like a shroud. I can see her body contorting, trying to escape the flames. It's horrible. She is screaming. Aha, look! Do you see? Some are turning away. They are not so bloodthirsty anymore, are they? The flames rise high into the air. She seems to waver and then falls limp. Only the cords hold her to the stake now. There is relief that this horrible business is over." Lysander's body stiffened, his hands clawing the seat, as though he were trying to get away.

"What is it? What do you see?"

"She is still alive. She was dead but now she is… this is not possible… She is glaring at us. She has no eyes, but she is glaring nevertheless."

"Glaring at who?"

"Us. The council. How is it she is not dead? She is saying something. A curse. But we cannot make it out. Now she is looking directly at me, and there is such hatred in her blackened face. I cannot look away. The smell of burning flesh is all around us. Like cooked swine. I can feel her anger, growing. I can almost see it spiraling around and above her. It was not supposed to turn out this way. Not like this. What have I done?"

"Tell me what happens now."

234

"The flames envelop her until there is nothing more to see. She is gone at last."

Avery could see thick droplets of sweat beading Lysander's forehead. His clipboard was on the desk and he picked it up now. Flipping through his notes, he spotted a discrepancy with the sessions he had given Reverend Small all those years ago. The reverend had mentioned only four council members, not five. After a few moments, he asked. "What are the names of the council members?"

"Parris Locke, John Endicott, Richard Bellingham, William Hibbins, Simon Bradstreet."

"Do you know any council members in your current life?"

"Yes."

"Who are they?"

"James McMurphy, Diane Crow."

A long pause.

"Peter Hume."

Avery glanced up from his notes. "Yes, that makes four. Who's the fifth, then?"

Silence.

"If you need a few moments—"

"Jack Avery."

Were Lysander fully in the here and now, he would have seen that Avery's face had become the color of curdled milk. He shuffled uncomfortably in his chair, overcome with a sudden coughing fit. The door to his office swung gently open as though a subtle gust of wind had caught hold of it and bent it to its mindless will. Even when part of Lysander realized that no wind had opened that door, that someone had entered the room, that Avery was scrambling out of his chair, still he couldn't move. The only way out of his hypnosis, Avery had told him during that first session, was to fall asleep, and when he woke up again, he'd feel like a million bucks.

He heard the sound of shuffling feet and then a swooshing sound as though a racquet had been swung through the air with great speed. A gurgling came next and the sound of something thudding heavily against the floor.

Now, someone was walking, no, limping, toward him. Although the lids of his eyes were firmly closed, he didn't need to see to know exactly who it was. He could hear him pulling something out of his pocket. Then the metallic snap as the top of a lighter was flipped back. A flame was billowing before him. He could feel a displaced patch of warm air tickling the front of his eyelids, swirling about as it rushed to escape the heat of the flame. Then a rough hand touched his face and pulled his left lid up over his eye. The reverend's gleeful face wavered in the semidarkness, orange in the flame's glow. He reached behind his ear and freed a cigarette tucked behind a patch of thinning gray hair. He clamped it between chapped lips and held the flame up to the end until it glowed red in the darkness. Then he held the glowing ember up to Lysander's eye.

"The book of Revelation," the reverend said. "Recite it for me."

Chapter 34

Lysander remained silent. His body was still so tightly held in that hypnotic trance that he couldn't have moved even if he'd wanted to. The cigarette inched toward his eye, so close now that it dried the thin layer of moisture surrounding his cornea. Sweat poured down Lysander's brow. The reverend giggled and pulled the cigarette away.

"Time to go night-night," he said. He flicked the lighter again and held the flame by Lysander's eye, the lid still propped open by the long nails of Small's right hand.

A shuddering jolt shot through his body, no less violent than if he'd stuck a finger into an electrical socket. His chest and hips surged upward with what felt like 10,000 volts of electricity. He hung there for a moment, wiggling, before falling back down into convulsions. The room went black and then returned a moment later somehow very different.

No longer was Lysander sitting, facing the reverend. He was above him now, looking down on them both. The reverend craned his head skyward and smiled. Lysander's spirit bobbed helplessly against the ceiling as the reverend reached out with his other hand, grasping both sides of Lysander's physical head and then slumped forward. Over by the desk, sprawled on the floor, was Avery—his hands nearly amputated. The handle of a kitchen knife

237

protruded from an empty eye socket. The sight filled his belly with a sick feeling.

He turned back just in time to see a long, wispy trail of dark vapor slither out from the reverend's solar plexus. It snaked its way along the floor and up the leather chair toward Lysander's body. The mist stopped momentarily and then crept into Lysander's nostrils the way smoke from a cigarette might hover before being drawn in.

Then Lysander saw his physical eyes flip open. Even floating as he was against the ceiling, he could see that his eyes had become milky white. The reverend extended a hand—one of Lysander's hands—and examined the arm stretched out before him.

A single terrified thought was jack hammering inside Lysander's weary mind:

If Reverend Small leaves with my body, it'll be the last time I see it.

Lysander drew his legs in and planted his feet against the ceiling. He would use it as a kind of springboard and shoot himself back into his body. If his momentum didn't fail him, he would jump back in and expel the reverend back to his own aging husk, now slumped in the chair, a red stain at his left knee. With a jerk, he launched himself straight for his forehead and bounced off it. The effect was like putting two negative ends of a magnet together. He couldn't even get close.

As the reverend rose and went to the phone, Lysander hovered over him, panic-stricken.

His body, the intricate webbing of tissue and liquid, the body that he had always taken for granted as his own, now belonged to someone else. Someone intent on throwing it off a cliff... or mutilating it... or—

Didn't that go against the rules of nature? he thought bitterly. *Think, goddammit. Think.*

The reverend hung up and dialed another number. Finally someone answered.

238

"Samantha, please."

The surreal quality of hearing his own voice in the third person was overshadowed by the sudden realization that he knew what the reverend was up to. Rank fear gripped him. Yes, there was a fate worse than death. That old fuck was going to kill Samantha and leave Lysander's battered and barely breathing frame at the scene of the crime, a bloodied knife in his hand. Charged, tried and convicted of a crime he did not commit. But what could he do?

"Listen very carefully, Samantha," Small was saying. "Meet me at James McMurphy's. I-I know, but there's not a lot of time." A tentative silence followed and Lysander sensed the apprehension on the other end of the line.

"Whadoyamean, I sound different?" Small laughed, but it had none of the qualities of Lysander's laugh. This laugh sounded flat and lifeless. "Of course it's me. Same as always. One hour?... No, I can't say over the..."

The crushing finality of Lysander's circumstance was becoming clear to him now. He was a ghost and would remain a ghost unless he did something fast.

Each frantic thought sent him careening around the room at quantum speed. He moved with the speed of thought. He could pass through walls, but controlling it was like being at the helm of a tall ship with no rudder and no compass, where up was down and down was up. His first order of business: learn to control this thing. His number one obstacle to doing that: frantic thought patterns.

Concentrate, Lysander!

Lysander tried to narrow his maelstrom of thoughts down to a single point. He pictured Avery's desk, and himself sitting at that desk, and when he opened his awareness to the room around him, he was there. Just when he thought he was getting somewhere panic seeped in again.

There had to be a way out of this! Had to be!

And he was sent reeling across the room toward the door. He stopped himself, floated up to the ceiling and searched...

The reverend, wearing Lysander's body, was still on the phone. Lysander glanced over at the reverend's shed skin. It lay slumped forward in the leather chair. A flap of his gray wispy hair had fallen into his face. Lysander examined the reverend's body. Why not? he wondered, turning the idea over and over the way a jeweler might appraise a precious stone. It had been done to him. Why would the reverse not be true? It wasn't pretty, he knew that, but no other solution came to mind. He shifted his awareness behind him.

Yes, still on the phone.

Lysander made the sign of the cross, stretched his hands out before him and dropped from the ceiling. He slid into the reverend, feeling no resistance, bracing himself as one might brace themselves entering a freezing lake.

His head and shoulders jerked upright at once. A terrible pain was suddenly throbbing in his left knee. His mouth, dry and pasty, tasted like... an ashtray. He opened his eyes. The room was darker than it had been a second ago.

He stood on legs that felt as though they had been dipped in concrete. He tried to walk across the room. Each step accompanied by a blast of pain in his left knee. He became dully aware that it was dragging behind him. Working the reverend's body meant a lot more effort, Lysander realized. It was much older than his own and stiffer in places he never even knew existed. Floating on the ceiling, his mind had been far clearer, but now a new layer of conscious thought was yammering away at him. It wanted him to kill and destroy. It knew that a new resident had entered and it was resentful of the intrusion. The reverend's body wanted him out.

He limped up behind the form just now hanging up the phone, unable to make his leg cooperate unless he pulled it along behind him. He saw himself—the real Lysander—turn around. The look of surprise and the sudden flash of fear in his eyes was unmistakable—worth the price of admission. That vivid display of fear excited him. Sexually. In that split nanosecond of time he was reminded of that first moment when Samantha had nudged her lips up against his own. His pants suddenly grew tighter, filling with an erection—a stubbier version of his own. That memory of his first night with Samantha was playing back to him, but not as it had actually happened. No, this was different. He was standing over her, slapping and biting. She was begging for him to stop. His hands, the reverend's hands, crawled up and clasped tightly around her tiny neck. Her body tensed as she slapped at his hands and dragged her nails across his face, across his neck. Those hands gave one final shuddering squeeze, and she folded like a rag doll beneath him.

He closed his eyes. These were *his* memories, cherished possessions, and now somehow, the reverend, or at least some part of him, had gotten his grimy hands on them and was remaking them to his liking.

In a dim pool of light, two shadowy forms faced one another: an older man, with a head of disheveled white hair, and a young man with a pale face and fine features.

In a blur of movement, the reverend clamped his hands around Lysander's neck. Except, the reverend had stolen his body, Lysander reminded himself, so these hands, surprisingly strong and powerful, actually belonged to him. Lysander was strangling himself.

"I hope you're enjoying all of this," the voice asked. It was his own, but mixed now with something more feminine. "I know how much McMurphy did. Should

241

have seen the look on his fat face when I gave him his body back—a wretched thing too, filled with perverted thoughts. Little boys in all manner of compromising positions. A pity really. Came to and found the whole family chopped up." An insane burst of laughter bellowed out of him. "And the best part? The poor sod thought *he* had done it. Million dollars if you can guess what he did then." He pulled a hand away long enough to mimic placing a gun in his mouth and pulling the trigger. He rocked his head back slightly and grinned.

The reverend's fingers found Lysander's throat again and his grip tightened. A low gurgle emanated from deep within Lysander's throat.

The reverend's voice dropped to a whisper. "None of this was my doing, I just want you to know. The incident with that Thomas boy was especially tragic. Derek, I think you called him. He had no part in this dirty business. By now I'm sure you know that. If you had only come through that door as you were supposed to, things would have turned out quite differently, I can assure you."

With lightning speed, Small retracted one of his hands and punched Lysander in the stomach. He doubled over. A string of saliva trailed from his mouth and dangled to the ground. The reverend lifted Lysander's head, wiped away the dribble with the back of his hand, combed back a plume of gray hair with his fingers, then socked him in the face, sending him reeling into one of the leather chairs.

The room was spinning in circles that threatened to swallow Lysander whole. A bolt of pain bore through the swirling confusion. His nose had been broken. No, correction: the reverend's nose had been broken.

Stay down! an internal voice cackled. You're beaten. Be a good boy and it'll all be over soon enough.

But this was not Lysander's own inner voice speaking

242

to him now. He knew the difference. This voice belonged to the reverend. Slipping into this body was a lot like renting a fully furnished apartment, piss-soaked carpet, bed bugs and all.

Regardless of what had happened in the past—actions he couldn't change even if he wanted to—he would not just roll over and play dead. No sirree. His face felt like a squashed tomato, but there was still some gas left in him. He tried to get up, his hands outstretched and ready to grapple, but something hard hit him on top of the head and the next thing he knew he was swimming again. Swimming in a sea of blackness.

Chapter 35

Samantha couldn't shake the uneasy feeling that had been bothering her ever since she arrived at the police station. Everything about her surroundings vouched for her safety. She was with her father and Deputy Morgan. They had picked her up, and her hands were curled, thankfully, around a hot cup of tea. But still something seemed terribly wrong. Lysander had called moments before and he had sounded strange. She had told her father and Alex what had happened that night, why they had broken into the reverend's house, but that sickening feeling would not go away. She looked down at her hands and saw that she had scratched the edges of her fingers raw.

Alex said, "I think it's time we picked this guy u—"

"I don't wanna hear anything out of you right now!" the sheriff roared. Alex recoiled. The sheriff was still steaming over the newspaper article that had appeared this morning in the

Millingham Gazette.
Serial Killer in Millingham?
Tobey Fallen

An anonymous source close to the sheriff's department today said Millingham police may be looking for a serial killer. For several

244

months now, the source alleges, Millingham's chief deputy, Alex Morgan, and Medical Examiner Dorothy Olsen, have been investigating the deaths of Derek Thomas, Peter Hume, and the purported suicide of the sheriff's own wife, Diane Crow, for the possibility they may have been the work of one man.

The source refused to comment on how they had come by the information, other than to say they had intimate knowledge of the inner workings of the investigation. This information contradicts Sheriff Crow's earlier assertion that none of the deaths were in any way related...

The fallout from the article had been cataclysmic. Within hours, Alex had seen the switchboard at the sheriff's office lit up like Yankee Stadium. The town had been a powder keg of tension for weeks, and now with their worst fears realized, the seams of civility and control were beginning to break down. Jack Frazier, a high school substitute teacher and gun enthusiast, had organized a vigilante force to hunt down the killer, only to find himself in a three-hour-stand-off with Crow, Alex and Jeff. Crow had been on the phone with the mayor three times today, and during more than one of those times, the blinds to his office had snapped closed. Still Alex had heard the shouting and knew that the worse it got for Steve, the worse it would be for him. At first Alex had been certain Jeff had sprung the leak, but even Jeff wasn't that stupid. An anonymous source close to the investigation could only mean one of three people—Crow, Jeff and himself. That was when it dawned on him who the real culprit was: Sheila Evans. Somehow she had gathered up all the rumors in town and spun them into a dark cloud over Steve's head. And was it any wonder? He had left her cold for Dorothy with hardly a word of explanation.

Sheriff Crow was still staring at him when Samantha spoke. "I've gotta meet Lysander in twenty minutes—" she began, battling that uncomfortable feeling that still

245

hadn't left.

"You'll do no such thing," her father barked. "Alex will go and pick him up. This is police business. You almost got yourself killed tonight."

"There's no fucking way I'm staying here!"

The room descended into a stony silence. All eyes turned to Sheriff Crow.

"You're already grounded for a year," he said with forced calm. "You wanna go for the rest of your life?" He looked over at Alex. "Go get Lysander and bring him back here. And you," he said, pointing at Samantha, "you're staying right here till we get back. I better not so much as find out you left that chair."

He stood up to leave the room.

Samantha crossed her arms over her chest defiantly. "And where are you going?"

"I'm gonna get Reverend Small."

"Dad, be careful, he's dangerous." Her voice sounded desperate. She was beginning to wonder if this was the last time she would see her father alive.

"So am I." He smiled and motioned for Jeff to follow him.

Jeff cocked his hand into the shape of a gun and pointed it at Alex. There was a gleeful look on his face. "We'll see you back here in one hour."

Samantha sprang to her feet. "Alex, you gotta take me with you. Lysander doesn't trust you. If you show up alone, he's liable to hide. It's a big house. You'll never find him."

Alex shook his head. "Can't do it."

"It's not like him to do something like this. He must be in danger."

She could feel his hesitation, and she thought if she pushed hard enough he would give in.

She put her hands together. "Pleasssssse—"

"Sam, I've betrayed your father enough for one

246

lifetime. You saw him. If I so happen to piss the wrong way, I'm through. And it doesn't exactly help that Jeff takes every chance he can to fill the old man's head with trash about how incompetent I am."

"My dad loves you, Alex. You're one of the family. You're like a son to him."

He went to the gun rack by the back wall and fumbled with the key. He was saying something as he unlatched the door, swinging it open, asking if there was anything she needed while he was getting Lysander. She eyed the nightstick on his desk. The same one he had reached for when Derek had resisted arrest. How long ago that seemed now.

She could not stay here another minute. Every second lost meant Lysander was in more danger. Sam made a decision; perhaps a decision she had made the moment her father had walked out that back door.

She picked up the nightstick and crept behind Alex. He was still unlocking his shotgun, waiting for her to answer his question. The room was so quiet, the fluorescent lights buzzed loudly overhead. He started to turn around when the aluminum made contact with the back of his skull. His legs gave out from under him, and he spilled onto the ground. There would be hell to pay, she knew, but the more she thought it over, the more she understood that Lysander was in serious trouble. She reached into Alex's pocket and pulled out a large key ring. She then unsnapped the leather strap on his belt and removed his revolver. She had never used a gun before, not even for target practice. Her fingers trembled as she held it. The steel was heavy and cold in her hand. Death at her fingertips. She hoped she would have no reason to use it, but if the reverend reared his ugly head, without the slightest hesitation, she would blow it off.

She hurried out to the parking lot behind the station.

Two police cruisers were parked side by side. The first

247

belonged to Alex, the other to Jeff. Her father would have taken his own cruiser for sure—he hated being chauffeured around. She slid behind the wheel of Alex's cruiser, laid the gun on the seat beside her and tried to think what to do next. Her father had always driven her around, had always chided her about not getting her license right away,

You never know when you might need it.

She tried to laugh, but her throat was dry and scratchy. How hard could this be really? she thought. She held down the brake and turned the ignition. The engine turned over.

Easy enough.

She draped an arm across the passenger seat—as she had seen her father do so many times before—stuck it in reverse and nudged the gas. The car began to back out of the parking spot. But in her excitement to leave, she had turned the wheel too soon. She winced at the sound of grinding metal as the fender raked the side of Jeff's cruiser.

"Shit!" Her hands fumbled to put the gear shift into drive. Suddenly the possibility occurred to her that Alex might wake up and cut her off before she could get to Lysander. She shoved the car into park, flung open the glove compartment and searched around frantically. Her hand touched something hard and she pulled it out. It was a switchblade. Samantha got out and slashed the tires of Jeff's car.

The cruiser hissed in defiance as it slowly sank onto four rims. She dashed back to the car and pulled out of the parking lot.

As she approached the McMurphy place, she sped up, snapping the long chain that blocked access to the dirt road leading to the house.

She came at last to the old McMurphy house. She could see soft light coming from one of the windows. A lantern

248

was on. She smiled in relief. Lysander had waited for her.

• • •

Lysander was rubbing his temples. His head was pounding. He felt as if someone had used it to bash down a great oaken door.

His fingers froze over a lump at the back of his skull.

He sprang to his feet with a start and scrambled over toward a full-length mirror, barely aware that he was dragging his left leg behind him.

He saw his reflection and screamed in despair. His voice was different now—deeper, raspier. He could feel the vibrato throughout his body. But there were other voices as well, voices clearly not his own still ringing inside his head. Like him, they too were stirring, and now with their slumber ended, they wanted him to do awful things. Unspeakable things.

"Shut up! Shut up!" he screamed.

For a brief moment they shrank away.

Think, Lysander. Think, goddammit.

He struggled to settle his mind.

"McMurphy's," he remembered. "He's gone to McMurphy's…"

There was a chance that Samantha had not fallen for the reverend's call. If he was lucky, she would have seen through the façade. But he knew that was wishful thinking. He knew that if a grenade had rolled in at their feet, she would have jumped on it in a heartbeat, if it meant saving his life.

He scanned the room and noticed something was missing. The area carpet where Avery had lain was saturated with blood, pooled in two great circular patterns. Another stain led from the carpet toward the

249

open office door and around the corner. But nowhere was Avery.

How long had he been out for? He looked up and saw that it was still dark outside. Surely he couldn't have been out more than thirty minutes. An hour tops. His left leg was as stiff as hell. He tried bending and stretching it back into shape, but every movement sent fiery bolts of pain coursing through his body—or more accurately, through the reverend's body.

Lysander ambled out of the room and up the stairs. He remembered Samantha's triumphant expression at having jabbed that knife into the reverend's leg, and the irony of that exhilaration came back to him now with every step.

The Honda in the driveway was gone. That meant for sure he was already at the McMurphy place, waiting for Samantha. Lysander rushed to the phone and dialed home. His father answered. The old man sounded irritable. Had he been drinking?

Lysander began to speak but trailed off.

"Hello?" his father said with annoyance. "Who's there?"

Lysander could hear the television blaring in the background. Sam wasn't there. He hung up and called the police station. It kept ringing. He switched the phone to his other ear. The left one, he had begun to notice, didn't hear so well. He let it ring about ten times and then hung up.

Shit.

There wasn't time to waste. How the hell was he going to get to McMurphy's before—

His eyes lit up.

The garage!

He hobbled though the kitchen, recalling how that first day Avery had been working on his MGB. He had even boasted that it was nearly finished. With growing anxiety, he swung open the door and snapped on the garage light.

250

There it was: low red frame, white racing stripes.

He filled with a hot panic as he searched for the keys.

Come on, come on!

The glove compartment was locked and they weren't in the ignition.

Of course not, why would they be?

Could they have been in Avery's pocket? he wondered. He hoped not, since that spot on the floor where Avery had fallen had been empty when he woke up.

He hobbled back inside. He would check by the front door for a key rack. But when that too came up empty he slumped to the ground in despair. Then something clicked.

On Lysander's first visit, Avery had taken him in through the garage, hadn't he?

He ran to the garage door and found a small wooden rack mounted on the wall. Two sets of key chains hung there, side by side. One of them bore three letters. MGB. He stood staring at it as a thirsty man might stare at a shimmering mirage. Then he snatched it from the rack.

Once he had heaved open the garage door, he maneuvered himself painfully into the front seat. His heart sank to the soles of his feet when he looked down at the stick. The car was standard. He barely knew how to drive an automatic, let alone a standard. His left foot went to the clutch and depressed it. He turned the ignition and the engine thundered back at him, deep and gorgeous.

Then a curious thing happened. He held down the clutch again, put it into first and shot out of the driveway. The road came up at him quickly and Lysander shifted into second before taking a hard right. With the sound of squealing tires, he left behind him a fading cloud of white exhaust.

He did it with the facility of someone who had driven all his life. Shifting from third to fourth, he caught his

251

reflection in the rearview mirror and saw the reverend's face staring back at him again. The very idea took some getting used to—something he didn't want to get used to. Speeding toward James McMurphy's crumbling excuse for a house, he realized it wasn't really him who knew how to drive standard. It was the reverend and the thought that he was drawing on that experience made him shudder.

Five minutes later, he came to a midnight blue pickup truck askew across the road. The driver's side door was ajar, a pair of legs sticking out. Lysander pulled up and got out. The scene looked fresh since the pickup's engine was still ticking. As he drew closer, he heard someone moaning from inside the cab. He stuck his head in and couldn't hide the look of surprise on his face. "Chad?"

The pale figure looked up at him, his face brightening at the sight of the reverend's trusted face.

"Reverend Sma… " He tried to get the words out, but his head fell back. His hands were cupping his right side. Thick matted blood oozed from between his fingers.

Two thoughts crossed Lysander's mind simultaneously. The first was that he didn't have time to help. If he left Chad here, surely someone would find him and bring him to a hospital. Right? The second thought, however, was strangely foreign. The shadowy parts were back again, clawing at the circuitry of his brain—no, it was the reverend's brain, he reminded himself—wanting him to stick his fingers into the fleshy wound and rip Chad's side open. That second thought, vile and disturbing as it was, helped to make up his mind.

Grunting and heaving, he wrenched Chad from the pickup. Lysander staggered to the MG with Chad's limp form in his arms. Blood had pooled by the pickup's accelerator in such a great quantity that Lysander wondered how Chad wasn't dead already.

"Chad! You gotta help. I need you to walk."

252

Chad nodded his head. But his eyes where rolling up into his skull. Lysander shouted at him and somehow that got his legs moving a little. They made it at last and Lysander flopped him over and into the backseat. There was no time for delicacy. He would drive him to his house and have his parents call an ambulance. As they pulled away, Lysander tried to keep him conscious.

"What happened? Chad! Look at me! What happened to you?"

Chad's cheeks were ashen, his lips cobalt blue. He was babbling incoherently.

Lysander reached back and slapped him in the face. He was surprised at how little pleasure he derived from the act, but that didn't stop the voices from demanding more.

Again! Harder!

STOP IT!

"Chad, what happened?"

"Was gonna teach that little freak a lesson... saw him... driving. Cut him off... Oh, I'm sorry, Ma, I'll clean it up, I promise. I'll be good, you'll see..." His voice was drowned out by the MG's engine.

Lysander reached back with one hand and grabbed Chad by the scruff of his neck. Chad's eyes grew wide for a moment.

"Lysander. Was that who you cut off?"

Chad nodded absently.

"If you get outta of this, you promise me you'll leave Lysander alone. He's never done anything to you. He's just different, that's all."

Chad's head lolled back, his eyes fluttered, then closed.

Lysander loaded Chad into the MGB and tore off.

A moment later, Lysander sped into the driveway of his house too fast to brake in time and rear-ended his father's Buick, slamming his head against the steering wheel. For a terrifying second he felt the world swimming away from him. He pulled Chad up and over his shoulder and

253

shuffled slowly, awkwardly toward his front door. Mercifully, the door was unlocked.

Inside, Lysander could see the blue glare from the television flickering in the other room. "Lysander, that you?" came his father's disembodied voice. "Where you been, son?"

"Help. I need help," Lysander shouted, cringing as he heard the deep unexpected bellow in his voice. He regretted now confessing to his father about the reverend. It was going to make this very complicated. He didn't have time for complicated.

His father came scrambling around the corner, eyes wide like saucers. His hair was off to one side, the fear and shock on his face turning to blazing anger.

Lysander had expected no less.

"You get away from him!" his father growled, his face suffusing with a crazed expression.

But before Lysander could respond, his father was on him, one hand clamped firmly around his neck, the other belting him in the face and stomach.

"Call an ambulance," Lysander was trying to say, but in actuality the words sounded more like "Curr 'n ambulass."

His father's eyes were glazed. His breath ripe with whiskey. Lysander was suddenly worried for his life.

His mother appeared on the top riser in her nightgown, her hair tied back for sleep, and she was shrieking.

"Stop! Glenn, stop, you're going to kill him!" Then she shrieked, for quite a different reason. Lysander would remember it afterward in spite of the pummeling being administered to him. "Oh, Glenn. Oh, God, I think my water. Glenn, oh God, my water... It's... Glenn! The baby!"

Glenn's grip slackened and his trembling hands came away. He was being torn by two almost impossibly strong drives—either pummel the shit out of the guy who had just brought his son home in a bloody mess, or tend to his wife, pregnant and about to give birth on the upstairs landing.

Glenn stood and bolted up the first two risers and then stopped, panting.

Lying on the ground, rubbing his throat, Lysander shouted. "Dad, will you call a fucking ambulance!" He pointed frantically at Chad. "He's gonna die."

Glenn turned to the crumpled, ashen-faced form on the ground, only dimly aware, it seemed, that Reverend Small, a man at least a decade older than he, had just called him "Dad."

Then a shift in Glenn's expression when he seemed to realize that the person lying in a pool of blood in his front hallway was not Lysander. Glenn blinked thickly up at his wife, perched above him, holding her belly, and then bolted for the phone in the kitchen, spilling over one of the dining room chairs in the process.

His mother's eyes were still fixed on him.

"Evelyn, I need to find Lysander. He's in terrible danger."

His mother's expression changed. "Lysander?" In that moment she seemed to realize as well that the boy sprawled on the ground wasn't her son. "Reverend Small, he was just here."

Lysander rose, albeit with some difficulty and ambled up the stairs feeling like a one legged pirate. Step, plant, step, plant. He could see his mother growing fearful as he approached, inching away from him as though the angel of death himself were coming for her.

"What do you mean, just here?" Lysander barked.

His mother was breathing heavily. Doing one of those fancy Lamaze exercises, sounding like a puffing train. "Lysander was here not ten minutes ago." Fear filled her eyes, and she looked unsure how much to reveal to this man covered in blood. "Lysander stormed in and ran up

255

to his room. God knows what for."

"The locket," he whispered and pushed passed her on the narrow stairway.

Lysander limped hard to his room and saw right away that it had been turned upside down. He went to his overturned night table, set it right side up again and pulled open the drawer. He reached a bloodied hand in and groped around until he found the locket, still taped to the underside of the drawer where he had hidden it. Battered and dented, but still in one piece. He slid it into his pocket and headed downstairs. He shuffled past his mother and out the front door toward the red sports car, growing more and more certain that he was already too late.

Chapter 36

Samantha pushed against the large oak door of the McMurphy place. It swung open with a quiet groan. In the shimmering moonlight, she could see that the thick bolt that kept the McMurphy house locked lay shattered on the front porch. She groped around inside her jacket pocket, feeling for the reassuring angles of the revolver. But that uneasy feeling wasn't going away. Could it have something to do with the awful smell that was making her nose wrinkle?

There had always been a certain foul quality to the air at the McMurphy house. It went hand in hand with a ruined old house, the way all old things gradually developed an odor of decay. But now the characteristic smell of mold had been replaced by something new and more vile. The olfactory force had hit her the minute she made it over the threshold—although she had caught small traces of it stepping from the cruiser.

What died in here? she wondered, holding a hand up to her nose.

She could see the light from the lantern glimmering in a room up ahead.

"Lysander!" she called out.

No answer.

"Lysa—"

257

A hand touched her shoulder and she let out a yelp of fright.

A smile was floating in the gloom. Eyes peered out at her from shadowy sockets.

"Don't be nervous," the voice said

Samantha clutched her heart.

"I coulda blown your fucking head off! Jesus Christ, Lysander, don't sneak up on me like that."

There had been a subtle transformation in his expression when she had cursed. A twitching kind of expression she had never seen in him before. It looked strangely like...

disapproval. The foul stench didn't seem to be bothering him at all. In fact, he seemed to be savoring it.

"What's that smell?" she asked. "It's fucking awful."

That disapproving look again.

Shivers trickled up her spine. Lysander's presence, normally comforting and soothing, was beginning to frighten her.

"Who did you come with?" he asked. His breath was bad. That was weird, his breath was never bad. It was stinging her eyes.

She hesitated. "I'm alone."

"That gun," he said. He was in front of her now, about to walk away. "Don't let it out of your sight."

She gave him a strange look.

"We may need it."

"We shouldn't," she said quickly. "My father and Jeff have gone to get Small. They say they have enough to nail his ass to the wall."

He stopped suddenly, baring his teeth. "That's good to hear."

"Why did you call me?"

He was nearly halfway down the hall when he spoke. "I wanted to show you something. You'll never believe it. It should tie things together quite nicely." He was whisking

258

his hands together with pride. "No loose ends."

His back was turned to her, but she could hear the smile in his voice.

She followed, one hand over her nose, the other clutching the handle of the gun in her pocket. If the reverend came out at them—correction: if he was stupid enough to come out at them—she was ready.

Off they headed toward the room with the soft fluttering light.

• • •

Dorothy was finishing up another late night of work when a young assistant named Catherine Stapen came into the room Dorothy called either her office or her cell, depending on the mood she was in.

"I think we may have a problem," the young woman said.

Dorothy peered up at her from under her reading glasses. "Nothing that can't be fixed, I'm sure."

But the panicked look on the assistant's face said it all. Something *was* wrong. Terribly wrong.

"It's Peter Hume," Catherine said as though the very name were explanation enough.

"Yes, what about him?" Dorothy barked.

The two women locked eyes, and fear passed from one to the other. "He's gone."

• • •

The floorboards moaned beneath Sam's feet as she walked. She and Lysander were headed toward the old dining room. Tall shadows wavered and broke against the far wall, stretched fiendishly tall by the light of the

259

lantern. Her heart beat like an ancient warship revved up to ramming speed.

"Lysander, I don't like this. What is it you're showing me?"

He disappeared into the room ahead of her.

She entered. The room was dim, webbed with pockets of deep shadow, but she could see enough.

In the center of the room was a long cherrywood table. Around it five chairs had been set. Seated clumsily in four of those were bodies in varying degrees of decomposition, all peering back at her. The two on the left were lipless.

On the far right was Avery, his corpse visibly bound to the seat with thick rope, looking very much alive except for his missing eyes and slashed throat. Lashed beside him was Peter Hume, his face pale gray. He was still wearing his tattered yellow cardigan. Next to him, with her head slumped on Hume's shoulder, like two high school sweethearts, was Samantha's mother. There were holes in her face where something had been nibbling at her cheek. The flesh flapped open like a can of half finished beans. The top of her scalp was missing, exposing a patch of grimy white bone. At the far end was a figure Samantha could only guess was James McMurphy, his features long since melted away, except for a set of crooked teeth, many of which were broken— presumably from the force of the shotgun going off in his mouth.

Her mind was spinning in dizzying circles...

The great big ship goes round and round... round and round... round and round... the great big ship goes round and...

... trying to shut down.

A horrible dream, that's all it is. Just a horrible dream.

Slowly, she became aware of the screaming. It was a distant thing at first and then grew as the sound of a train might grow, bearing down on her, about to tear her in half. She took a half step and stumbled backward. Her shoulder blades sank into the moistened, decaying wall, and with the shocking touch came the realization that the one screaming had been her.

Lysander was gone.

From the hallway came the sound of the front door creaking open. A voice called out to her. Her instincts told her to run away from that voice, that it had come to hurt her. She spun toward the doorway, yanking the silver .357 from her pocket. She held it out in front of her, arms straight, hands trembling, barely aware anymore of the horrible stench.

Heavy footsteps traced down the hallway.

She backed away, hoping that there was nothing waiting behind her. The lantern, hung by the door, teetered ever so slightly. The shadow corpses swayed in time, back and forth, back and forth. The steps drew closer. She cocked the gun's heavy metal hammer. Out of the darkened hallway came the reverend.

"Saman—"

Samantha closed her eyes and shot. The room exploded with a thunderous boom. A second later, she opened them and saw a man fall to his knees. He was not the reverend, and it took a moment for the reality of what she had done to sink in.

Alex looked up at her in surprise, a dark patch spreading out from the center of his chest. Then, with her ears still ringing from the gunshot, she heard another set of footsteps.

The gun drooped to her side. *What have I done?* she thought numbly.

The staggered rhythm of these new footsteps was one she would have recognized, but she felt her hold on the world slipping away. On they came. Step, then drag. Step, then drag.

This is all a bad dream is what it is, just a bad terrible dream.

261

This time it was the reverend. His face a mask of pain. Blood streaked his right cheek. He was pulling his left leg behind him and he opened his mouth to say something when his eyes fell to the man on the floor. Alex's chest was jerking in tiny, shallow gasps of air.

"Oh, my God," he said in a gravelly voice. "What have you done?"

Samantha raised the gun. "Get away from him!"

The reverend held out his arms. "Sam, I'm not who you think I am." The sincerity in his face was distracting her. "I'm Lysander."

Her head tilted, the way a dog might tilt its head trying to understand the gibberish of its master's voice. This was a trick, she thought. Her head was spinning out of control.

"Shoot him, Sam!" a voice ordered from behind her. "What are you waiting for? Shoot!"

She glanced over her shoulder. Lysander emerged from the shadows. There was something wrong with his eyes. In that split second of doubt and confusion, she wondered if it might not be a trick of the light, but from here they looked sliver and dead.

That was when she saw his hand slip into his pocket and reappear a second later with a chain hanging between his webbed fingers. At the end of it was a locket. The locket.

The expression on the reverend's face—his own, he kept reminding

himself—suddenly shifted. His milky white eyes had grown a size larger, and the lower half of his jaw was flapping open.

"You were human once," Lysander shouted. "And maybe not so long ago. I know now what we did to you and it was wrong. We didn't understand then, you're right, but I do now. I know what it's like to be hated. And judged. I know all too well."

262

For a moment the reverend's face wavered between seething hatred and something else, something softer. His head slumped between his shoulders as though some great weight had bore it down, and there it stayed. When it came back up, all the uncertainty had gone out of him. The cords in his neck had drawn tight. His nostrils flared. His hands were working like a child furious at having been fooled.

"Shoot him!" the reverend said to Samantha, his voice quavering.

A drop of perspiration tumbled into her eye, and the reverend's form before her blurred.

"Shoot him now!" he commanded behind her.

She looked at Lysander and then at the reverend—his arms still held out protectively before him. She wanted nothing more than to shoot him, but Lysander was acting so unlike himself she wasn't sure anymore.

The reverend said to her, "Sam, remember when you asked me if I'd ever been in love?" His voice was nearly a whisper. The gun trembled in her hands. "Remember? We were sitting over there." He pointed down the hall to the room where Derek had been staying. "It was raining outside and you asked me if I'd ever been in love. Do you remember?"

Samantha's hands were not just trembling, they were quaking, the gun still poised at the reverend's head.

"And I said no, never have, never would. You asked me and I said no way. That wasn't true, Sam. I lied that day."

She half smiled, still not entirely sure what to believe, but then she saw the reverend's face tense and his mouth fall open.

"Sam! Watch—"

She turned just in time to see Lysander, his right hand raised above his head. In that hand was the long blade of a knife. His lips were stretched wide with elation. She held the gun tightly in her hands. There was a moment

263

when she could have pulled the trigger and torn away the right side of Lysander's face. He was close enough that she could have closed her eyes so she wouldn't have seen it happen. Only the spatter of blood hitting her cheek would have told her she had hit her mark, but she couldn't bring herself to do it.

The knife tore through Samantha's shirt and buried itself into her chest. Her mouth gaped open with a shocking jolt of pain. She tried to turn and run away, but the knife would not let her go, jammed as it was just inside her collarbone. The gun flopped out of her hand and thumped onto the floor. She tried to pull herself free, but he was too strong, this demon in front of her, his arms pumping up and down viciously. He was tearing her apart. Strangely, after that initial explosion of searing pain and agony she had felt only numbness from her waist down. Lysander, the real Lysander—she could hear him stumbling forward. She wanted so badly to stand and fight, but her legs had become strands of jelly. The knife was wrenched violently from her chest and then her legs gave out completely. She crumpled to the floor, making a muffled thud as her head landed on a section of wet planking. A burst of starlight bloomed before her eyes and when it cleared, she saw two forms struggling above her. She could hear a rattling sound in her chest as she tried to breathe. A sharp blast of pain ignited whenever she gasped for air. Ten feet away was Alex. His eyes were glassy and still. She wanted to call out to him, but each breath, each rasp, was coming shorter and shorter. Her breathing became shallow. Lysander heard it too because she could see his eyes become wide with fear as he looked down at her—dressed as he was in the reverend's skin—his arms locked in his own struggle not far above her. She wanted to smile to him. To give him courage. She willed herself to focus on his eyes to let him know she was okay.

264

Ignore Small's monstrous face. Ignore that Halloween mask he was wearing.

Smile, goddammit!

But her face refused. It was like forcing a smile onto a lump of hardened clay, and after a few futile moments, she abandoned the effort. She had to conserve her energy. She would need it if she wanted to keep breathing, shallow and partial though her breaths had become.

What Samantha Crow did not yet know was that she had already been dead for over sixty-three seconds.

Chapter 37

At first, neither did Lysander. He was weaponless and locked in a struggle against, of all people in the world, himself. It was worse than any nightmare he had ever known. The knife Reverend Small held came swishing through the air barely an inch from his face. He could feel the rush of air brush his cheek. Somehow in their scuffling, Small had managed to free his right arm from Lysander's grip, and he was swinging the knife wildly, that maniacal expression of pleasure plastered across his face. They spun in circles. One of them kicked the gun across the floor, and it slid under the table of seated corpses. Lysander caught the sleeve of his arm and stayed the horrible hacking motions at least temporarily. He could see Samantha lying on the floor, her right leg curled under her, her clothes saturated with blood. The reverend was struggling to get the knife free. He was trying to knee him in the balls. He missed by a hair and sank his knee instead into Lysander's left thigh. Grimacing, Lysander tightened his grip. If that knife got loose again, he would be finished.

He looked at Samantha again. Her chest, jerking before in shallow spasms, had stilled. Her blood glistened from the blade's edge. Lysander's vision fogged as hot tears filled his eyes and tumbled down his cheeks. She couldn't be dead.

The reverend was laughing now. That bastard knew. But she could be brought back. It had happened before. Dead wasn't always forever, and the thought filled him with hope and then something else, a feeling almost alien to him: rage. The world stretched out before him into a long narrow corridor. At the far end of it was the reverend. And beyond that, Samantha alive and well.

Lysander snapped his head forward and brought it down on the reverend's nose. He saw his own nose, the nose he had looked at in the mirror for seventeen years, explode before him in a gush of red. The reverend's eyes watered from the pain. Lysander maneuvered him over to the table and whacked the knife out of his hand against the table's edge. It fell away and he kicked it into the corner of the room. He went to work then, letting fly a hail of fists. Bashing the reverend's face... bashing his own face. Past was the time for thoughts of self-preservation. He would continue until he was dead, damn the consequences. He was turning that face, still smiling, into a red pulp. The tears on Lysander's cheeks had dried, and now there was only hate. Now there was only loathing. He spun the reverend in a circle like a discus thrower, gaining speed and momentum, and then released him toward the doorway. The wall trembled and the lantern that was hanging precariously from a hook beside him, swung wildly. On the floor, Alex let out a quiet moan and rolled over onto his side.

Lysander's eyes flared. If the lantern fell, he realized, they would all be engulfed in flames. That thought seemed to strike both men at once: Lysander, from the other end of the room and the reverend, leaning against the wall beside it, his eyes little more than puffy slits. The grin on the reverend's face returned. With surprising agility, he snatched the lantern off the hook and flung it at Lysander's feet. Lysander had tried to leap out of the way, but he was too slow. An explosion of glass and metal engulfed him as the kerosene in the lamp ignited and burst into flames. A thick yellow inferno clamored up his pant legs. He slapped at the flames, but the suit jacket he was wearing had also caught. The pain was excruciating, like a thousand stinging bees. As he flung himself to the ground, trying to beat out the flames, a single thought coursed through his mind: No one should ever have to feel this much pain. From a great distance, he could hear himself screaming. Through the flames he could see the reverend, convulsing. He was dimly aware that the fire had triggered a seizure, and Lysander's body had flopped to the ground, jerking and twitching. As Lysander tried to fight free of his burning clothes, everything went black. Slowly, the room grew still, and the world was suffused with an orange glow. The distinct lack of pain was the next thing he noticed. The third was the reverend's body below him.

Lysander hovered above the body dressed in what had once been a gray flannel suit. It was now mostly charcoal strips, exposing areas of blackened and charred skin. The muscles in his left leg, the wounded leg he had been dragging behind him, tensed and released in spastic fits. Near the door he saw his body—his real body—lying face up on the ground. He recognized it only because of where it lay. The face was so mashed he couldn't have spotted himself in a crowd.

The fire ignited by the lantern was spreading fast. He floated toward his body. He would get back in, if he could, and drag Samantha and Alex to safety. He was crossing the room when he noticed the tiny black dot against the far wall. He paused for a moment. The dot, which seemed to be hanging in midair, was growing. In the split second in which he'd stopped, it became the size of a beach ball. A voice was calling his name. It sounded a lot like Samantha's. The hole was reaching out in all directions, and Lysander could see swirling movement within it. Tiny pinpricks of light were turning over like some great cosmic whirlwind. From here they looked like tiny galaxies. Then he felt the tugging, a strangely curious sensation at first, like holding your hair up to the end of a vacuum. And as the black mass stretched to the ceiling, the pull grew stronger.

Lysander, get to your body fast!

The thought thundered in his head like an order from a drill sergeant.

Samantha, is that you?

He started to move toward the doorway, but each step was becoming tougher and tougher—like wading up to his armpits in a tidal pool.

Someone was standing close to his body. He couldn't see them so much as feel them. They were disoriented, confused. He increased his pace, fighting every step of the way, leaning forward as if battling a great wind. Behind him, the churning mass had turned into a vortex. Oddly enough, nothing in the room was affected by the suction, which was growing more powerful by the second. The table with the corpses was perfectly still. The remains of tattered curtains against the far wall lay undisturbed. The flames, however, were bending toward the vortex, as though some black hole were greedily devouring every last ounce of light.

As he approached his crumpled form on the ground, he caught the reverend, now a dark shadow, scrambling to reenter Lysander's unconscious body. Lysander grabbed him by the ankles and jerked him back. He was surprised to find substance there, surprised that his hands did not just pass through him. The reverend fell forward, his legs and arms pumping furiously. He was crawling crablike on his hands and knees. Lysander yanked harder on his ankles, careful not to let go of his grip and be sucked into the vortex. The flames had begun climbing up the far

269

wall, only feet now from Samantha's body.

Come on! he shouted.

With a final jerk Lysander sent the reverend smashing against the back wall.

The edges of that violent black mass had disappeared beyond the floor and ceiling, but the pull it was exerting was like being in a wind tunnel. The elastic flesh of their nonphysical bodies flapped away from them, dangling before that gaping mouth. Lysander's legs flopped out behind him. Even the reverend was having difficulty. It was then that he saw Samantha's dead body. He knew for sure she had passed since he could see her soul coming slowly unhinged from her body and spilling out onto the floor. She was sliding for that open mouth and she was picking up speed. If he went physical now, she would surely be sucked into the jaws of that churning beast and be lost forever. He turned away from his body and clambered to cut her off. Small would have it any minute now, but he had never had a choice in the matter, had he? She was less than five feet away and moving fast.

"Samantha!" he cried.

She stirred slightly but did not look at him. He lunged for her as shadowy tendrils began lashing about her ankles. He could see her squirming, trying to free them.

"Stay calm, Sam. Stay calm."

She looked up and found him, her face a mask of fear. She held out her hands, and by the time he found them, her knees had disappeared.

Her expression flickered. "I can feel it draining me," she said. Tears were spilling over her lids and down her cheeks. "Let me go, Lysander or it'll take both of us."

Lysander pulled with everything he had. The force sucking her in was so great. Then she screamed. When he looked back, Small was slinking toward them. He had forsaken the safety of Lysander's body as well for one last chance to dispose of them both forever. He scrambled

270

onto Lysander's back, slithering up his spine until he was level with his head. His lips peeled back, revealing a set of crooked teeth, and he sank them into Lysander's right hand. Lysander felt a strange burst of electrical energy and his grip slackened. Sam screamed. She was gone from the mid-chest now, her eyes looking vacant and dull.

"I can't hold on much longer," Lysander said desperately.

Sam found his eyes, and in them he saw she was defeated. "I love you, Lysander. I have since the very beginning. But you knew that all along, didn't you?"

Small's jaw unhinged for another go at Lysander's hand when suddenly his eyes bulged from their sockets. His mouth fell open, not with sadistic delight this time, but in agony. A set of hands had closed around his neck. Alex's spirit loomed over them, free now from his body. Leaning heavily against the tidal forces, he hoisted the reverend up by his neck. Ripping his hands, finger by finger, off Lysander. But the reverend wasn't done, not by a long shot. With his arms and legs coiling around Alex's frame like a boa constrictor, he sank his teeth into the fleshy part of the man's abdomen. Alex crashed to the floor, writhing, the reverend clawing at him with everything he had.

Lysander tightened his grip on Samantha. "This is our last chance. You have to help me or we're finished."

Sam's sleepy eyes met his. "Okay," she whispered.

Lysander knew now that everything centered on how well he had learned to maneuver in this new environment. The lessons had already started in that very first moment, hovering in Hume's living room. He would have to concentrate. Block out all of the turbulence; the fire raging all around their physical bodies, Alex's bellowing as the reverend tore at him. Most important and difficult of all, he had to block out the sight of Samantha as her soul was being devoured wholesale. He

271

tried thinking of his dog Sandy and the strings of drool that dribbled from her mouth and how it had sent him into fits of laughter. Then he thought of Sam and how tightly they had held each other the night before. How warm her naked body had felt next to his.

"Lysander!" Sam squealed, excitement in her voice.

Lysander opened his eyes. The blackness had receded to somewhere around her hips. It was letting her go. From behind them they could hear grunting and groaning. A ferocious battle was going on, and by the sounds of it, Alex was losing. And why wouldn't he be? They were operating in a reality where physical strength meant next to nothing.

The reverend straddled Alex and began sinking his thumbs into his eyes.

Samantha screamed, and with that the vortex shuddered and grew stronger.

Sam's face contorted. She was slipping away again. "Hurry, Lysander!"

The light that went on in Lysander's head felt brighter than all the suns that had ever lived. The realization was so sudden and intense that he had nearly burst out laughing. How had he not seen it before? The churning black hole wasn't after their souls. It was negativity it wanted.

He turned to Samantha. "It's the fear and the hate in you. That's what it's feeding on, the dark stuff you keep buried down deep. The poison that consumed Rebecca Goodman all those years ago. Clear it away. Clear it all away and think of something else. Think of your mother and how much you loved her. Think about you and me, Sam. Think about us. In the hallway at school when you pushed me against the locker and you kissed me. How nice it felt." The black mass seemed to be throbbing.

"That's right. Stay in that moment. Hold it and don't let it go!"

272

The great mouth pulsated faster now, gathering more and more speed until it seemed to reach a kind of critical mass. At last it gave a final shudder and expelled Samantha clear across the room, past the table of seated corpses. Lysander rose, keeping his mind clear of as much negativity as possible. Because of that the torrential wind that had nearly killed him and Sam was little more than a stiff breeze. The reverend and Alex were struggling only a few yards away. Alex was screaming in agony and Lysander felt the wind picking up. Their hatred was still feeding it, he realized. It wasn't over yet. Lysander hooked an arm around the reverend's neck and bent his head back.

"You were right all along," Lysander whispered into his ear. "It was coming. It's waited all these years and it's finally come. But not for me. It's here for you." With a half twist he sent him spinning across the room and straight into the vortex. Reverend Small landed as a man would in a vat of thick tar. There was enough time for Lysander to see Small's wide-eyed face as the last of him was consumed. The expression on his face was one of astonishment and above all, terror.

Behind them, the vortex was already shrinking. The edges came together, closing back down to a single black speck on the wall. Then, slowly, with a flicker, the dot blinked and disappeared altogether.

Back in the room, the fire was raging out of control. Lysander went to Sam, but when he got there, she had already rolled back into her body. He turned to help Alex and knew at once there was a problem. Alex's body lay slumped on its side. Lysander could see he was trying to slide back in. But it wasn't working. Every time he rose up, his body remained on the ground.

"Something's wrong," Alex said, confusion registering on his face.

Lysander looked at Alex's prone body and a well of

emotions sprung up from within him. In spite of everything Alex had done, he couldn't bear seeing him like this.

Lysander crossed to help him.

"There isn't time for that now," Alex barked. "We gotta pull Sam free. Don't worry about me, Lysander, just go. Get out there and get us out. That's our only chance."

Lysander hesitated. He wanted to say thank you. Alex had saved them.

"Go!"

Reluctantly, Lysander went to his body. A moment later he sat up into the physical world with a violent jerk. He was squinting like a newborn baby, half expecting the raging fire to trigger the first signs of a seizure. It didn't happen. The top three-quarters of the room, however, had filled with a thick cloud of black smoke. His eyes stung as he crawled toward Samantha. Her boot was on fire. He pulled her along the floor. Through the open front door he could see flashing lights racing down the dirt road. He pulled her several feet from the house. Blood from his nose dripped onto her forehead. His face was pure agony, but he had no time for that now. He staggered back inside and emerged a minute later with Alex. Dragging the deputy the same way he'd done with Samantha.

Sheriff Crow and Jeff were coming at a full run, guns drawn. They had come after a neighbor had reported seeing a police cruiser barreling down the street on four flat tires. On his way from the police station, Alex had twisted the rims of Jeff's cruiser completely out of shape.

"We need a doctor!" Lysander shouted. They stared at him in horror. "Hurry! Call for help," he shouted again. His plea finally registered with Jeff. He bolted back to the cruiser and fumbled for the radio. Lysander studied Alex's supine form for a moment. Neither he nor Sam was breathing.

274

Lysander tilted Samantha's head back. He clamped her nose shut, ignoring the blood that trickled through his fingers. His other hand he slid under the back of her neck. Her lips parted and he blew deeply into her open mouth. With laced fingers he began pumping her chest rhythmically. He blew air into her lungs again and then pushed against her chest, trying to kick-start her heart.

"Lemme try!" Sheriff Crow shouted. "She's my daughter, for God's sake."

Lysander moved aside. Steve wiped Lysander's blood from her mouth with the sleeve of his uniform and continued trying to revive her.

Lysander gazed down at Alex. His skin looked almost translucent. Sheriff Crow had done his best to revive him, Lysander could see that. He would keep going until the paramedics arrived. Even though a growing part of him knew it wouldn't do any good.

Behind him, Sheriff Crow was chanting, "Come on, Sam! Come on, girl, you can do it! Wake up, Sam. Wake up!"

Epilogue

A big, slobbery tongue licked Lysander awake. He came to, talking to Sandy, certain that her large head and sad eyes were resting on his stomach, only to find himself alone. They had given him a tranquilizer at the hospital. A deflated-looking Sheriff Crow had come by, but he had been too drowsy to answer any questions. He wouldn't have known what to say anyway. Many questions of his own were left unanswered. Not long ago, a fat nurse, her hair done up in tight ringlets, had fed him something intravenously and it had helped him forget what had happened, but it hadn't taken long for those memories to begin elbowing their way back in. Samantha was foremost on his mind. She hovered before him, a stinging reminder that he had lost the love of his life, again. The first time around, as Parris Locke, his thirst for power had blinded him. And now, as Lysander, his conquest of Summer had nearly landed him in the same boat. But, in the end, he had seen that vacuous path for what it was and he had found Sam at last.

He dared to wonder if she was still alive. The last time he'd seen her, she was sprawled on the ground, paramedics swarming around her like tiny insects.

His hope turned to dread and Lysander's face contorted painfully.

276

Bandages were wrapped around his face, save for his eyes, and his hands were bound. Burned in the fire.

He had made the decision not to think about Samantha anymore when a muffled exchange between a doctor and a nurse drifted in from somewhere outside his room.

"... Crow's gonna need 10 milligrams of Trizioline. Twice a day and..."

"Yes, doctor..."

"Oh, and nurse. Go ahead and leave her in 3B for now..."

"All right, doctor..."

Lysander's heart surged. He unplugged the IV and swung his legs off the bed. The tiles were cold on his feet. He stood up and nearly fell over again. He stumbled out of his room, aware that his left leg wasn't dragging behind him.

A young doctor materialized before him and Lysander asked him where Room 3B was. The doctor pointed down the hallway and told him to make a right at the corner. Lysander then asked if he knew anything about Alex Morgan, Deputy Alex Morgan and the doctor's expression changed at once. Lysander understood the implication well enough.

He shuffled down the hall and turned as the doctor had told him to. Ten more steps and he was at Room 3B. The door was open. A nurse was inside, injecting a syringe into an IV.

"I'm sorry, but this is a private—"

"She's my girlfriend," he said awkwardly, the idea still feeling somehow foreign.

Girlfriend. I have a girlfriend?

They had never discussed their status, but his love for her was so overwhelming, he could not refer to her any other way.

The nurse slipped past him and out of the room.

Samantha lay perfectly still. Bandages covered her face

and chest and hands. Tubes curled from her mouth and nose. Her chest rose and fell in a steady, delicate rhythm. The heart monitor beside her showed a steady pulse.

Lysander pushed a chair next to her and slowly sat down. He reached out and took her hand into his. Her skin was cold. He brought it to his lips and kissed her knuckles, her fingers, the palm of her hand.

"Samantha," he whispered, "I know you can hear me. I want you back. I want you back more than anything. I've made mistakes, I know that, but you and I have a second chance now and I can't lose you, not again. What was it you tried to say to me in the hospital that time? You better come to, or I'm gonna beat you back into consciousness?" His face broke into a smile and somehow he could feel her smiling back at him.

The moment was broken by a faraway sound. An alarm clock was going off in the distance, and for a split second he thought he was back in his bedroom. Then he understood that that was impossible. He had smashed that damn clock months ago. He peered through the bandages that covered his face. Someone nearby was sobbing. He kissed Sam's hand again, laid it carefully at her side and left the room. The crying grew louder.

The sound was coming from down the hall. He followed it until he found the source. He could hear the gasps of the people there as he entered. They were gathered around the bed. His mother's eyes were blood red. Glenn was beside her, his face the color of old linen. At the foot of the bed, two nurses worked feverishly on a baby. His mother's baby, he realized distantly. His little sister. Judging by her current condition, he might never get a chance to meet that little sister.

A third nurse came in and whispered to his mother. His mother's face was washed out and labor-worn. The baby deathly silent...

"Little angel just stopped breathing," one of the nurses

278

was saying as they plied their skills.

His mother's mouth was bent open at a queer angle, on the verge of wailing again, when a tiny noise brought the room to a screeching standstill. A low gurgle, barely audible—a noise that could just as easily have come from the back of his mother's throat. But this was most definitely not his mother. Lysander was certain because her eyes grew to the size of dinner plates. Her lips parted with hope and surprise. The baby coughed and started crying. Lysander's mind suddenly filled with a horrible, unthinkable thought. Was that really his baby sister, or had something else snuck inside during that brief vacancy?

His mother held her arms out, and in them the nurse placed the baby. She was red and squirmy and wrapped in a little blanket. Tears were streaking down Glenn's face and spilling over his smiling lips. He was laughing now, as though this had all been some terrible prank and the pranksters had come clean.

"This kind of thing does happen," one of the nurses was saying. The others stood by, beaming, careful not to leave for fear of a relapse.

"Lysander, dear," his mother said, sniffling. She held the baby up carefully, concerned but unable to hide her swelling pride. "I want you to meet your baby sister, Jessica."

The baby wiggled in his mother's arms and then opened its eyes.

"Isn't she the most gorgeous thing you've ever seen?" his mother said blissfully.

Baby Jessica regarded Lysander. The baby's mouth drew open, and Lysander half expected it to say something demonic. Something awful.

I'm coming!

But instead the child's tiny pink face dissolved into a lusty cry. His mother and father were all broad smiles and

279

teary laughter.

Lysander felt his heart fill with a longing that had been almost completely alien to him before Samantha.

Hope.

Baby Jessica wiggled again. And a new thought began to take form.

She is beautiful, isn't she?

Also by Griffin Hayes

Novels
Malice
Dark Passage

Novellas
Hive I
Hive II
Hive III
Bird of Prey
The Neighbors

Short Stories
The Second Coming
The Grip
Fatherland

Collections
Night Terror
Nightfall